STARFALL

Book Three in the Chronicles of Fid

David H. Reiss

THE LONELY WARDEN
A POEM BY ALAIN MATHESON

Eden echoes in every leaf,
And in creatures great and small.
Homed upon an endangered reef,
Blue marble circling Sol.

Oasis held in strained balance,
Since an age when seas were young,
Imperiled not by hate or malice
But by progress' snake-like tongue.

A future bought without care for cost,
The children's world, betrayed.
Glories by right inherited, lost
And all their hopes decayed.

Treasuring life, the warden rises; he stands and does
   not balk,

Lest that blue effulgent marble still and turn to
    barren rock.

And so.

The grizzled warden, twisted,
Strains towards the grand abyss,
Racked with pain, enlisted
To shield life 'gainst artifice.

To oppose they who try advance,
Not knowing 'pon whom they tread,
To press their dreams and apply a lance,
Lest best intentions turn blood red.

The weary conscript, vigilant,
Stands wary at the border,
'tween what blooms and bleeds, grandiloquent,
And dull incarnate order.

The lonely warden dare not flag; he knows his cause
    is just.
The battle be eternal, to stave off a world of dust.

1

———

"I GENERALLY PREFER TO AVOID KILLING," I INFORMED MY struggling captive, "but I AM a murderer. Please keep that in mind as you answer my questions."

"I'm not going to tell you a damned thing," the young superhero grunted. "Let me go!"

My train of thought derailed.

The powered armor that I was wearing was arguably the most dangerous ever constructed during my long supervillainous career. The fourteen-foot-tall (unfortunately damaged beyond repair) Mk 35 heavy-combat model had boasted greater raw strength, but the technological innovations concealed within this more-compact design were legion. Reinforced with layered forcefields, fitted with powerful energy weapons and framed with the remarkable orichalcum alloy that only my missing adopted-sister could manufacture, the Mk 39 was more than sufficient to intimidate even the bravest of foes.

As with all of my armors, the surface did not reflect light in the slightest. Distant stars sparkled inside that darkness, granting the disorienting effect that I was naught but a man-shaped opening into deep space. A crimson glow seeped from the armor's joints—an angry wireframe wrapped around empty night.

"Are you insane?" I asked, incredulous. "What in Tesla's name are they teaching you?"

The youth tried again to tug his arm free from my grip. "What d'you mean?"

I considered my teen-aged opponent: clad in a black body-suit with white-stripes and cobalt trim, he'd put on a bit of muscle since the last time I'd hospitalized him. Whatever flaws might exist in the Junior Shield training program, their physical instruction was top notch. Reluctantly, I had to admit that the way he'd turned his wrist during his escape attempt had been textbook perfect. If not for the invisible shaped forcefields that I was using to wrap around his arm, he might have pulled away. His manual skills were not in question. His reasoning, on the other hand...

"I just implied the willingness to end your life," I growled, "and you responded with open defiance. That's foolishness."

I released my grip and he floated a few feet away. As always, his hair and eyes flickered to glow cerulean as his powers activated. Once, he'd only been able to fly relatively low to the ground. Practice and training had improved his control and he now could maintain his altitude even though I'd dragged him more than a thousand feet over the Hudson river.

"It was a judgment call," Cherenkov yelped defensively. His hands gathered into fists and glowed electric blue but he knew better than to loose those energy blasts at me.

"It was reckless! You were defenseless and laughably overpowered-"

("...I'm not laughing," he mumbled.)

"- and yet you were willing to provoke me instead of deescalating!" I gestured at his aching wrists to imply that the threat had been real. "What if all I wanted was to know the capital city of New Mexico? Would that have been worth challenging a hardened killer?"

"Is it Albuquerque?"

"Santa Fe. That's not the point," I sighed, but the vocoder that disguised my voice struck the weariness from my tone. "You should have attempted appeasement...to draw out the conversation while looking for opportunities. The subject is covered extensively in your Escape and Evasion text."

"Like I said," he rubbed at his wrists, "it was a judgment call. You've had me cornered before, I thought we could talk this out. And we're talking, right?"

"...you made a conscious decision to disrupt my expectations, in the hopes that it would alter the conversation's flow. Intriguing."

"If it's stupid, but it works-"

"Then it's still stupid," I interrupted.

"But it works," he chuckled, and I saw evidence of his mentor's influence in his impish smile. "So...Doctor Fid. What d'you want?"

"Originally, I wanted information about your unfortunately humorous teacher, Cloner," I answered dryly, "but now I mostly just want to break your legs."

He gulped and reflexively floated a few feet backwards. Over the last several years I'd generated a bit of reputation for fracturing the limbs of heroes I liked. "I don't know anything you could use against him."

"Relax. I don't think that anything that I intended to ask would count as a betrayal of trust."

"Okaaaay," he replied, transparently unwilling to take me at my word. I approved of his wariness. "What d'you want to know?"

"Cloner had seemed receptive to a treaty between myself and the New York Shield, and had been willing to trade access to certain captured technology in return for concessions on my part."

"I haven't heard anything about that."

"Negotiations were still in progress," I waved dismissively. "Recently, however, I have been unable to make contact. I came to ask if anything was amiss with the leader of the New York Shield."

"So you grabbed me mid-patrol and threatened to kill me, just to ask if my boss is okay?"

In retrospect, the approach I'd chosen did seem unnecessarily confrontational. Several recent experiments had resulted in failure and I was, perhaps, becoming overly eager to pursue other options. I had no intention, however, of allowing any hint of my growing desperation to be disclosed to the heroes, so I answered only with a stony silence.

"...all right," Cherenkov finally said, looking unnerved.

"It's probably nothing. Our internal system has been wonky lately, lots of messages getting lost."

"Your external security has been unaffected." Behind my armor's emotionless and featureless faceplate, I frowned. "I'd been under the impression that the New York Shield's network infrastructure is maintained by Cuboid."

Fixing an internal networking issue should have been a simple task for the android hero; Cuboid was, after all, the only currently-active artificial intelligence on Earth. All of my recent investigations had been aimed at returning that number to two: my adopted little sister had been the world's second A.I.. Her emotional growth had (by design) been limited to mature at human rates, and thus she'd had the mind and android body of an adorable eleven-year-old girl... but she had been technically more advanced than Cuboid and had evolved so thoroughly that a villainous sorcerer's spell had recognized her as being a living, sentient being. The servers still functioned, but her personality—her psyche—was missing, stolen by the strange extra-dimensional effects of so-called 'magic'. Gaining access to technology key to her rescue was the sole reason for bargaining with the New York Shield in the first place.

Whisper had had a childish crush on the young hero before me. Her artificial eyes glowed the same color as did his. My little sister liked this boy and I'd threatened his life.

It was very possible that I'd miscalculated the dosages of anti-psychotics in the pharmacological regimen that had been keeping me awake for the last week.

"Cuboid is busy designing a new body for himself,"

Cherenkov explained, interrupting my reverie. "Cloner thinks things'll get back to normal in a week or so."

I didn't want to wait a week or so.

"Tell Cloner that he owes me a beer," I instructed the young hero. "Friday. He'll know where to meet me."

Cherenkov looked positively boggled by the idea that his mentor—the leader of the East Coast's premiere superhero team—shared drinks with the world's most feared supervillain, but I was unwilling to waste time upon further explanation. The technology hidden by the New York Shield was promising but there was other research I could be performing. Other tests and other experiments to run, just in case. Whisper needed me.

I shot into the sky and disappeared among the stars.

❧ ❧ ❧

The attack had been a show of power on Skullface's part. A significant percentage of the city of Boston—my city—had been abducted and held in mystic stasis. When I'd slaughtered the sorcerous supervillain and broken his spell, the city's residents had been returned home none the worse for wear. All residents save for my sister.

One theory I believed to be promising was that Whisper had become something akin to a disembodied spirit. She'd been a unique creature, a new life form...clever and kind and perfect! The 'spell' hadn't been designed with a wonder like her in mind, and thus the effect that separated her psyche from her circuits may have been flawed. If this conjecture could be verified, then I would be one step closer to rescuing my sister.

Unfortunately, the literature on disembodied spirits was limited and it was difficult to separate fact from fiction. The mystical arts had been mere fantasy in the ages before the alien Legion had fundamentally altered the boundaries between universes, and yet many of the most accurate tomes had been written centuries prior to changes in the laws of physics sweeping over the Earth. Belief had reshaped reality and super-stitions shifted into verifiable facts. But not all superstitions had made that transition, and only those with the correct inborn talent were able to sense the difference between truth and fable.

I did not have said talent...but I had science. And if Whisper was a disembodied spirit, then there was every chance that her psychic essence had become anchored in the vicinity of the quantum-connected servers that had once housed her consciousness.

The server-farm was vast—she'd had access to my entire infrastructure, a hidden network that had taken decades to build (or steal). My armor's sensors had been modified to identify akashic fields, but range was limited and the devices required time to function. I'd already checked the most-likely locations to no avail, but an exhaustive search would take months.

(According to what lore I'd been able to acquire, the energy-signature known as 'spirits' dissipate if outside their body too long. The moon's cycle supposedly had a powerful influence and Whisper had now been missing for seventy-four nights...but my sister was strong. I was going to find her and she was going to be fine. Her little android body was going to wake up, then she'd hug her puppy and we'd go to the beach and make sand castles. No other outcome was acceptable.)

Another theory was that displaced akashic fields might have a measurable effect on the operation of nearby quantum computers. If this proved true, then an analysis of past error logs might be able to pinpoint Whisper's location. Sadly, locating disembodied spirits to experiment upon had thus far been unsuccessful.

Most of my mystical knowledge had been gathered from the library of a supervillain who'd been known as the Ancient. Even under the effects of sleep deprivation, neural pruning and psychochemical reshaping, however, I was not so dehumanized as to believe that the Ancient's methods of procuring test subjects were morally justifiable. He'd been a monster! Hundreds had been kidnapped and murdered to further his grand experiments.

I was not so far gone. Not yet. Fortunately, if all that was required was an akashic field separated from a body, then other options were available.

My construction automatons had been tasked with moving a vast array of sensors and computing power to my ocean-floor laboratory. In the lonely deep, there were no other higher life-forms that might pollute my data. There was only me: one willing test subject, ready for the upcoming procedure.

Whisper had loved the ocean, loved the look and sound of the waves, and adored everything that lived under the water's surface. She loved accompanying me to this laboratory. A very thorough cleaning would be necessary before Whisper could join me here again.

I thought of siblings whom I'd failed and raised the handgun to my mouth.

❦ ❦ ❦

"Terry. Terrrrrrry. Wake up!"

A small hand nudges at my shoulder. I keep my eyes closed and try not to react; I'm certain that it's too early for Bobby to be waking me up. I'm still far too exhausted for this.

The first time that I'd made the bus-ride home from college had seemed like an adventure. My first real unchaperoned trip. There was something magical about the anonymity. Inside that foul-smelling, overheating compartment we were all of us awkwardly alone. The enchantment faded quickly. Last night's journey had left me aching and tired and irritable.

The hand withdraws, and then the bed shifts as a skinny eight-year-old climbs up to pat at my face. "Wake uuuuup!"

I flinch reflexively and my little brother giggles.

"I'm tired," I whine, rolling over onto my other side.

After a few moments, I feel the bed shift again as my little brother circles around. Small hands once again pat at my cheeks, molding my lips to make a funny fish-face. "It's breakfast time."

"It's too early." I sit up and glance at the clock across the room then recoil. "Or not. Okay, I'm sorry. Do you want cereal?"

"Uh-huh. With raisins."

"Okay, okay. Lemme up."

Bobby crawls off the bed and I pull on my clothes. I'm supposed to be babysitting today because our parents are visiting a gallery owner who'd hosted one of Mom's showings. So far, I wasn't off to a great start.

Trudging to the kitchen saps what is left of my energy, and the bowls, milk and cereal all seem unnaturally heavy as I fumble to arrange a meal. Bobby has already climbed into his chair and is gripping his spoon eagerly.

"Here y'go." I set his bowl down and he dives in. My own breakfast is picked at more slowly. My need for coffee is growing to epic proportions.

Mom 'n Dad don't like when I drink coffee. I have two PhD's now and they still treat me like a kid. I'm eighteen! But they don't keep coffee in the house even though they both drink it when they're out. It's stupid. It's not fair.

"I need help with my homework," Bobby pipes up, and I wince when I notice the mess that he's making at the table. Milk spatters and soggy corn flakes are strewn about haphazardly.

"What subject?"

Everyone drinks coffee at the university. I have my own coffee maker in my office. Next time, I'm going to bring it home with me.

"Math," Bobby replies. "You're a good math person, you can help me, right?"

Despite my discomfort, I can't help but smile. I'm going to post that label on my door before office hours. Dr. Terrance Markham: Good math person. "What chapter are you on?"

"Six!"

"Ok. Ten, three, nine, ten, five, two, five, four, eight, six, eight, and four."

Bobby stared at me, confused.

"Those are the answers for chapter six's homework. I read your textbooks last time I was home, remember?"

He runs off to find writing utensils and I clean the mess left behind. Bobby is taking a while, so I sit down and rest my eyes for just a moment.

My arm is poked again, this time with the back of a pencil. "Wake uuuup!"

"I was awake," I lie, grimacing as a wave of pain pulses behind my eyes. "What was the question?"

"The first one."

"Ten," I reply quickly. The headache is caused by caffeine withdrawal, I'm certain.

"Okay, but why?"

"Why what?"

"Why's the answer ten?" The hint of impatience in my little brother's voice is becoming more pronounced.

I sigh, "It just is."

"That's not a real answer."

"It's sixty divided by six," I bite out. "If you had sixty apples and divided them into groups of six apples each, you'd end up with ten piles of apples. Six times ten is sixty. It's basic! Only a moron needs help with this stuff!"

My little brother's eyes are filled with such hurt and betrayal that my chest aches from the sight of it.

"Bobby, wait, that isn't what I-"

He doesn't sob aloud—he just darts away from the table faster than I can react, and by the time I'm on my feet he's made it around the corner. The sound of his bedroom door slamming shut echoes throughout the house and, like a puppet with snipped strings, I collapse back into my chair and rest my head on my forearms.

"I'm sorry," I whisper even though I know that my brother

can't hear me.

In my mind's eye, I flip the sign on my office door. Dr. Terrance Markham: Mean math person.

※ ※ ※

My new body's hair was still wet from the liquid in the clone-tank and I felt chilled even though the undersea laboratory was maintained at its usual temperature. There had been sufficient clothing stored on-site—before my adopted sister came into my life, I'd spent more evenings in my laboratories than in my civilian identity's home and I'd often needed a change of outfits prior to returning to my 'day job' as CEO of a multinational biotechnology firm—but this fresh skin was overly sensitive at the moment.

I tried to ignore the shivering and focus on the test results.

Full neural realignment would take hours, I knew. My spare clone-bodies were maintained in a ready state by the medical nanites flowing through their veins and my memories were kept updated via my quantum-network-connected neural link. The actual 'soul transfer' was a more recent innovation: the first major piece of technology that I'd created utilizing information taken from the Ancient's library. He'd been an academically rigorous sorcerer and his lab notes had been sufficiently detailed that I had hopes of mimicking many so-called 'magical' effects using pure science.

The initial test results were promising. When my previous body had been rendered inoperable, my 'spirit' had been temporarily disembodied and then (manipulated by my akashic relocation device) thrust through a complicated array of sensors before being homed inside this new flesh.

Akashic fields are a multidimensional phenomenon, and (exactly as I'd predicted) their movement produced a measurable effect on the fields present within a quantum computer. Error correction algorithms prevented such variations from altering the computers' operation, but there were logs when those error corrections were performed. A disembodied spirit located near one of my server farms could be tracked!

And so my heart was pounding with eager optimism as I sorted through mountains of information. I remained still and calm as surgical automatons administered their final modifications upon my person, certain that at any moment I would find my sister and be able to begin the arduous effort of bringing her home. Even when the second pass resulted in no tangible results and I was forced to modify my data models, I was still buoyed with hope.

When that faith finally failed, it struck like a physical blow. The urge to howl, to lash out and destroy, to climb into my powered armor and lay waste to anything that crossed my field of vision was overwhelming. But that would be counterproductive.

Pain and I were old friends and I dared not allow this setback to delay additional labors. I'd wasted resources—creating and maintaining spare clone-bodies was expensive and I had fewer than a dozen stashed in hidden laboratories around the world—but this had been only one theory among many. It could now be stated with certainty that my sister's spirit had not become anchored near to any of my own laboratories...but there were entire worlds of possibilities still to be examined.

Slow, deep breaths helped to focus my thoughts. Bobby was dead, and in my heart of hearts I knew that I was to blame. If Whisper was dead then that too would be my fault, and that was not a possibility that I was willing to entertain. Whisper was out there, somewhere. Whisper needed me. And thus, there was more work to be done.

Fortunately, this body was well-rested and I could restart the clock on the pharmacological regimen required to stay awake and active for long periods of time. I ordered a few drones to clean the gory mess that still lay at the center of my lab and settled in to perform further analysis.

🕸 🕸 🕸

It was a pleasantly raucous night at Lassiter's Den. The FTW —the hacktivist collective once helmed by my deceased friend, Starnyx—had recently performed an infiltration of a major import-export company and were gathered here to celebrate.

Idealist non-violent anti-capitalists, members of their coalition never stole anything for themselves. Instead, they used their computer skills (and in some cases, superhuman abilities) in less-than-legal manners to combat corporate malfeasance. Their online broadcasts were viewed by millions and CEO's trembled in fear whenever rumors of a new FTW show were spread.

Lassiter's Den was a bar that catered to villains and

outlaws. The FTW may have been relatively innocuous as such organizations go, but they were more than welcome here. Root and Colonel Panic had brought a crowd of their non-powered fellow members, toasting their successful heist. The FTW's current leader, LuckySeven, was holding court at a table towards the back of the bar, explaining a timing-based software exploit to an eager audience of less experienced hackers. They were a clever, friendly group and their tendency to buy beers for other patrons had earned them a favorable reputation.

There were other colorful patrons present as well. Loose Cannon and Jynx were sidled up at the bar, and Minotaur and the Amazon were sharing a quiet drink over candlelight in the corner. Blackjack was here (did he ever go home?) surrounded by costumed minions. Unusually, no one in his crew seemed injured; that fact would explain their good cheer and loud laughter.

It was a busy Friday night, and it was here that Cloner was to meet with me.

A hush fell when I (as always, fully hidden within my iconic powered armor) floated smoothly into the room. Most of those here gathered were among the lower echelons of the superpowered criminal community. Doctor Fid might as well have been royalty. Also, I'd recently slaughtered several other high-powered villains, so the mixed reactions were understandable.

"Bill." I nodded in acknowledgment to the bartender. "A pint of Starnyx' favorite."

If the FTW was here en masse, it was inevitable that the barman would have ensured a reliable supply of the microbrew that their former leader had preferred. William Wasserman had been a fixture at Lassiter's for longer than I'd been a customer here and he was disturbingly competent at his job.

Lassiter's Den was a charming bar with a rich history. Decades past, the bar had been on the border of two organized-crime families' territories and members of both gangs came here to discuss peace between their organizations. Over time, the bar became accepted as neutral ground among the New York criminal community.

The location still maintained much of its old-world charm: the decor was all polished hardwood and warm tones, with lighting provided by candles and simulated gaslight. Violent, vicious criminals came here and were lulled into friendly camaraderie. If not for this place, I would likely never have had the opportunity to befriend Starnyx.

Starnyx had watched Whisper while I was indisposed. He read to her and jokingly called her his favorite shell script. If he were still alive, he would be mourning her absence. I missed my friend, and it now occurred to me that it had been foolhardy to remind Cloner to meet me here.

The leader of the New York Shield (arguably the most powerful superhero team on the East Coast) was aware of this place...but he'd evidently kept that knowledge close to his chest. No other heroes had performed raids and no vigilantes had arrived to break Lassiter's Truce. I could only hope that my choice in inviting Cloner back here would not motivate him to alter his hands-off policy.

Bill slid a pint glass into my armored hand and a snake-like tube extended from my forearm into the cool fluid. It wasn't so simple a mechanism as a straw. The beer was pumped up into a separate temperature-regulated reservoir within my armor and carried up to a mouthpiece hidden inside my faceless helm. I'd never bothered to figure out a means of eating solid food while masked, but imbibing liquid refreshments when among peers was...pleasant.

My sensors identified a familiar akashic field.

Cloner's power was the ability to create additional bodies. If there were a limit to the number or variety of forms that he could form, I had not been able to detect it. He'd once filled football fields standing shoulder to shoulder with himself and charged as one towards danger. Today, he had arrived as an attractive middle-aged woman of Filipino descent.

I waved her over as she entered, and she startled. Cloner was, I was sure, used to a certain amount of anonymity. The vast majority of his clones were nondescript and disappeared into a crowd.

As a hero, he was effective. As a spy, he was extraordinary.

In how many battles, I wondered, had the New York Shield triumphed only because Cloner had spent days exploring the battleground ahead of time? There were rumors that at one point he'd had thousands of active clones spread across the globe, each with their own careers and families and lives...Accountants and lawyers and pizza delivery guys and bank tellers. He supposedly had embedded his selves throughout society in order to gather gossip and information on a grand scale.

I hadn't created the technology to confirm the rumors,

then. But when Cloner had fallen under Legion control, it stood to reason that the entire hive-mind had been taken. Sorting through missing-persons cases from that time period did lend credence to the tale.

I claimed a table and the Filipino woman joined me. At my silent command, a secondary forcefield sprung up in a sphere around us, modulated such that it would not block physical movement but that any sound from within would be muffled. It would not do for any to eavesdrop on this conversation.

"Hey doc," she grinned, her expression shifting to that of the irreverent jokester persona that Cloner had hidden behind for years. The smile looked unnatural on her face. "You wanted to talk with me?"

I resisted the urge to order him not to call me 'Doc'. That had been Starnyx' nickname for me and I disliked hearing it from any other lips. But Cloner wouldn't obey and letting him know that he had a means to needle me seemed ill-planned. Given his sense of humor, I was certain that every hero in the U.S. would be addressing me in that manner within a week's time.

"I do," I replied with forced calm. "I was hoping to complete our negotiations."

"And I'm thinking that I should call the deal off," she retorted, still smiling despite the forceful tone that had crept into her voice. "You threatened one of my kids. That makes me wonder if'n you're really planning on keeping up your end of the bargain."

"You and I hadn't agreed to terms yet," I answered. "Also, Cherenkov was unharmed."

"And then you told him that I owed you a beer. Thanks for that, by the way. He has his teammates following every one of me that he knows about to see what bars they go to."

Outwardly, I was immobile, an implacable powered-armor shaped silhouette of the night sky with dim crimson accents. Unseen and unheard within that fearsome suit, I couldn't help but laugh as I realized that—as we spoke—Cloner was likely leading his students on a wild goose chase...or rather, several wild goose chases. I made a note to check the local news first thing tomorrow morning for any particularly amusing stories.

"You scared him," Cloner added, his voice deadly serious.

"Good. He's right to be wary," I chuckled darkly. "I'm agreeing to peace, not to pacifism."

Cloner frowned, tilting her head to glance towards the crowd of cheerful hacktivists. "That ship's sailed, huh?"

"It has."

After Starnyx's death, I'd joined the FTW and taken the same pledge of non-violence that all their members had sworn. I'd kept to the oaths while I was a member but when I'd been framed for murder, they had disavowed me none-theless. I had no regrets. My intention had been to honor my friend's memory, but the truth was that Doctor Fid was a poor fit for the organization that Starnyx had left behind. The FTW was better off without me.

"So, if you're still a scary villain...why should I trust you?"

"I've never broken my word," I answered gravely. "And you've trusted me in the past. After I saved you from the Legion. After I saved the Earth."

" 'n now you're askin' for access to tech that could wreck the world all over again."

I laughed, "You've seen me in battle. Do you really believe Dr. Chaise's technology to be more dangerous than my own?"

"No," she smiled resignedly. "I suppose I don't. But you threatened one of my kids to get to me. I'm not okay with that."

"Then allow me access to the device Skullface used when he attacked the United Nations. Negotiate terms and protect your trainees."

"All right." She closed her eyes for a moment, and when she opened them her expression was fiercely serious. "Yeah. Awright. Your last offer still valid?"

"It is."

"I'm adding one caveat. You stay away from the Junior Shield." Her voice held a strong tone of finality. "You don't use them to send messages anymore. Got it?"

"I do. And your terms are acceptable."

"Then we have a deal. I'll let you know when 'n where to pick up your loot."

I nodded and silently finished my beer before leaving Cloner and Lassiter's Den behind.

2

———

With the Mk 39 safely stored in the ocean-floor laboratory, I returned home via teleportation platform to my personal office where I was greeted by a hopeful puppy.

"Good girl." I forced a convincing smile and knelt to ruffle the wagging little black Labrador's fur. She rolled to her back and squirmed eagerly, so I petted her stomach as well. "Good girl. You want to go for a walk?"

Nyx (named in honor of Starnyx) yipped in what I interpreted to be an affirmative response, so I play-wrestled with her for a while before standing to grab her leash.

Most of the available literature suggested that canines of this age required significant emotional support and social feedback, so I'd rarely spent more than a few hours away from home. The majority of my research had been done here rather than in the laboratories that I'd hidden around the world. Whisper's pet needed to be well-cared-for when she returned or else she'd be sad.

It was only loud or potentially messy experiments that were relegated to the remote laboratories.

"Okay," I told the dog, calling upon well-trained acting experience to maintain a cheerful tone. "Let's go!"

Nyx barked again and bounced sideways, tail lashing back and forth with so much force that it looked like the gawky, adorable thing was going to injure itself. The pleasant volunteer at the adoption center had assured Whisper and me that the puppy would eventually grow into her oversized paws and lose that awkward gait. For now, though, she still tripped and tumbled when she got too excited while following at my heels. I made the appropriate happy noises and led my little sister's puppy out of my office.

Nyx slowed to a halt as we passed Whisper's room, tail lowered nervously. Ears folded down, she nosed into the room as if hopeful that her mistress might sit up and join us. But no. Whisper remained prone, her delicate android shell bereft of any consciousness.

This had been her second body and she'd only been occupying it for a few months before the incident, but Nyx had never known her in another form. We could have made her look completely human but that would have meant abandoning the aesthetic chosen by her creator. As such, we'd worked to make sure that this new body was more graceful with far more sensory capabilities so that she could interact pleasantly among her friends…but still with the pale too-perfect skin, elfin features and complete lack of hair that had been characteristic of her original body. When she was awake, her eyes glowed a pleasant robins-egg blue.

Her eyes were dim now, and for a moment I thought that

it was Nyx who was whimpering. I coughed to quiet the sound.

"It's all right," I shakily reassured the puppy. "She's just resting. She'll wake up soon, I promise. C'mon, let's go play fetch."

Nyx resisted being pulled away from the door at first, pining, then followed after me with less joyous abandon than before.

It was some time before the puppy became fully involved in her play. We jogged and played tug-of-war with furry toys and I threw dog-slobber-covered tennis balls. I wasn't a young man but this highly-modified body was well-rested and only a few hours old. My little sister's dog was kept entertained until dusk began to fall, and even if my face were streaked with tears I played the role that was required of me.

🐛 🐛 🐛

The Face of Mourning

Trouble looms for embattled company AH Biotech while former CEO grieves the loss of a child. Can the company he founded survive without him?

By Russel Carre and Thomas Granger
Photo by Brian Ferris
Oct 6, 12:01 a.m. ET

It's been more than two months since

Terrance Markham stepped down as CEO of AH Biotech, and rumors of internal strife and lost productivity abound. Early hopes that the stock price would quickly rebound have proved unfounded, and investors who'd become used to the company's reliably meteoric growth are becoming nervous.

The new top man, former CIO Aaron Schwartz, has large boots to fill.

A Nobel prize-winning physicist turned businessman, Dr. Markham launched AH Biotech with bigger-than-life ideals. Long term employees treasure the t-shirts that proudly declared: "There is no goal two!".

Goal one was to save the world.

The early days of AHBT were characterized by big risks and bigger rewards, with funding put towards innovative lifesaving technologies and massive ecological engineering projects. The company's non-scarring quick-clot medicated bandages—apparently derived from the biological process that certain marine invertebrates use to form their exoskeleton—have saved thousands of lives, and other advances have led to the complete rehabilitation of two toxic Superfund sites. A diverse range of genetically engineered food crops have brought relief to famine-riddled regions. The promise of working on interesting and truly worthwhile projects lured top researchers away from many more well-established competitors, and the company named in honor of Dr. Markham's own mentor flourished.

"Aaron's a great guy," commented one AH Biotech employee who spoke of Dr. Markham's replacement under the condition of anonymity. "He's been with the company forever and he'll keep the lights on, for sure. He just doesn't know the science is all."

And a culture of scientific innovation is what top employees had come to expect. Two department heads have left AH Biotech in the last month, and whispers spread that a further exodus is inevitable.

Says current CEO Aaron Schwartz, "Some teething pains are unavoidable, but I have every confidence that we'll endure, heal and grow. Goal one hasn't changed!"

Bold, optimistic words, but many fear that the lack of scientific savvy at the executive level will hamper innovation. At a recent earnings call, investors pressed Mr. Schwartz for details on (cont'd page 18)

❀ ❀ ❀

Cloner had been true to his word. The waterfront warehouse was secured but unguarded, and the remnants of the Dimension Bomb designed by the late Dr. Chaise (weapons designer and second-in-command to the sorcerous criminal, Skullface) were packed in crates, ready for transport. With the Mk 39's stealth systems enabled and a swarm of micro-drones providing sensory data, I explored carefully before entering to examine my prize.

I should have simply left. My larger utility drones could easily have carried the crates aloft and flown them to the site of my choosing where I would be able to study their workings at my leisure. The truth, however, was that I didn't really need the majority of materials. The power supply and interfaces were inferior to my own, and the field augmentation module was of a design that I'd long since abandoned.

There was, however, a spark of genius buried amongst the dross. Dr. Chaise had used a massive energy dump to create space-time ripples, carefully modulated to increase the area affected by his weapon. It was a brilliant innovation. He and his employer would have truly become a force to be reckoned with had he recognized some of the other ways in which the method could have been utilized. But in the end... he'd primarily been a weapons designer rather than a scientist. What a terrible waste of skill and intellect.

Yet another reason why I, in retrospect, felt justified in tearing his spine from his corpse.

(In truth, it had been pure rage that had guided me. That, and the need to take something irreplaceable from Skullface. I'd found Chaise only hours after laying Whisper's empty body in her bed and placing her favorite doll in her arms. The brutality had been...unnecessary. Someday—when my sister was home safe and all this was behind us—I would come to regret that act, I was sure. Remorse was a luxury in which I had no time to indulge, hence the neurosurgery and chemical treatment intended to focus my attention appropriately.)

Given sufficient time and energy, I was certain that I could have mimicked Dr. Chaise's accomplishment without seeing the remnants in person. Time was not, however, a resource that I had in abundance. So...I opened crates and carefully sifted through the wreckage, sorting through components until I could isolate pieces of the puzzle that would aid in the next device that I needed to craft: an expanded sensor array that would be able to detect disembodied akashic fields at range.

I was just beginning to develop a theory as to how the mechanism functioned when a blast of iridescent purple energy struck my back and crates exploded into kindling as I plowed through them. The armor's forcefields and other automated defensive capabilities responded automatically, however, long before I hit the far wall.

That energy attack was familiar to me, and I supposed that I should have expected this interruption. This warehouse was located in Brooklyn, and Brooklyn's local heroes were actually refugees from an alternate dimension. They'd been brought here by the effects of this very device: an interdimensional rift that had torn them from an Earth in ruins and carried them here instead.

Fate has an odd sense of humor. I've done the statistical analysis to demonstrate it.

"Psion!" I roared, relaying my digitally altered voice through the microdrones' external speakers so that my anger echoed throughout the structure. "This is not a good time. Leave me to my work and you and yours can escape unharmed!"

The leader of the Brooklyn Knights, Psion was a slender woman of Korean descent whose energy blasts were characterized by their vivid purple coloration. Her costume consisted of a burnt-orange bodysuit with dull yellow accents, but I could not see her now. None of my sensors were able to locate the source of the attack.

Another member of their team—Wildcard—had an extraordinary array of powers available to him but could only manifest three at a time; he must have sacrificed one of his combat-related abilities to generate an invisibility field so thorough that even the radar, liDAR and sonar modes of my threat-detectors had been fooled.

I floated a few inches above the ground, waiting, hopeful that perhaps the Brooklyn Knights had heeded my warning. Hopeful, but not optimistic. I'd fought them before, after all.

And then my wait was at an end. White Tigress—a nine-foot-tall humanoid feline behemoth—snarled a challenge, seeming to blink into existence only inches from connecting with a vicious swipe of her claws to the side of my head. She was powerful and brutal, but my forcefields were more than sufficient to resist cutting damage and I'd been punched by heroes far stronger than she. While I was rocked back from the force of the blow, my inertial displacement field minimized any significant trauma.

"You just couldn't leave well enough alone," the unseen

Psion accused as her teammate set upon me in murderous frenzy. Impressively, Wildcard's invisibility was so thorough that I could not pinpoint her location by the direction of her voice. "That weapon is too dangerous for anyone to use ever again. Even you!"

Hm. If the Brooklyn Knights were aware of the crates' contents, then their presence here was not an improbable coincidence after all. Annoyingly, neither was it betrayal: the contract that I'd offered Cloner stated only that the New York Shield would not interfere when I came to collect my prize.

The smirking annoyance had found a loophole and sent another team in his stead.

The Brooklyn Knights were a good choice. Given their connection to the device in question, it was more likely that they would be willing to risk battle against the notorious Doctor Fid. And it was well-known that I'd spared the Knights any serious injury in our prior conflicts. After I'd saved this world from the menace that had ravaged their own, they'd made a point of carrying a chilled six-pack on their patrols, on the off chance that they might run into me so they could offer a bottle in gratitude.

That had been a good beer.

Sending the Knights might have been a rational choice but it was poor strategy on Cloner's part. I was in no mood to be gentle.

"I'm not making a weapon," I grunted, floating a few feet off the ground so that I was eye level with the White Tigress as we fought. "I need this for personal research only."

The felinoid heroine was fast and agile. She kept close

and battered at me with strike after strike, attempting to keep me occupied while her teammates repositioned. I allowed my armor's combat algorithms to fight with minimal piloting input on my own part. Focused martial arts training and decades of battle had honed my own fighting skills but the Mk 39's automated systems had quicker reflexes. My own focus was directed upon re-programming sensors to detect air movement, unexpected energy signatures...no cloaking method I'd ever encountered had been absolute and Wildcard's would be no exception.

"We can't trust you." Shrike called, a hint of hurt betrayal creeping into his voice. "Not after you started killing again."

Shrike and I had come to an accord on more than one occasion and I supposed that he'd believed in (and supported) my short-lived attempt at rehabilitation. The efforts had been honest at the time, but Skullface's excesses had forced me to loosen the chains holding back the more monstrous portions of my soul. The kinder, gentler Fid could not have done what had been necessary to save the city of Boston. The kinder, gentler Fid might balk at what might be necessary to rescue Whisper. Unacceptable.

Tail lashing, the massive anthropomorphic tigress roared and flipped and leapt about, and I blocked and countered as though we were partners in a smooth, violent dance. I kept close. Several of White Tigress' teammates had ranged attacks but any barrage that might be capable of damaging my armor would do far worse to the furred fighter if she were accidentally struck. It was a race to see which would occur first: the Brooklyn Knights setting up what they believed might be an overwhelming assault, or my technology unveiling their precise locations.

"I had cause," I graveled in belated reply to Shrike's accusation. "Chaise and Skullface needed to die."

"Not your place to judge," White Tigress yowled, eyes glowing fiercely.

"I don't enjoy taking on that responsibility," I replied seriously, "but I will if I must."

Given that White Tigress' response consisted of an attempt to bite my face off, I supposed that my argument had been unconvincing.

Of the Brooklyn Knights, only Shrike and Wildcard were serious threats. The former, because the yellow-white spikes and planes of force that he could summon were impossibly hard, immovable, and sharp (Shrike had accidentally cut my arm off, once), and the latter because I could never quite be certain what powerset I was facing when Wildcard was on the field (surprises were always dangerous.) Psion, Blizzard and the White Tigress were fine heroes. Against a lesser opponent they would be an extremely formidable team.

Doctor Fid was no lesser opponent.

I laughed, loud and mocking, and shifted to a more aggressive stance, adding kinetic energy blasts to my repertoire and pummeling White Tigress with powerful physical attacks. I had the Brooklyn Knights' measure now; spectral chromatography was able to detect the carbon dioxide the hidden heroes exhaled, and I could see that they'd spread out to box me in.

The Tigress reared back reflexively when a backfist bloodied her muzzle and I shot forward to grab her massive wrist in one hand. My other fist slammed into her elbow with a resounding crack.

"No!" shouted an unseen Blizzard and a swirling cone of superchilled air and sleet poured towards me. The thick sheet of ice that had instantaneously encased my upper body shrieked and crackled as I shrugged it away, and I replied with a subsonic pulse that shook the soft tissue of Blizzard's lungs so thoroughly that it would be half a minute before he could draw a breath.

Two down and three to go. Unfortunately, the White Tigress had taken advantage of the brief moment when I'd been slowed by ice to leap away and nurse her broken arm. Without a hostage, there was nothing staying the remainder of the knights' attacks.

Psion and Shrike launched their assault: dozens of yellow-white needles of impenetrable force sprung up from the ground as Shrike tried to pierce my armor (or perhaps merely to entrap me). I swiveled and danced through the increasingly dense, dangerous maze while Psion poured energy blast after vivid purple energy blast upon me. I retaliated with weak energy blasts of my own, intended more to keep them moving than to inflict injury. I had no objections to breaking a few of their bones, but they hadn't earned any more permanent damage.

Wildcard also revealed the second of his currently-available powers: a localized electro-magnetic pulse to disable electronic devices. Unfortunately for him, the Mk 39 was very well shielded. His choice had been tactically sound, but in the end he'd chosen a power that would be of no use.

It's rare, but sometimes chance does actually work in my favor.

"It didn't work!" Wildcard called, voice rising with the first hints of fear. I'd left him unconscious in all of our prior battles, and that was before my more recent violent excesses had become public knowledge.

"Get ready for a retreat," Psion ordered grimly.

I laughed louder, victorious. Wildcard's final power must be transportation-based! Teleportation, perhaps? In any case, it seemed likely that I could dismiss him as a threat. Whatever Cloner had planned by sending the Brooklyn Knights to interfere, his plot had failed.

Another bright purple stream of energy splattered off my helm, but my shields were operating at full capacity. So long as I was able to weave through the maelstrom of pillars and spikes that Shrike was calling forth in an attempt to cage me, there was nothing to fear. I sent carefully-controlled bursts of plasma in Shrike and Psion's direction, but was careful to allow White Tigress time to pick up the fallen Blizzard, to hasten their inevitable 'escape'.

"Wall him off!" Psion ordered, and Shrike summoned an impenetrable barrier between myself and the gathering heroes.

And then Psion aimed one final blast, more powerful than any she'd thrown thus far. Despite the intensity, my forcefields would have easily withstood the flood of purple power...had the attack been directed towards me.

"No!" I howled, jerking sideways and unleashing a torrent of emerald-hued gyrating energies at the retreating heroes. A deluge of pulsing force-field needles sprayed forth.

For a moment, it seemed as though time itself had stopped and I stared at my own outstretched hand, disbelieving.

And then the bodies fell and blood began to flow. Shrike's guttural rasp as he collapsed was going to haunt me, I knew.

A desperate, plaintive mewling filled the air and the White Tigress stepped protectively in front of her companions. She could barely stand. That particular weapon had never been intended for use against any but those with the most powerful regenerative capabilities.

It was an ugly tool.

"They're alive," I told her. "For now. Take them and go."

The giant humanoid tigress kept wary eyes upon me as she quickly gathered her injured and groaning friends and brought them closer to Wildcard. I watched impassively. I should have moved to help, but I couldn't find the will to step forward.

There were puncture wounds all along Wildcard's left side and one that looked to have pierced his jawbone, but his expression was fiercely focused even as he struggled to breathe. He closed his eyes in concentration, and all five critically wounded heroes disappeared in a flash.

"Damn it all," I whispered, hands shaking. Some of the Knights' blood had aerosoled from the initial impact. Even as I watched, the gory mist was settling into uneven, messy splotches on the warehouse floor.

They'd live, I told myself, and wished that I felt more certain of that judgement. It would take only a handful of minutes for Wildcard to shift his powerset to regeneration and healing. In a half hour's time the Brooklyn Knights' pain would be only a memory, while mine was only beginning.

The crates of components—the last remnants of technology that I'd hoped would locate Whisper—had been rendered into unusable scrap in one tsunami of vivid purple power.

❧ ❧ ❧

"It's all right," I told Nyx, my hands shaking from the effort of restraining my rage. I tried to pet the puppy, but she squirmed away and licked at my fingers. To comfort me, I imagined. "I can still bring her home. I have partial scans, that will be enough."

There was a part of me that wanted nothing more than to declare war upon Cloner. To gather up my most powerful combat drones and every scrap of offensive weaponry I'd ever designed and to rain destruction on the New York Shield headquarters. But I could slaughter them all and salt the Earth and the effort would not get me one second closer to finding my sister.

My internal medical systems were quickly reprogrammed to synthesize benzodiazepines and antipsychotics. I needed to calm down and I needed to work. I needed to concentrate.

It was not, I decided, the Brookyn Knights' fault. There was further punishment in store whenever we next crossed paths, of course, but I recognized that they were only obeying their nature. They were heroes, and letting children suffer was what heroes did. Sometimes on purpose, sometimes by accident...they couldn't help themselves. If the so-called 'heroes' were actually a positive force within society, there never would have been a need for Doctor Fid.

I'd forgotten that. I'd treated the Knights as though they were worthy of respect simply because they were honest, noble, and dedicated to their ideals. That wasn't a mistake I would make again.

The superhero named Bronze had let Bobby die, a conscious choice to protect his own secret identity rather than to protect the innocent. The Knights' crime was not so severe. Their self-righteous refusal to allow me to complete my research in peace may have slowed progress, but I would persevere. Whisper was strong and she'd be able to wait the extra time.

(According to intercepted radio communications, none of the Brooklyn Knights had perished. Wildcard had tele-ported the group to a hospital where all team members were stabilized until superpowered healing could be applied. Damn them all.)

It was Cloner who I didn't understand. I'd reached out to him and offered far more than had been required of him in return. He had to suspect that my motivations were personal. He had to suspect that I was desperate. Was he actively attempting to incite me to further violence?

If so, I would need to be wary. Cloner's joking, irreverent mien was a facade; there was a fiendishly devious mind hiding behind that annoying smile. If he thought to provoke me then calm evaluation would be the safer choice. Unless, perhaps, this had been stage one of a risky double bluff...an attempt to force me to second guess my future interactions with him.

I could not know for certain. In any case, the leader of the New York Shield may not have violated the word of our agreement, but he had certainly violated its spirit. There would be no further negotiations between us, no deals and no forgiveness.

I'd never claimed to be a hero, so I would (of course) be the better man. The letter of the law would be my guide, and someday I'd find an entertaining loophole...for now, though, Cloner was the least of my concerns.

"It's all right," I reassured Nyx again. I could feel the psychoactive drugs streaming throughout my system working. "I have an idea. C'mon, let's go to my lab."

Whisper's puppy followed at my heels as I headed to the teleportation platform hidden in my home office.

3

Nyx was settled comfortably in makeshift bedding
thrown together from old towels and I donned the Mk 39
once more. The medical devices hidden beneath my ribcage
and the nanites flowing through my veins were effective at
certain tasks, but their resources were limited. The systems
built into my armors would be more efficient for long-term
usage. The Brooklyn Knights' exploits had cost me time, and
I did not intend to lose any more to inconsequentials like
sleep. Psychoactive compounds poured into my brain and I
immersed myself fully into my studies.

I had yet to fully complete my evaluation of the Dimension Bomb's fragments, but what concepts I'd been able to
unearth thus far were intriguing, and I had to admit that the
math was elegant. It was surprising that a hack like Chaise
had stumbled across so exceptional a theory. The practical
application relied upon universal constants that had been
shifted due to the Legion's tampering more than a century

past, and the echoes of the interstellar event that had created their own telepaths...and the emergence of superpowers on this planet.

Using a variation of this discovery, I could predict other regions of the universe in which superpowered beings might also have come to exist. They were distant, certainly, but the existence of the Legion's space-faring armada indicated that distant entities could still be a threat. I made a note to study the implications in greater detail another time. For now, my attention was riveted upon a very specific problem: dramatically expanding the range of my akashic identification sensors.

I poked and prodded at the formulas for hours, heart racing and mind swirling with the possibilities. After a time, I stepped out of the Mk 39 armor to do my work by hand; even though my neural tap allowed for an intuitive and simple interface with my quantum computer farms, for some things an array of blackboards was still superior.

In a strange way, my time in academia—as a student and later as a professor—was likely the happiest period of my life. I was a lonely outcast, of course, but I had my studies. My world was pure math and pure science then. The feel of chalk in my fingers, the dry taste of dust on my lips...it felt like coming home.

I paused occasionally, using my neural tap to route calculations to remote computer systems, to confirm results or to run simulations based upon quickly jotted estimates...but the greater part of the work was struck in white scribbles on slate while I wandered from board to board. Every quirk was compared against existing data, whether from previous experiments or from the decades of compiled sensor read-ings either gathered myself or stolen from researchers around the world. That one simple finding could be applied to the study of physics in so many ways...it was magnificent. It was rapturous.

It was useless.

I stood, as still as a statue, as I re-ran the calculations in my head. Programs checked and re-checked my results, and each outcome was the same: this new discovery could not be used for the purpose that I desired. My civilian identity could, perhaps, squeeze another Nobel prize from these findings, but it would not help me locate Whisper.

Energy and enthusiasm fled.

The chalk was put away and a towel dampened to clean the blackboards. The work was done at a slow, deliberate pace, and when it was completed I picked up a sleeping puppy and activated the teleportation platform.

If I'd stayed in the lab with the Mk 39 only feet away, I was reasonably certain that the evening would have ended in murder. I was not yet so far gone that such a choice seemed an appealing option, so I returned home and laid the little black Labrador next to her unmoving mistress.

"I'll bring her back." I was careful not to wake the puppy as I stroked her sable fur, "I don't know how, but I will."

Numb and listless, I stumbled back to my room. There was no plan, no next step in mind, so the use of psychoactive chemical stimulants to stay awake would have served no purpose. Instead, I decided to allow myself a handful of hours of rest and embark into a new approach the following day. This was a setback, not an ending. Violence was painfully tempting...though in the end, unnecessary.

But I tasked a few search programs to locate the Brooklyn Knights civilian identities' homes just in case I changed my mind.

❧ ❧ ❧

That it was the doorbell that awakened me was testament to how exhausted I'd allowed my recently-decanted body to become. Layers upon layers of alerts had been transmitted directly into my sleeping brain via neural tap...one when a familiar vehicle approached my estate's driveway, another when attempts were made to contact me via the intercom at the gate, and still another when the appropriate code was entered to bypass the gate's security. I hadn't stirred, not until the insistent chime startled me from my slumber.

I used my neural tap to review streamed security footage and groaned. There wasn't anything on my schedule and I didn't recall making plans to meet...but I couldn't simply pretend not to be home. My visitor would know better.

Pulling on loose-fitting clothes was the work of a few seconds, then I half-stumbled half-jogged to the door.

"Aaron," I forced a shaky approximation of a smile. "It's good to see you."

As I spoke the words aloud, I was surprised to find that they felt true.

Aaron Schwartz was the closest thing that Terry Markham—my civilian persona—had to a friend. He knew nothing of my dual identity, of course, but he'd worked alongside me for the better part of a decade and his daughter had been Whisper's closest companion.

I accepted his offered hand gratefully and then stepped aside and gestured for him to enter. "How's Dinah doing?"

"Not great. Not terrible. She's sad, but she's coping. She misses her friend." He paused, then smiled sadly as though he already knew the answer to the question he was about to ask. "How's Whisper?"

I couldn't respond aloud, so I just shook my head. Aaron blinked away tears and awkwardly gripped at my shoulder in silent sympathy.

My status as a respected CEO had been used to lobby for the bill that had allowed AIs to be accepted as United States citizens, and as the first completely artificial being to be recognized under the Synthetic Americans Rights act my ward/sister had become something of a minor celebrity. Aaron and Dinah's loyalty and acceptance had helped Whisper through a confusing, stressful time.

After Skullface's spell, I'd told him that I needed time away from our company to try and save Whisper, to wake her up. He'd had no understanding of the technical aspects of my quest but had simply offered whatever support he could provide.

(The public aspect of Whisper's link to Dr. Terrance Markham complicated Doctor Fid's conduct. If the actions I took when behind the starfield mask were too overt—if it became obvious that the armored villain were searching for a means to help a little android girl—then my secret identity would be revealed. Fortunately, I knew of no one who might make that connection.)

"Do you want something to drink?" I asked when I could speak again.

"No, thank you," he shook his head. "I just wanted to check in on you and see how you were doing."

"I've...had a few setbacks," I looked away, avoiding his sympathetic gaze. "But I'm still hopeful."

"It's been more than two months," he noted. "And you don't look well."

"I'm...not," I admitted.

"I know. I wouldn't be, either. But if there's anything I can do..."

"Just take good care of our company," I managed a half-smile.

He winced. "It's not as easy as you made it look."

"What's going on?"

"Frank Tierney put in his two weeks' notice today," my friend sighed.

Thoughts swirled. "Is another company poaching from our employee list?"

"No, he's retiring." Aaron shrugged helplessly.

Dr. Tierney was passionate about his work; retirement wasn't going to be a comfortable fit. I imagined that he'd be seeking a new berth within six months, and Frank was smart enough to know it. If he was leaving, then something had gone terribly wrong with the company that I'd founded. And that implied that Aaron's visit had a secondary purpose beyond merely to offer sympathy.

"I can't come back," I told AH Biotech's current CEO in a desperate rush. "I can't. I'm needed here, you have no idea how complicated this is. Whisper needs me."

"Just come in and shake some hands, see if you can figure out why the researcher groups are so unhappy," Aaron cajoled. "Everyone would love to see you."

"I can't, Aaron."

"We're hemorrhaging talent and I have no idea why!" He waved a hand irritably, "I may be warming your seat, but it's still your company. You're the largest individual shareholder. Just...come in. Help me get a handle on things."

"You want help? Tell Frank he's funded for the kelp carbon sequestration project, he'll show up to work on Monday like nothing happened. It'll lose money for a few years, but it'll keep him around and that means keeping Annette and Xing. Qiangguo will want in on the project but make sure he stays on radiation cleanup, he's close to a breakthrough. Have Natalie replace Reyansh on plastic-metabolizing plankton and put Reyansh on Frank's project. And tell William in Microbiology that he's doing a great job but if he talks to a reporter again, he's fired."

"What the hell?" Aaron stared at me. "Were you just sitting on that and watching me fail? If you knew how to fix this, why didn't you tell me?"

"I trusted you to figure it out on your-"

"How the hell am I supposed to figure it out if you don't tell me anything?" Aaron gestured expressively, "Damnit, Terry, the people who're still alive need your help too!"

I stared, and Aaron recoiled from whatever he saw in my gaze.

"I...I didn't mean that Whisper is dea-" he backtracked.

"Get out of my house."

"I'm sorry," he begged. "Please, Terry, you have to know I wouldn't-"

"Wouldn't try and blame me for your failures just because you forgot how to pick up a phone when you got my job? Wouldn't show up on my doorstep begging for my help while my ward is sick?" I glared, "Please, tell me what you wouldn't do!"

"I'm your friend, Terry."

"Right now, it doesn't feel like it. Get out!"

"Yeah. Okay, fine." His earlier annoyance had faded, leaving only weary sadness. "Any other last bits of wisdom you care to offer before I leave?"

I considered. "Get Theo back. I know he quit...call him, give him whatever he wants, just get him back and make him Chief Strategy Officer. He's as good as I am at identifying promising projects, and the folks in R&D will respect his opinion if he shoots them down."

"The Board will need to approve any new executive positions..." Aaron noted quietly.

"I'll take care of it. Just get out and leave me alone!"

"All right." He paused by the door and his sad sincerity was painful to look upon. "I *am* your friend. And I'm sorry."

Dr. Terrance Markham: Mean ex-CEO person, I thought to myself miserably, watching Aaron walk to his car. But I didn't call him back.

There was still work to be done.

❧ ❧ ❧

Annoyingly, I was beginning to believe that the Brooklyn Knights had been correct in their desire to keep the Dimension Bomb's workings hidden. With fresh, well-rested eyes, I'd returned to examine the prior night's data. Thus far, six separate means to use the discoveries to construct doomsday devices had been posited and not a single method which would help in my quest to locate Whisper.

And that suggested another avenue of investigation.

The Brooklyn Knights were straightforward and heroic. They worked well as a team. None of them, however, were experts in high-energy inter-dimensional physics. Why had they been so certain that the wreckage held dangerous clues? The device that Dr. Chaise and Skullface had used in their ill-fated assault upon the United Nations building had caused some level of destruction, but not so much that a casual observer would be aware of the existential threat that this technology represented.

Someone else must have analyzed the machine and informed them of the dangers.

There weren't a great many people in the world who were mentally equipped and sufficiently educated to have understood the physics involved. The lion's share of those who could were academics and thus not particularly well-trained in the practical skills of weapons design. Some others were villains: inventors or geniuses looking to use their talents for grand goals or self-enrichment. Finally, a much smaller number were heroes. I doubted that the Knights had any contacts among the first group nor would they have taken advice from the second, so it was likely a member of the last group who had provided analysis of the

Bomb that had cracked inter-dimensional barriers and brought the Brooklyn Knights from their own post alien-invasion apocalyptic universe to this one.

I suspected that the Knights had consulted with Professor Paradigm.

Paradigm was a west-coast based inventor/hero who'd been one of the founding members of San Francisco's premier superhero team. I imagined that he just liked the alliteration when introducing himself as Professor Paradigm of the Paragons. Although he'd long since retired from active duty, he was still well connected to the cape-and-cowl community. His fortune was maintained by providing non-lethal weapons, protective gear and transportation for super-heroes around the world.

Several of his designs were adequate and he was rumored to be a thorough researcher. It was entirely possible —given that he'd had longer to study the device—that he'd uncovered some aspect of its workings that eluded me. If I could gain access to his research then I might find a hint at what I was missing.

The Professor's security was legendary. Rumor had it that the Gray Cat, one of the world's most talented burglars, had tried and failed to break into Paradigm's sanctum, and Whisper and I working together had been unable to find a flaw in his computer system's integrity. Furthermore, he put as much effort as I did to ensure that his work could not be reverse engineered.

After my dealings with Cloner, the idea of negotiating with a hero left a bitter taste in my mouth. If any better option was available to me, however, I did not see it. And so,

I swallowed my pride and sent a carefully worded e-mail. And then, there was nothing to do but to wait for a response.

And, perhaps, to respond to requests made by others.

※ ※ ※

There was no subtlety to my landing. The crash echoed in the dimly lit abandoned warehouse and debris and dust scattered in a chaotic haze around me. The impact was no strain upon the Mk 39's frame and the cacophony was useful in alerting my quarry of my presence.

The Red Ghost's scarlet cowl hid the majority of his face, but my sensors were able to reveal a cautious frown that touched the corners of his lips and that his brows were furrowed in intense observation. His hands were close to (but not quite touching) the high-tech batons that hung at his hips.

The Mk 39 had been designed to withstand battle against powerhouses like Titan or Majestic, but it would have been beyond foolish to ignore the threat. The crimson-clad hero's raw offensive capabilities were not nearly so potent, but his quick mind (and tendency to repurpose weapons confiscated from villains) made him a dangerous adversary. Mentally, I ran a quick diagnostic to ensure that my predictive combat algorithms were operating at peak efficiency.

"What?" I growled. The armor's vocoder usually stripped emotion from my voice but this time lost its battle to disguise my impatience.

"I didn't think that you'd arrive so soon," the Red Ghost

replied guardedly. "My invitation was sent less than a half hour ago."

"You summoned me and I came." I gestured with both hands to our surroundings. "What do you need?"

To arrest you for nearly killing the Brooklyn Knights, his expression said. But his voice was calm: "A shipment of control boards arrived damaged. I thought that I should get your input first rather than reaching out to my supplier."

So. We were going to avoid mentioning the elephant in the room, then. No matter.

More than a year ago, the Ghost and I had agreed to work together to bring some of my life-saving technologies to the world-at-large. The public narrative was that the crimson cloak-wearing hero had reverse engineered a device that he'd captured after one of our many battles; in actuality, my condition had been that I maintained control of manufacturing key components in order to keep the technology from being stolen and mis-used. Many of my inventions could be used to catastrophic effect if ever they fell into the wrong hands.

(Some would argue that my hands already were the wrong hands. The sentiment is understandable...but given that I've never accidentally torn cities off the face of the earth by mis-calibrating a forcefield, I contended that the safest hands were still my own.)

The first mechanism we'd conspired to deploy had been a modified inertial displacement system to be installed in motor vehicles. At first, the devices had been so expensive to produce that only high-end luxury cars could afford them. With mass production, the cost was coming down.

When last I'd checked, there'd only been a single fatality caused by impact in one of the vehicles thus equipped: a small sportscar struck by a freight train. The inertial displacement field had been overwhelmed then disrupted when the frame buckled. My armor would have survived such a blow, but the amount of power, layered protections, and structural augmentation necessary to create that level of safety was well beyond the capability of anything that could be mass produced.

"I'll look into it," I informed the Ghost. I'd already figured out what had caused the issue. A quick check via my neural tap found a notification that my automated factory had run low on supplies. I should have caught that. Whisper, whose multitasking and information-gathering capabilities bordered on the ludicrous, would have reminded me if I had let that slip. But Whisper was gone and I'd been understandably distracted. "The problem will be fixed shortly."

The Red Ghost's shoulders relaxed only slightly. "Thank you."

"If I decide to change our agreement, I'll tell you to your face." I sighed exasperatedly. And then, because I was feeling petty, I added: "I'm not a hero, after all."

"Cloner told me what he'd done," he shook his head. "Honestly, I'd been worried that you'd sabotaged the shipment in retaliation. I should have known better."

I barked in laughter, and my vocoder made the sound sinister. "That's kind of you to say, but now that you've mentioned it I have to admit that I find the idea tempting."

"Please don't," the Hispanic hero asked gently. "We're

saving lives. Despite how things ended with the Brooklyn Knights, I know that you still value that."

While I wanted to believe that he was correct, that priority felt academic when measured against my need to see my sister safe. In the end, I simply sighed. "I am...grateful...that you are willing to continue our dealings. I had half-expected for this meeting to end in violence."

"For what you did to the Brooklyn Knights?"

"And for what I did to Skullface and Dr. Chaise," I replied. "You were angry when you discovered that I'd killed Imperator Rex."

"I was angry because I'd believed that you'd killed Imperator Rex for personal reasons," he shook his head slowly. "Skullface and Dr. Chaise were killed to save our city. I'm not going to lie...I'm not happy that you chose to commit murder, but I do understand. My wife was among those who were kidnapped by Skullface's spell. As was I. And as for the Knights...You hurt them badly, but you also let them go. I think Cloner can claim as much blame as can you."

I found myself oddly touched.

"That having been said," the Red Ghost continued, a hint of steel sneaking into his tone. "I don't condone your recent actions."

And now came the expected righteous judgment. I cut my external speakers so that he could not hear my exasperated sigh.

"I'm serious," he said crossly. Somehow, he must have guessed that I'd rolled my eyes; I checked my body-language control algorithms and suit telemetry but did not discover any anomalies.

It was possible that I'd spent too much time conversing with the Red Ghost rather than simply fighting against him, and he'd grown able to interpret my sudden silences. A worrying proposition.

"You've become more aggressive in the months since Skullface," he continued, "and if you didn't sabotage the delivery on purpose then you made a mistake you wouldn't have made three months ago."

"We're done here," I bit out. "I'll ensure that another shipment of control boards arrives within five business days."

"Don't dismiss this," he frowned. "Titan has recovered and the Boston Guardians are back to full strength. We're grateful to you for saving our city, but that doesn't grant you immunity if you continue down this dark path. We'll stop you."

"You won't." I stated evenly, though my blood felt as if it were boiling in my veins. "Not this time. There are tasks I need to accomplish, and you and yours had best stay out of my way."

"We won't do that. We can't."

"Then I suggest that you train someone at the manufacturing facility to take over in the event of your untimely demise!"

For a long moment, there was silence.

"You and I have fought for nearly a decade," the Red Ghost frowned. "Yet I think that is the first time that you've directly threatened my life."

In a secret bunker I kept a series of crayon drawings produced by my dead brother's hand, comic strips detailing our imaginary adventures as heroes with him starring as the titular "Strongboy" and I as the sidekick Doctor Fid ("because you're a P-H-D doctor and 'P-H' is pronounced 'fffff'."). In the same vacuum-sealed and UV-resistant glass case rested an action figure depicting the red cloaked person who stood before me. I often imagined Bobby playing with that toy, expression focused but smiling nonetheless. He would have loved it. My little brother would have worshiped the Red Ghost, and the rational part of me could not fault him for it. There was an annoyingly intelligent, moral, and dedicated man hiding behind that crimson mask.

I took a slow breath to steady my pinwheeling emotions.

"Don't interfere," I warned, suddenly weary. "For a little while longer. Please."

His expression turned sympathetic and he had the look of a man about to wonder aloud if I was well. If I let him ask, I was worried that I might break down and tell him the truth.

To avoid that embarrassing scenario, I flew upwards through the ceiling and into the night sky at maximum boost. Afterburners really were the most effective method to avoid uncomfortable conversations.

❁ ❁ ❁

The majority of my infrastructure resided in the northeastern United States. California might as well have been a foreign country. Certainly, I'd never shifted sufficient resources to build a teleportation platform on the West Coast. I dared not operate at the Mk 39's full power lest I attract attention and—even with my latest advances in flight speed and with forcefields shaped and modulated to eliminate air friction—travel time to California and back would take hours. Even so, I plotted a sub-orbital ballistic arc and took to the sky.

Professor Paradigm had sent word that he wanted to meet in person.

In any other circumstance, I would have enjoyed watching the tableau passing beneath me. I rarely traveled long distances during daylight hours, and from a few hundred-thousand feet of altitude the world was a lovely marble. There were sprawling metropolises etched into the landscape, scars torn into the Earth from mining and industry and pollution...and yet, there was glory, too. Smaller picturesque villages, rolling hills, vast forests, empty plains, mountains and lakes and rivers and a world that felt alive. Everything connected, all part of a greater whole.

Overhead, the stars...the deep black of empty vacuum and the countless pinpricks of vibrant light scattered throughout grand expanse. Above the majority of the Earth's atmosphere, the view was clear. Sadly, my mind was focused elsewhere.

I used my neural tap to turn off my eyes and slaved my body to an autopilot function so that I could concentrate fully upon the formulas that I'd begun exploring earlier. Mentally, I utilized the quantum-networked link to reach out to dozens of computers and trigger simulations and calculations, to hack university systems and gain access to a promising doctoral student's thesis, and to download relevant texts from libraries around the world.

Even with my heavy combat drones left behind, any time I was cocooned within Doctor Fid's armor I was primed for battle. Being ready to match wits against a hero who claimed to be a scientist was another thing entirely.

Oblivious to the void above and the grand panorama below, I submerged myself in math and engineering schematics to prepare.

4

———————

THE AREA SURROUNDING PROFESSOR PARADIGM'S manufacturing complex was parched: fields of dried grass bleached nearly white, broken by patches of sun-baked earth and clay. The facility was located in the foothills at the south edge of town: a straight road to highways but with few neighbors. There was a ranch a ways up the hill with fewer than a dozen horses wandering the property, grazing upon withered vegetation. A lonely business park stood down the street with only tumbleweeds populating its parking lot. It was a quiet region, stark but picturesque.

The only bustling activity in line of sight was within Paradigm Labs. Twenty-one cars were present in the lot and two trucks preparing to depart with the day's shipments, and one sleek, elegant aircraft rested on the main building's helipad. Silver and white with electric-blue trim, there was something eager about its shape, something playful. Even powered-down and still, the craft looked like it desperately wanted to explode from the surface and leave the Earth behind. Professor Paradigm's personal vehicle.

With my cloaking systems fully engaged, I descended from the heavens.

Despite the manufacturing facility's nondescript appearance, there was ample evidence that the location was well-defended. Equipment sheds and fake air-conditioning units were spread across the buildings' rooftops, and they could easily house hidden weapon turrets and an impressive array of threat-detecting sensors. I bypassed active and passive radar, sonar, and two frequencies of LiDAR as I approached.

My own scans were able to determine which building was being used for research and which buildings were used for manufacturing. Professor Paradigm had indicated that I should meet him within the former, so I deactivated my stealth field as I neared the tall smoked-glass entryway. The translucent doors swung open automatically and I floated forward to the front desk towards an increasingly distressed security guard.

"I am expected," I explained calmly, keeping my hands relaxed at my side. The body-language modification algorithms that I'd designed into my suits had been intended for intimidation purposes. Fortunately, those programs could be turned off if a less threatening demeanor was desired.

The security officer—a slim, mid-twenties blond wearing a professional-appearing suit—took a moment to gather his voice. Facial recognition confirmed that the name on his employee badge—Keith Henrickson—was accurate. "Wh- who are you meeting today?"

"Professor Paradigm. Inform him that I have arrived."

"And, uh, who should I say is calling?"

Even with the Mk 39's body-language modification algorithms disabled, the security guard wilted under the force of my faceless and expressionless glare. He tapped at the switchboard to make the appropriate call.

"Professor? You have a visitor waiting in the lobby. He says that you were expecting him?"

There was a pause. The communications equipment on-site was annoyingly secure; I wasn't able to intercept the response.

"It appears to be Doctor Fid, sir." Another pause, followed by a strangled chuckle: "Yes, sir, I'm pretty sure."

Keith Henrickson developed a queasy expression and dove to take cover behind his desk.

The floor-to-ceiling windows that I'd passed while entering into the lobby went opaque, and I could hear what sounded like heavy blast doors slamming into place throughout the building. A fraction of a second later, the lighting flickered and shifted to an angry red hue and an alarm began to blare.

The level of melodrama seemed unnecessary for a consultation, but I had to admit that I was in no position to throw stones. Similar theatricality had awaited more than one superhero who'd burst into one of my decoy lairs.

To allay boredom, I took the opportunity to perform more detailed scans of the building's security. The exterior fortifications looked to be adequate—force-fields and structural integrity fields layered upon the armor plating that had sprung up about the building—but the internal defenses were woefully insufficient. The desk that the security guard was huddling behind, for example, was constructed of material that would barely stop a high-powered rifle. It felt oddly cruel—to me, at least—to leave an employee so poorly defended.

I was still designing theoretical improvements when my armor issued a series of high-level alerts. Faster even than my augmented reflexes and automated systems could react, gravity itself was twisted around me and the breath was driven from my lungs. There was a moment of vertiginous, wild spinning followed by a shock of impact that overwhelmed my inertial dampeners.

Darkness.

🕸 🕸 🕸

"I have some design ideas for my next body," Whisper smiles shyly.

"We just finished building your current body, sweetheart." I don't look up from my worktable. The majority of the rosin fumes are captured by a desktop air-cleaner, but still the familiar piney scent wafts over me as I solder a component into place.

The component I'm building will be miniaturized and refactored and optimized before the final automated fabrication...but I still prefer making basic proof-of-concept prototypes by hand whenever possible. There is something viscerally satisfying about feeling an idea grow into physical form within my grasp. And so the table has been co-opted for the act of creation, covered in an eclectic mass of breadboards and wiring harnesses and assorted components. Eventually, this will hopefully evolve into a more efficient (and significantly less expensive) controller for the inertial-displacement devices being sold to car manufacturers.

The currently-existing iteration of control board is over-engineered for what it needs to accomplish. An automotive safety device doesn't require the same tuning as a suit of powered armor. And if I can safely lower costs, then the mechanisms might find their way into more inexpensive vehicles…and thus once more prove that so-called "heroes" are unnecessary. Scientific improvements save more lives than spandex-clad do-gooders every day of the week.

(Annoyingly, this system is only being made available to the community via my secret alliance with the Red Ghost. That a superhero was the public face of the project certainly muddies the message. Still, in the end, I'm certain that it will be the technological marvel that is lauded, not the masked hero.)

"I know. I like this body," the adorable little android replies. "I'm talking about my **next** body, for when I'm older."

"All right." I'm still distracted by circuit-board optimization ideas. A car's frame forms an enclosed cabin, and that simplifies the number of variables significantly when compared to the movements involved for a form-fitting suit of mechanical armor. The math can be streamlined, entire functions relegated to dedicated hardware that will outperform even the most powerful microprocessor. "Send me the design specs, I'll have a look."

She uses her connection to my neural tap to insert the files directly into my brain. It's a detailed, significant download so I pause in my work as I digest the data.

"No," I finally say, setting down my soldering iron and

turning to face my adopted sister. "Also, you're grounded until you turn forty."

"What? But why?"

"Because these modifications are inappropriate. You're an eleven-year-old girl!"

"I'm twenty-three," she objects, pouting petulantly.

"Only if you count from your first line of code. It took your father half of a decade before he was ready to bring you on-line."

"Then...I'm eighteen!"

"Sweetheart, your father designed you to mature at a human rate. He loved you and he wanted to raise you as his own. When he died—"

"I don't wanna talk about that."

"When your father died, your processes went mostly idle. Whisper, you're extraordinary...but you're an eleven-year-old girl," I explain patiently. "And these modifications aren't for little girls. How do you even know about these things?"

"I read the Internet," Whisper replies in a sotto voice. "All of it, every day."

I take a moment to ponder the futility of designing a safe-search algorithm to guard against a curious pre-teen super-intelligence, then shake my head. "We can talk about your next body another time, okay?"

"Okay." She hugs me, then looks hesitant before continuing: "I'm not going to be eleven forever, Terry."

"I know."

"It's just...sometimes it feels like you only want a **little** sibling. Like Bobby was."

"I don't want to talk about that," I say mechanically, throat tight with emotion.

"Bobby would have grown up. And you wouldn't have stopped him from thinking about the future."

"You'll grow up too," I chuckle. "One year at a time. And I'll always want you to be my sister, even if we make your next body twenty feet tall. For now, though...play with Nyx and call Dinah. Enjoy being a little android girl."

"Dinah's my age, and she thinks that Cherenkov is dreamy too," Whisper comments conspiratorially.

Cherenkov's limbs, I decide, are in urgent need of a shattering. I should visit New York again after I deal with Skullface.

❧ ❧ ❧

I blinked, aghast at the level of destruction that a single attack had wrought. The once-pleasant foyer had been rendered into rubble, granite floors shattered into fist-sized chunks and simple-yet-comfortable furniture shredded to the point of being unidentifiable. I double-checked my math; the Professor had thrown me into a tight orbit around an artificial singularity and that kind of force was difficult to contain.

It seemed strangely sacrilegious to unleash weapons this dangerous when only a stone's throw from a working laboratory. If my own inertial displacement fields hadn't reduced the effects of the attack, who knew how much experimental data would have been corrupted? Professor Paradigm's force-fields had done a great deal to limit the damage, but even then I imagined that the entire building would have shaken to its foundations.

The front desk had been torn into kindling and I saw no sign of the hapless security guard. For a moment, I thought that the former leader of the San Francisco Paragons had murdered his own employee. A quick sensor sweep, however, found the remains of a very effectively hidden trapdoor and a localized stasis field. Keith would be trapped outside of spacetime for a while, but he would (eventually) be fine.

"That was uncalled for, Professor," I called to any microphones that were surely within range. The Mk 39's self-repair utilities had already mended any surface damage and the medical nanites coursing through my veins were hard at work patching ruptured internal organs and torn ligaments. My flesh-and-blood limbs were too damaged to obey my commands, but the armor's movement was controlled by neural link. I stood up smoothly and brushed a bit of debris from my shoulder mockingly. "Care to try again?"

Now that I was aware of the threat, I could launch an interdiction field before the singularity could be formed. Sadly, Professor Paradigm changed tactics.

The exterior forcefields dissipated, trailing into nothingness like vapor off the surface of a still pond at sunrise. A cascade of neutron beams poured into the building. The remains of the smoked-glass windows splattered across the room's wreckage in glowing molten globules, but I was already moving. My armor's automated combat algorithms seized control and guided me to dance—laughing mockingly—between the energy blasts.

Elegant, gorgeously curved floating remote-controlled

tanks had gathered around the parking lot. They shimmered in the light, somehow creating the impression of unearthly power and intent. I was reluctantly forced to admit that Professor Paradigm's aesthetic sense far outstripped my own.

But I was Doctor Fid. These pretty toys could not stand against the Mk 39's full strength, and I was in no mood to be gentle.

I launched through the gaping remnants of what had once been a pleasant building entrance into the open sky, clenched fists flowing with gathered power, and streamed plasma blast after plasma blast upon my attackers. The air itself roared in complaint, billowing smoke twisting around torrents of energy as I rained desolation from above.

A warning blared across my consciousness as my sensors detected additional threats. Further energy weapon emplacements were being deployed from atop other buildings in the campus. I darted low to grab one of the tanks' neutron-cannon barrels, tore it away from its turret, and hurled it at the largest of the weapon platforms. The resulting explosion was glorious.

The rooftop weaponry, I realized, had been a decoy. Emitters hidden beneath the now-devastated parking lot asphalt erected a fiery dome above the battleground: a mountain's worth of simulated mass hanging overhead, flickering and dancing like roiling flame.

I was still analyzing the sheer volume of the creation when the emitters shifted polarity with a bone-shaking crack. Instantly, the twisting mass of emulated weight was tugged downward with the force of a hundred gravities, a Pyrrhic apocalypse pulled down upon themselves that sandwiched the remaining tanks and me amidst the carnage.

The impact was phenomenal. Breath was crushed from my lungs in a choked and bloody gasp, and a litany of alerts indicated that my medical nanites would be kept busy for hours to come...but the Mk 39's orichalcum sub-frame held strong. Any other material would have buckled, disrupting the protective inertial dampening field that protected my body from fatal harm, but the remarkable orichalcum—that alloy created by Whisper's deceased father, that extraordinary metal that only she could create—was all but indestructible.

(I could steal the secret from her now. It would take a few hours, but I could pry open the sections of her still-operating memory banks that connected her to her creator's foundry. With a ready source of orichalcum I would have been able to build new armors, new drones, new weapons...and all that it would cost would be the ultimate violation of my sister's trust. No.)

My armor was the only operable technology remaining in the affected area; of my attackers, nothing survived. Shedding the ruined remnants of what had once been an automated tank, I floated regally to my feet.

"End this!" I roared, shaped forcefields vibrating the very air to enhance the volume of my armor's external speakers. Smoke and dust trembled in the wake of my shouted demand, and for a moment all was eerily silent. "This can only end in your tears, Paradigm!"

If this battle continued then the destruction would surely spread. Whatever reason Professor Paradigm had had for initiating conflict, it apparently wasn't worth his employees' lives. The remaining weapons platforms powered down with an audible hum.

"I'm coming out!" Professor Paradigm sounded defeated, his voice was emitted from a tinny loudspeaker atop one of the unharmed buildings.

I hovered silently, idly programming invisible forcefield pseudopods to snuff grassfires that had sprung up along the parking lot's periphery. In a handful of minutes, millions of dollars' worth of damage had been done here: no employee cars remained intact, the road and parking lot were beyond salvaging, and several of the surrounding buildings would require significant repair.

For what? I'd threatened no one! The sense of smug satisfaction for having defeated the superheroic inventor on his own turf, at least, was enjoyable enough to offset any feeling of annoyance that arose when I considered the amount of labor that would need to be put towards repairing the Mk 39 before it could once more operate at full capabilities.

❦ ❦ ❦

"Terry...I can't access your current project files," Whisper accuses, blue eyes glowing fiercely.

This android body—her second since I adopted her as my ward slash little sister— is not so elfin as was her previous form, but she is still a slim, small-framed creature. Even with all the advancements that I'd instructed a team at AH Biotech to make in creating human-like artificial flesh, Whisper still chose an embodi-

ment that echoes the design ethos her father had granted her: high cheekbones and delicate features made otherworldly by her pale, too-smooth skin, and completely hairless from the tip of her toes to the top of her bare skull. The nuanced way she moves, the way she smiles...she doesn't look artificial. She looks alien. A strange angel missing its wings.

The attempt to intimidate me with the force of her glare is, quite frankly, adorable.

"It's still in the experimental phase," I explain, coughing and covering my lips to hide my amused smile. "The Ancient was a brilliant researcher, but his grasp of quantum mechanics was perfunctory at best."

Recently, I'd acquired an entire library's worth of notes from a long-deceased supervillain; he'd been a powerful sorcerer with the heart of a scientist and had spent years (and, admittedly committed no small number of atrocities) while attempting to make logical sense of his talents. I do not have the Ancient's innate ability to sense and manipulate so-called 'magical' energies, but I am beginning to believe that I can construct a model to offset that lack.

It is, I suppose, a good thing that the Ancient hadn't had a proper grounding in applied mathematics. Even among villains, the Ancient had been a horror. A deeper understanding of the concepts that his journals explore could have made him a nigh unstoppable monster.

Nigh unstoppable was not the same as being actually unstoppable, of course. Science would have eventually prevailed.

"I can help run simulations," Whisper offers hopefully.

"I'll need your help later," I promise. "I want to test and verify a few theories before I'm ready to throw you at this."

"Okay," she smiles, then lowers her eyes. "It's just...you've never locked me out of your files before. I thought I must have done something wrong."

"Oh, sweetheart, I'm so sorry." I scoop the little android up into a gentle hug. "That isn't what I meant at all."

"Then why be all secret-y?"

"Some of the experiments the Ancient performed were...ugly. I want this to be clean science before you get to look at it."

"I've read every case-file from the Ancient's trials," Whisper says softly. "I know what he did."

"The investigators didn't uncover even half of the experiments he performed. He kidnapped kids, Whisper—little boys and girls, the same age as you and Dinah—and he did bad things to them."

The little android shivers. The relatively-recent changes that we'd made to her programming allow for her to emulate sleep and dreaming. Nightmares are still a new and frightening experience for my little sister. "Then why are you using his research?"

"After reading all this, I'm glad that the Ancient is dead and I wish someone had stopped him earlier," I sigh, "but knowledge isn't inherently good or evil. It can be used for either cause. I think I can use this knowledge to do good."

"Yay!" she cheered.

Created by one supervillain and adopted by another...I often wonder how such a tremendously gentle creature managed to thrive with such role-models. But then, perhaps it's no mystery at all: Whisper is smart enough to see our flaws and to learn from our mistakes. She'll grow into the kind of person we failed to become...better than us in every way.

"So," I say, blatantly changing the subject, "I may not be

ready to ask for your help on this project, but I can at least explain what I'm working on. If you're still curious?"

"Mm!"

"The Ancient spent years studying Akashic records..." I began, and the little android tilted her head and listened attentively. I couldn't help but smile.

It's going to be heartbreaking when she eventually outgrows me.

❧ ❧ ❧

The subject of my ire appeared, emerging from somewhere deeper inside the laboratory building and hobbling carefully through the broken glass and rubble. Professor Paradigm had aged since the last promotional photos that I'd seen. He was stooped and unhealthily slender, his wispy hair bleached to the color of snow and his skin pale and wrinkled. The former hero's steel-blue eyes were clear, however, and his gaze hinted at a fierce intellect that missed nothing.

"This was wasteful," I stated scornfully as he approached.

"I'm insured," was his dry reply.

"If you initiated all of this violence as part of an insurance fraud attempt, you should know that this armor records all of my conversations." To the best of my knowledge, there was only one company that offered a policy against 'acts of Fid' and they performed a significant amount of research before issuing payment...but they did pay well. "I'll want a cut, donated to the charity of my choice."

"I don't commit fraud," he shook his head, seeming somewhat bemused even by the suggestion.

"Then, why?"

"The only new technology for you to steal was in those hovertank drones," he waved at the shiny twisted piles of scrap spread across what had once been his laboratory's parking lot. "Nothing left for you to take now, is there?"

"Technically true," I began. His willingness to see his work destroyed rather than taken was admirable and drawing me outside into the cross-hairs of his means of destruction had been a well-considered strategy. Even so, I was unable to withhold my exasperation, "except that I wasn't here to steal anything!"

The older man stared up at my faceless mask. "What?"

"I hadn't even been aware of your new tanks' existence." I crossed my arms. "I came here to talk."

He snorted, "What makes you think that I'd be willing to talk to a murderer?"

"We're talking right now," I replied dryly.

"We both know that I'm just stalling until the Paragons arrive," Professor Paradigm smirked. "Appeasement to draw out the conversation while looking for opportunities, right?"

I refused to flinch as my own words to Cherenkov were thrown back in my face. Still, satellite footage showed that the San Francisco-based team's shuttle was only just leaving their headquarters. Really, their reaction time was embarrassing. It was tempting to offer Professor Paradigm my teleportation platform technology purely for charitable purposes.

"They are still minutes away," I sighed. "I'd hoped for a

longer discussion, but I suppose that a few minutes will have to do."

"I'll give you nothing," the old man lifted his chin defiantly, and given the intensity of his gaze I could not help but believe in his commitment. Eventually, I was certain that I could find a chip in his moral defenses, some bribe or threat that would break his will...but such an effort would take time. I did not possess an abundance of that particular resource.

"Then why send me an invitation, if you weren't willing to talk?"

"... what?" He looked honestly gobsmacked.

"An e-mail! Telling me to meet you at this location!"

"I never sent you a damned thing," he spat as though annoyed even at the concept. "Not a damned thing."

I used a holographic projector mounted on my shoulder to display the message in question. He read it twice, shook his head in disbelief.

"That's an auto-response message I send to members of my physics think-tank," the former leader of the San Francisco Paragons chuckled darkly. "We don't invite murderers to our weekly coffee."

"Oh, for the love of Tesla," I sighed. "Let me guess: Cuboid is responsible for aspects of your network infrastructure, and some communications have gone awry while his attention is focused upon building a new body?"

"You destroyed his old one." Scorn dripped from his voice like a viscous ichor.

"That was more than a year ago," I scowled, though he

couldn't see my face behind the Mk 39's faceplate. "And I was busy saving the world at the time."

"You may have saved the world," the old inventor turned to stare across the wreckage that had once been the entrance to his workplace, "but you've left a lot of destruction in your wake. You've hurt people I care about. And your time is almost up."

I could have stayed. Could have fought the Paragons, could have attempted to subdue them without doing any permanent injury and then continued my attempts to wheedle information from the recalcitrant Paradigm...but the odds were not in my favor. Already, hours had been wasted in traveling. How much more time was I willing to spend, chasing after what might well be another dead end?

My hand closed into a fist and I fired a modified stunner blast into the slender man's chest. Blue energies crackled and danced across his frame and he collapsed with a strangled gurgle.

Standing in vigilance over his convulsing form, I found myself musing whether or not I should feel guilty for his obvious pain. Foam formed at the corners of his lips and tears were squeezed from eyes clenched tight. Professor Paradigm had attacked without provocation and that last self-destructive high-gravity energy-dome collapse could easily have been fatal if not for the Mk 39's orichalcum subframe. Surely such excessive aggression should be punished! And yet...He didn't look like a proud, stubborn hero any longer. Pale skin was scraped raw against the rubble, and the only sounds he could manage were pitiful wheezes.

His thrashing began to wane, so I tagged him again while

I considered. Finally—unable to come to a decision—I engaged my flight systems and lifted a few feet from the ground.

"Tell your tin-plated tech-support to get back to work," I sneered. "That's the second time his failings have inconvenienced me. If it happens again, someone might be harmed."

I left the moaning inventor behind and launched towards the heavens.

5

—————

Cuboid (Android)

From the Online Encyclopedia

Cuboid is a superhumanly strong artificially-sentient gun-metal gray android created by the reclusive inventor <u>Christopher Perry</u> and is a member of the <u>Department of Metahuman Affairs</u> licensed superhero team, the <u>New York Shield</u>. There is some controversy over Cuboid's date of origin. Cuboid's first public appearance was on December 11, 2006, but it has been suggested that Dr. Perry began construction more than three decades earlier. Although early press releases implied that Cuboid's android body was self-contained, it has since been confirmed that Cuboid's brain is located in a secure server farm and that his body has been controlled remotely.

Even though all who worked alongside Cuboid <u>were convinced</u> that the android was a unique individual, for legal purposes Cuboid was initially considered to be Christopher Perry's property, and it was Dr. Perry who applied for (and received) license to operate as a hero in January of 2007.

Between January 2007 and June 2009, Cuboid was deployed only to assist in major superhero battles. In July 2009, Dr. Perry was offered membership in the New York Shield with the stipulation that Cuboid would act in Dr. Perry's stead. Cuboid has remained a staple of the New York Shield ever since. In addition, Cuboid has been employed to administrate the communications and data systems maintained by several superhero and government organizations.

Cuboid's body was completely destroyed by <u>Doctor Fid</u> during <u>the Battle at Mercer-Tallon</u> on January 24, 2018 and has not appeared in physical form since. Even without a body, Cuboid's autonomy was legally recognized with the passage of the <u>Synthetic Americans' Rights act</u> and all his contracts re-written, which led to team-leader <u>Cloner</u> joking that Cuboid was 'both the newest and the longest continuously-active member' of the team.

Contents

Personal Life

Although the android has no physical gender, Cuboid has always claimed to identify as male and prefers the use of the masculine pronoun.

Cuboid has been described as being gentle and infinitely patient but difficult to draw into social contact. Cuboid rarely speaks publicly or makes public appearances, instead choosing to release statements directly to the media or publishing

<u>essays</u> that convey his opinions. Despite this general reserve, he is known to have formed a few well-documented friendships.

Even before joining the N.Y. Shield, Cuboid had initiated a long-running friendship with then-team-leader (and now disgraced ex-heroine) <u>Sphinx</u>. In addition, Cuboid is known to have maintained relationships with several well-known scientists, philosophers, and writers.

According to Dr. Christopher Perry's <u>memoir</u>, Cuboid expressed a curiosity about (and reverence for) biological life even before being given a physical body. He has often demonstrated an encyclopedic knowledge of insect, animal, and plant species and is known to be a strident supporter of environmentalist campaigns. Although no images or footage has ever been released to the public, several of Cuboid's peers have stated that the android designs and maintains elaborate self-sustaining ecospheres as a hobby.

In addition, Cuboid has written two award-winning books of <u>pastoral poetry</u> under the pen-name of <u>Alain Matheson</u>, both of which are noted for recurring themes of natural harmony, the interconnection of all living things, and the importance of vigilant stewardship over both communities and

environments. Alain Matheson's true identity was only discovered when his second
book, <u>Blue Marble</u>, was nominated for the
James Laughlin Award in 2011. Despite
support from the current United States Poet
Laureate, Cuboid was determined to be inel-
igible to receive the prize by the <u>Academy
of American Poets</u> due to the fact that
Cuboid was not (at that time) considered to
be a United States citizen.

❋ ❋ ❋

It took several hours of meticulous research to confirm that
Professor Paradigm's technology represented the most likely
opportunity to significantly expand the range of my akashic
identity detector. He'd published academic papers with
tantalizing implications and applied for relevant patents
shortly after he'd spent time studying the remains of Dr.
Chaise's Dimension Bomb. Gaining surreptitious access to
the patent office's computer system was no help. The docu-
ments were missing key technical details that made reverse
engineering the proposed devices impossible.

According to gossip that I'd gleaned from the supposedly
'secure' chat-software the Paragons used, Professor Paradigm
had valid reason for his unwillingness to bargain: he'd been
on friendly terms with both Clash and Lycan. I'd badly
injured the former and murdered the latter. I regretted those
actions and had performed neurosurgery upon myself to
ensure that I would not easily make similar mistakes, but the

damage had been done long ago. Professor Paradigm would resist by any means available to him and his resources were substantial.

A cadre of my drones were dispatched to the West coast to construct and hide teleportation platforms in useful locations. In the future, at least, I wouldn't be forced to waste so much time traveling before initiating a confrontation. But Professor Paradigm was on his guard now, surrounded constantly by worried members of his former team. It would be some time until I could gain access to the elderly inventor without declaring war on the West Coast superhero community.

With every failed simulation or experiment, the option of war became more tempting. If Valiant—the most powerful superhuman in all of history—hadn't been observed visiting the San Francisco Paragons' base, then I would already have been preparing for battle. The Mk 39 was sufficiently well-designed that it would be able to survive hand-to-hand combat with Valiant, but it was highly unlikely that I would prevail in a physical brawl. My only chance of victory would be resorting to exotic weaponry.

The research contained in the Ancient's library had suggested several methodologies that would completely bypass the mighty hero's legendary invulnerability. Unfortunately, every one of those would be immediately fatal.

Valiant was a worthy hero, kind, generous, and deserving of respect. His tireless devotion to disaster relief saved tens of thousands of lives each year, and his mere existence served to limit the chaos that superpowered criminals were willing to entertain. Both Bobby and Whisper had liked Valiant. So long as other options remained available, I would prefer to avoid his slaughter.

Fortunately, it occurred to me that there might be another way.

❦ ❦ ❦

```
To: "Aaron Schwartz"
   <aaron.schwartz@ahbt.com>
From: "Terrance Markham" <terrance.-
   markham@ahbt.com>
```

Subject: Apologies and a request

Aaron,

There can be no excuse for the way I treated you the other day. You're always welcome in my home. All that I can say is that it has been a stressful time, and that you deserved better from me. I'm sorry.

I've reached out to the members of the Board and they've agreed to support establishing a Chief Strategy Officer position. I haven't spoken to Theo but I do believe that he'd be interested.

Attached is a document that includes my observations about recent technological trends, about existing projects and suggestions for possible future paths, and about staffing issues that I foresee further down the line. Something like this should have been written and handed off before your first day. Again, I apologize.

For now, I'm afraid that I need another favor.

I am going to be traveling and I was hoping that I could leave Nyx with you. I know that you already have three dogs, but I would very much prefer for Whisper's puppy to be with someone I trust while I'm away.

Thank you,

- Dr. Terrance Markham

To: "Terrance Markham" <terrance.-markham@ahbt.com>

From: "Aaron Schwartz" <aaron.schwartz@ahbt.com>

Subject: Re: Apologies and a request

Terry,

Of course! Dinah and I would be happy to take care of Nyx. Bring her by any time.

Thank you for the document. I shared some of your suggestions with Theo and he's raring to go. It's great to have him back on board. You were right about Frank Tierney, too…he's returned to the office like nothing's happened.

You do whatever you need to in order to

take care of Whisper and yourself. We'll be
here whenever you're ready.
    Aaron Schwartz, CEO

❀ ❀ ❀

Cocooned within my armors, I have felt at ease in the most extraordinary of circumstances. I've faced the deadliest of foes and endured the harshest of environments with confidence. And yet, a strange tension touched my heart as I approached New Orleans airspace, as though the city itself had noticed me and that it disapproved of Doctor Fid's presence.

It was a psychosomatic reaction, I was certain. A few tweaks to my pharmacological regimen and the feeling faded. Still, it was telling that my quarry had chosen this region as his home. A place that I very rarely had cause to visit, a place where my initial sense was one of discomfort. He'd relocated to New Orleans for a reason: to hide from me.

With cloaking system engaged, I hovered several thousand feet above the city—invisible against the night sky—and commanded a swarm of microdrones to explore. Tiny machines the size of insects, they silently spread out to map the buildings that surrounded my prey. Only when I was certain of the surroundings did I descend.

Overconfidence when visiting Professor Paradigm's facility had cost me precious time. There was no reason to allow a repeat of that debacle. The man I intended to confront this evening had fewer resources at his disposal than had the former leader of the Paragons, but that was no excuse to be incautious.

As silent as a ghost, I drifted lower through layers of anxiety and waves of doubt. I'd been wrong...this strange sense of unease was not merely in my mind.

There are no human psychics, and the alien invaders—the Legion—were no more. This was something else. Fortunately, facing the Legion mind-controlling telepaths had taught me many a hard lesson.

I braced myself for the headache to come, but still the intensity was blinding. Electro-stimulation applied directly to carefully selected regions of my brain drove away the outside influence, and the armor's neural interface made quick work of leveling my emotional state.

A genuine psionic attack! Here, on Earth! How extraordinary.

Someday (when Whisper was safe and I had the luxury of time) I was going to spend a month investigating why this city hated me. And why this effect hadn't plagued me on my one prior visit to New Orleans to assist with disaster relief. For now, however, Doctor Fid had a mission and my target was in sight. He was in costume, patrolling near a series of dilapidated dock-front warehouses.

I discarded stealth and dropped like a stone. Twice, I'd attempted to make civilized contact with a hero and twice I'd been punished for the attempt. I might have been a slow learner but some patterns were difficult to ignore.

I slammed into the ground like a meteorite striking the Earth, cratering the pavement and raising an impenetrable cloud of dust. It was only with sonar and radar that I was able to observe my agile target leap to safety in a series of elegant flips. My target's natural athleticism was supposedly the product of advanced genetic engineering, but the skill itself had been earned through hard training. Even without his high-tech toys and innate (albeit limited) ability to hasten and slow time, he would have been more than a match for any muggers or thieves that he might have happened upon during his nightly vigil. He had, in fact, proved himself a worthy opponent against no small number of lesser super-powered villains as well.

"Blueshift!" I intoned, pulsing my forcefield to drive the dust from around myself in an expanding sphere of clear air. "Stand down!"

What followed was a frenzied litany of high-speed cursing and energy blasts, both cast at such a remarkable rate that I could not follow it. Fortunately, the Mk 39's combat algorithms took control and could maintain reaction speeds far superior to that which could be managed by flesh and blood. I was a mere passenger within my armor as it smoothly danced between flashing attacks, parrying some and riposting with bursts of my own.

The hero was wearing a dark navy bodysuit wrapped in black body armor plates and wielded an ion-pistol in each hand. Blueshift leapt about violently in an attempt to outrace my armor's programming. The fiery blue-white halo of energy that arced after him intensified as he strained his power's capacity to alter his own localized space-time, and his rate of fire was so rapid that it seemed a constant stream of light, a roaring deluge of thunderous barks as the blasts boiled pencil-thin lines of air into plasma.

His movements were a blur. I could only see freeze-frame images captured by my sensors, a stuttered perception of combat too fast for human observation. At some point, my scepter had been summoned and I was batting brilliant beams of energy out of the air while closing towards the frantic Blueshift. He attempted a fighting retreat but was no match for the Mk 39's speed; the battle ended as quickly as it had begun.

My hand had seized his wrist and a shaped forcefield curled up his arm and around his torso, locking him firmly in place.

"Welcome to New Awlins," Blueshift managed an only-slightly-nervous approximation of a bright smile. "If you here for th' Jazz Fest, you a bit lost. Head lake on Pontchartrain-"

"I'm here for you," I interrupted. Blueshift had a reputation for being a loquacious opponent, and if I'd let him build up a head of steam, he was perfectly capable of blathering on indefinitely to waste time. Local supervillain Don Voudon had once visited Lassiters and complained incessantly about Blueshift's habit. It only took Don Voudon the time to down one beer to finish lamenting the failure of his latest scheme. He was still bellyaching about Blueshift's monologues, however, when William Wasserman announced last call.

"I'm flattered, but I'm in a committed relationship," Blueshift attempted to continue, momentarily blurring as he tried (and failed) to twist out of my grasp. "I can maybe put in a good word wit Valiant if you want t' hook up. The man knows his jazz. He was at the festival three years ago, I got him front-row seats for-"

I let my forcefield constrict around the hero's chest and the verbal deluge was cut off by a strangled cough.

"I'm here for you," I repeated, vocoder making the pronouncement resonate in an intimidatingly final manner. "You have something that I require. Cease interrupting and we can conclude our business peacefully."

"Keeping quiet don't seem like something I'm likely t' do," he half-chuckled, forlorn, when he could again speak. "And 'peaceful' don't sound much like your thing, neither."

"I'm willing to make the effort," I replied dryly, "since the alternative could include a great deal of unnecessary pain and suffering. Are you willing to do the same?"

"When you put it like that the idea does seem awful tempting."

"Excellent." I relaxed only slightly. Heroes were a perplexing bunch. If you gave them enough rope, some were often remarkably eager to hang themselves. I could only hope that the latitude that I was offering would not be abused. "I require access to your 'time machine'."

"It's not really a time machine, y'know." His forced smile cracked. "If you want t' visit the future, you're goin' have to do it the slow way: one-minute o' travel per minute."

"I understand the basic gist as to how your transport functions. I wish to examine it more thoroughly."

When he'd first publicly debuted as a hero, Blueshift had announced that he was a traveler from several hundred years in the future. The truth was eventually revealed to be more complicated: he was (unknowingly) an immigrant from an alternate dimension whose history had closely matched this one, to remarkable accuracy. The chances of every single action and reaction of every particle in two separate universes occurring in so similar a manner were incalculably low...but—given an infinite number of universes— inevitable. In fact, there were an infinite number of universes that just happened to be nearly identical to my own. Also, an infinite number of universes that were wildly different. And that was the problem. Locating a specific universe from among all those possibilities was extraordinarily complicated.

And yet, that was one of the capabilities of the craft the hero had arrived in.

"I don't think you'd be welcome on my home dimension," Blueshift noted, his expression troubled. "We remember our Doctor Fid. And, honestly, there ain't much technology there you can't replicate here."

"I have a different destination in mind."

"Yeah?" he looked skeptical.

"A dimension that the Red Ghost visited. I have no intention of visiting your homeworld."

The hero looked thoughtful and it was a while before he responded. "So, we negotiating or you just goin' threaten me 'til I give you what you want?"

"My plan was to attempt bribery, first."

"Tomorrow's megalottery numbers gonna be eight, fourteen, twenty-seven, fifty-seven, sixty-four, an' five for the lucky ball. I want money, it never gonna be a problem. But I got another idea."

"Oh?"

"Red Ghost 'n Valiant, they tell me there a person under that armor. I got a story maybe that person needs t' hear." He exhaled shakily. "You stand still 'n let me talk a bit, maybe I let you have a look at my ship."

The option of resorting to mindless violence was more appealing, but I nodded nonetheless.

❧ ❧ ❧

The sun hung low on the horizon and shallow wispy clouds glowed like hot embers as they poured over the distant mountain ridges. The scent of the nearby orchard washed over the camp, a pleasantly warm breeze that gathered and waned in patient waves. Jackson could watch the wheat fields ripple with each swell from his vantage point. The growing season had ended. For the first time in as long as he could remember, Jackson wouldn't be helping his family take in the harvest.

"Tell me again," he requested, refusing to turn towards the researcher who'd ascended the ladder to give him the news.

"They've narrowed it down to three names," the slender man grinned, still panting from the climb. "We have the go ahead to proceed."

The old watchtower had the best view in the facility, and everyone knew where Jackson preferred to spend his free evenings. If he'd gone to the town like Lois had wanted, maybe no one from the center would have been able to find him. Maybe he'd have had one more evening free from doubt and sorrow, one extra dinner spent smiling instead of making somber farewells.

It wasn't exactly unexpected; Jackson had been training for this his whole life. Countless procedures at the Center, endless drills and interminable lectures...it had felt like such an honor when the council announced his name. More than two hundred applicants and he'd eked out the win! The farm was paid for now, free and clear, because of his oath to serve. That was something to be proud of, something worthy. But when the eggheads at the Center started narrowing the list, reality settled in: this was real. This was going to happen.

Jackson Pierce was going to be a hero.

"I thought we weren't planning on moving forward until we'd narrowed it down to one," the young man commented, standing up and arching his back in a slow stretch. The watchtower was old and the footing unsteady, but Jackson had absolute faith in his balance.

The slim man in the lab-coat, on the other hand, was still holding to the ladder with a death grip despite his eager exuberance. "The records aren't as clear as we'd hoped. We lost a lot in the Long Dark...but the council is certain he's one of these three."

"How certain?"

"As certain as we can be," the researcher shrugged tightly. "We're only going to get one shot at this. I wouldn't be on this ladder if the council wasn't sure."

"All right," Jackson nodded and wished that his own conviction was as strong, but he was a soldier and he knew what orders awaited. "Climb down, I'll follow. The Commander is going to want to see me."

The smaller man flashed Jackson a grateful smile and began his slow and shaky descent. Jackson savored one last moment staring over the fields and croplands, and beyond that the rolling hills covered in a dense forest where he'd played as a child. And further out to the foothills that housed the reservoir and then the mountains whose ice-covered peaks fed the grand river that wove its way towards the facility. The sun was visibly lower now, blazing fiercely as if it resented leaving the day behind, and the snow-covered mountain peaks glistened as though on fire.

The Long Dark had stolen billions of lives and cost humanity centuries of progress, but the survivors had eventually rebuilt much of the world. This place was beautiful, and Jackson was going to miss it.

The soldier straightened his back, inevitability solidifying in his spine like an icicle. His own climb down was much faster than that of the man who'd preceded him.

Jackson wasn't one of the big brains, but he wasn't a dumb grunt either. There was too much at stake for the Council to trust a lesser soldier for the job. He'd need to think on his feet, to investigate and make entirely new plans based on whatever he found on the other side. He'd need to study, to learn, to mimic accents and blend in, to make executive decisions. Taking on this mission meant shouldering a heavy responsibility, and Jackson was as prepared as the entirety of the Center's resources could make him.

He'd be happier if it was only one name. One name was easy to justify: travel back in time and cross the name off, save billions of lives. Kill one man before he became an immortal monster, and with that death bring back the golden age of civilization.

Three names on the list meant that two were probably innocent. Jackson wasn't one of the big brains but that math, at least, seemed fairly simple. If the mission were successful, Jackson would never know which two. He'd just cross off the names and know that humanity had been saved. Centuries of music and culture and literature, rescued. And technology, of course. So much had been lost to the Long Dark.

To Fid's Revenge.

It was going to be a one-way trip—a sacrifice of everything he'd ever known—but Jackson Pierce was going to be a hero. A hero with blood on his hands, true, but a hero nonetheless.

The soldier shook the researcher's hand then took off at a jog to report for duty.

❧ ❧ ❧

"So that what I did," Blueshift continued in a flat monotone, his voice devoid of emotion even as silent tears spilled below his mask. "I got here 'n somethin' 'bout the trip give me powers. I cross off the names and I hid, got a job, live a quiet life. My entire world mighta been lost t' me, but I knew my sacrifice wasn't in vain. I built a better world, saved billions of lives 'n all it cost was a piece a my soul. Didn't mind making that trade, not a bit.

"But all three names was wrong.

"I didn't know, not for a long time. I ain't immortal like you, but I age slow; lived here nine years afore you show up. Spent more 'n a bit o' time hatin' myself after that, but eventually I decide t' soldier on. I hid here 'cause history say you never come to New Awlins, but I use my powers, become a hero proper. Reach out to other heroes, see if maybe I find someone who stop you afore the Long Dark."

"But now maybe I have a chance to stop you myself, because I tell you this story: according to what we piece together, Doctor Fid was searching for something 'n the world's heroes stopped him. And Doctor Fid went mad.

"He built a machine that undid whatever th' Legion did

hundreds years back, 'n superpowers suddenly stop working. Did something else, 'cause electronics stop working too. Planes fall out of the sky, satellites go dark, cars 'n trucks 'n trains stop movin'. All th' infrastructure what keeps th' world spinning, gone at the press of a button. Only person knew how ta build modern tech wit the new laws o' physics was Doctor Fid, 'n he kept punishing my world for more 'n a century. No one could stop him.

"But eventually he stopped bein' crazy. He wrote science books for our eggheads so they start rebuilding what was lost, and then Doctor Fid die real ugly by his own hand.

"So I let you look at my ship, but I need you t' know: if you do this thing, if you start the Long Dark, you end up hatin' yourself. F'true."

Blueshift fell silent, and I said nothing for a long time. Thoughts swirled, mathematical models exploding into my mind as I contemplated the enormity of what the faux time-traveler described: the sheer volume of death and destruction that his world's Doctor Fid had caused. It was mind-boggling. But (if my calculations were correct) I was fairly certain that I knew how he'd done it.

The so-called hero before me had more innocent blood on his hands than I did. The list of dead I'd compiled over the course of my violent career might have been longer, but the names I'd chosen to cross off were monsters and villains! The other Fid—the other Terrance Markham, my other-worldly analogue—had chosen to shatter that ratio, to pile so heavy a weight of horrors upon his soul that the ground must have shaken when he walked. And yet, I understood.

I remembered the hot, slick feel of Bobby's lifeblood

between my fingers, the stench of smoke and gore, and my baby brother's expression of bewildered disillusionment as he realized his favorite superhero, Bronze, had decided not to come to the rescue. I remembered that moment, that infinitely stretched nanosecond when the light left his eyes, and I remembered how incredibly heavy Bobby had felt in my arms as he finally fell limp.

I remembered guilt and I remembered rage. I remembered hate. And then I imagined feeling all that over again as the world's 'heroes', the brightly clad champions that this world practically worshipped, standing against me as my adopted little sister slipped beyond my reach.

I imagined the public cheering for them and could not fathom why my counterpart had been so merciful.

"I'm searching for something," I finally stated, the intensity of my purpose burning cold. "It is, in fact, very possible that I'm on a similar quest to the one your world's Fid was engaged in. As such, the power to stop a Long Dark is in your hands: convince them all to stand aside. You tell them the truth of what you've done and you make them believe it. Because if I fail, I'll already hate myself and...well...billions of lives and the tattered remains of my soul doesn't seem like a trade I would mind making, either."

"Everyone here scared of you," Blueshift whispered, eyes wide with horror. "But no one scared enough."

I was terrified too, but Whisper's need was greater than my own need for sanity.

"Show me to your ship," I ordered. Troubled and silent, the hero complied.

6

My creation bore little resemblance to the one Blueshift had displayed. His craft had been a sleek airship with an admittedly-impressive stealth field in addition to its supposed 'time-travel' capabilities. It had been outfitted as a platform from which to embark upon a covert mission: quick and silent. The ship's workings had been easy to reverse engineer; his world's Doctor Fid had written the texts that had been the basis of much of the technology. There had been more than a few new innovations to explore and the programming for the inter-dimensional energy sequencer would have been the work of years to reproduce on my own...but I recognized the design ethos and found it simple to unravel.

My own transport was no elegant aircraft. It was, instead, constructed from an oversized armored tank that I'd liberated from the now-incarcerated supervillain named Technos.

Improving upon the vehicle's offensive and defensive capabilities had been a hobby that I'd dabbled in over the last year or so. If ever I'd had the opportunity to talk Whisper into adding orichalcum frame supports and armor, the tank would have been impregnable. Even in its current state, it was a fortress. The exterior had been modified to match my armor's aesthetic—an unearthly silhouette of a clear night's sky given an intimidating three-dimensional form by an angry red glowing wireframe—and the machine's profile bristled with weapons and sensors and other field-manipulation tools.

It was the latter aspect which made this vehicle trivially easy to modify to my purposes.

Technos' original design had included a quantum-ripple emitter that he'd used to disrupt my flight systems. The created aura interfered with many devices, including several that were intrinsic to the workings of this very tank. The core framework, therefor, had been cleverly designed to isolate the interior from the effects of its own weapon. The shielding had been integral to the entire structure, and I could use that sheath to shape the required energies for inter-dimensional transit.

I'd already had most of the components available in my laboratories. A simpler transportation device had once been built for the Red Ghost when it had become plain that his own superhuman ability to transform into a red mist could be strained until he slipped from this dimension altogether, and the prototypes I'd kept in storage could be employed with almost no modifications necessary. It was only a question of fabricating the final pieces and putting them all together. Automated construction drones made quick work of it. My neural interface had allowed me to begin directing their labor before I'd even left New Orleans. And so it was only hours until I was ready to embark.

But I hadn't flown to the laboratory where my interdimensional transportation device was homed. I'd had another destination in mind, someplace I needed to be first.

Upon arriving via teleportation platform hidden in my office, I was seared by the overwhelming quiet; it cut deep, twisting through my innards like an ice-cold blade. Gone were the sounds of a puppy's claws scraping at the floor as the little creature scrambled in to investigate my arrival. Gone were the sounds of laughter, of children playing, of gentle song.

My home was devoid of life. The rooms formed a cavernous crypt and I was only one more ghost wandering its halls.

Whisper's room was...orderly. That had been my doing, putting her belongings back in their theoretical place to await her return. She had such an extraordinary mind—the most elegant artificial intelligence ever conceived—but she was also a child. When she'd fallen, books and toys had been strewn about randomly, a blanket surrounded by chew toys thrown in the corner for Nyx to lay upon, dolls and statues and other nicknacks arrayed haphazardly on the shelves in a system that made sense only to her.

I wished I hadn't tidied. The room no longer looked lived-in, and the thought tore at my heart.

When I'd met her, there had been one doll in particular that Whisper had treasured. She never let me see her play with dolls anymore—she was too old now, she always said—but somehow that specific doll had always been moved to another location whenever I visited this room. Every time but this one: it remained where I'd left it. My hands barely shook at all as I took the doll from its place and sat gingerly on the edge of the bed.

Whisper remained where I'd left her, too. Silent and terribly still.

"I have Amelia here for you," I said, throat tight. "I thought she could keep you company while I'm away."

I placed the doll in Whisper's arms as though it were the most precious thing in the world.

"I'm going on a trip. I need Professor Paradigm's help to… to save you. There are certain things that he's better at than I am. Things he's studied at length that I've only begun to explore, but with our history there's no way he'll ever help me.

"So I'm going to another dimension to seek out an alternate version of Professor Paradigm…a Professor Paradigm who's never heard of Doctor Fid. With the tech I borrowed from Blueshift, I can find the dimension that the Red Ghost visited…" I turned away, unable even to look at Whisper's still form lest I break down. "Please wait for me. Be safe."

I stood up and risked one last glance at my adopted little sister's android body. It was easy to imagine that she was only sleeping. And then I straightened my back and took a deep breath.

It was time.

(Cont'd from page 7) at Stanford Memorial Medical Center where Professor Paradigm is recovering. A spokesman for Paradigm Labs issued a brief prepared statement:

"Yesterday, our place of business was subject to a vicious and unprovoked attack from the notorious criminal, Doctor Fid. Fortunately, due to our founder's foresight and quick thinking, we were able to escape with minimal injuries. The damage to our primary campus is significant, but our greatest assets—our employees—remain intact. Repairs will begin within seven days, and the majority of our fabrication has already been offloaded to other facilities. We do not expect any serious delays in delivering outstanding orders.

"Unfortunately, our founder was injured in Doctor Fid's assault and remains in critical care. His prognosis is good and we are hopeful that he will make a quick and complete recovery. I spoke to him briefly before he was returned to surgery, and he asked me to convey his deepest gratitude for the outpouring of support and sympathy that he has received."

Several well-known heroes have been to the Medical Center to pay their respects to the wounded Professor Paradigm.

"It's a shame," said Valiant. The world's

most powerful superhero looked visibly shaken as he was leaving the hospital. "My battles against Doctor Fid have been well-documented, but I'd truly come to believe that he was changing his ways. Doctor Fid single-handedly saved the world from alien invasion, and he helped me save dozens of schoolchildren in Chile. This doesn't seem like the same person that I talked to, only a few months ago."

"He's gone off the deep end." The leader of the Boston Guardians, Titan, was less forgiving. "He's always been dangerous, but something's changed. Doctor Fid's become more violent and more aggressive, and he's appearing with a frequency that we've never seen from this particular villain. Of course I'm grateful that he saved the Earth, and I'm grateful that he more recently saved my home city…but that gratitude is not without limits. Once again, he has demonstrated that he is a clear and present danger to the public. Now more than ever, we heroes need to come together as a community and work to capture Doctor Fid once and for all. I've already received written approval from the Department of Metahuman Affairs to establish a strike force. I'll be announcing details within the next few days."

"Doctor Fid saved my life," commented the heroine Regrowth, another member of the Boston Guardians. "I was badly injured and buried under several tons of dirt and rock, and he dug me out and made sure my injuries were treated. He wasn't cruel, and I think that the person he was that day would be horrified by how he's acting now. Something happened during his fight against Skullface three months ago, and I agree with Titan's assessment. Doctor Fid has gone mad and needs to be stopped, for the public's sake and for his own."

The devastation at Paradigm Labs is beyond belief. A broad swathe of the property has been rendered into rubble; standing at the edge of the effected region, one can't help but be reminded how fragile our lives can be, and how brave our costumed protectors must be in order to oppose so terrible a menace.

Doctor Fid remains at large.

❦ ❦ ❦

The transition was dizzying.

There was an odd hum of building energies and a moment of strange pressure before activation, and then there was a cacophonous crackle of ionized plasma pouring off the transport's surface as I arrived. The period between those two instants was indescribable, a synesthetic deluge of flickering colors and shapes that flooded every one of my senses. Even within the Mk 39—with all the recording and analysis tools even my own technology could cram into my neural interface—I could make no real sense of it.

As the last of the rumbling faded, I imagined that I could still taste the platonic ideal of 'sphere' on the tip of my tongue. And then it was gone and I was someplace new.

The wrong place.

Dozens of alarms flickered, planted directly into my awareness via neural interface. Reflexively, I triggered my transdimensional battle-tank's cloaking field and raised forcefields to full power. For the space of several carefully-slowed breaths, I could only wait and hope that my arrival hadn't gathered undue attention.

A massive low-floating starship continued on its original course, slicing through the dingy clouds overhead and heading east towards the rising sun. It hadn't been optimized for travel inside an atmosphere, all sharp edges and unsymmetrical protuberances. The dark ship was an ugly thing, brutally utilitarian.

I recognized the craft's make. In my own dimension, a similar ship—laden with desperate alien refugees—had crash-landed in Colorado a few years back. That analogue had been stolen by rebels and damaged in a daring escape for freedom, barely functional before its unfortunate tumble into the Earth's atmosphere. According to my readings, however, this vessel was in excellent repair and bristled with weapons. A battlecarrier.

These were no refugees. This was the Legion.

I dared not risk aggressive scanning until I'd developed a better handle on the alien invaders' technology, so I relied upon visual observation as the great starship trudged across the sky. Turbulent anti-grav fields quivered below the ship's mass, twisting and compacting the heavy plumes of ash that polluted the air and gathering them into clods that fell like black snow.

This was a world in ruin.

As I'd limited my journey's possible destination to alternate universes which had had recent contact with my own, I could only surmise that this had been the dimension the Brooklyn Knights had fled.

It was no wonder that they'd never made any attempt to return.

I'd arrived near the edge of a city, unrecognizable by any visible landmarks. Many structures had been rendered into rubble, and others twisted into dilapidated wrecks, and every building in line of sight was scarred by fire and neglect.

Once, this region had been green. Sensors displayed the savaged skeletons of what had previously been a forest, and the murky sludge where a pond had lay. This Earth was faring as poorly as its inhabitants.

The atmosphere was breathable—if only barely. I doubted that I would have cause to step outside of my own vessel without my wholly self-sufficient environmentally-controlled armor but it was good to know that the option existed. Finding naturally-potable water would be more difficult. Fortunately, there were materials on board that could be used to build a simple desalinization and purification rig. The inter-dimensional ripples caused by my arrival would only take twelve hours to fade so that my next jump could be safely managed. Perhaps I could use some of that time to resupply.

Ash had formed a blanket upon the ground, and in it I could identify trails of footprints. There were survivors nearby. Scavengers, most likely...desperate men and women, struggling to survive the end of humanity. It seemed probable that Legion had been patrolling the region specifically looking for even so minor a lingering pocket of civilization.

From what I'd been told, the Legion took their genocides seriously. They would not withdraw their forces until all that remained was dust. Dust, and a handful of carefully-chosen mind-controlled puppet-slaves.

Visibly, there was no hint that any resistance persisted. I could, however, detect a few highly encrypted radio broadcasts, hints of chatter from the last remnants of what had once been a vibrant society. That there was even this much infrastructure remaining was a pleasant surprise. On the off chance that the data might be relevant, I started a program to decrypt the signals.

The alien starship continued towards the horizon and, for a moment, I truly believed that luck had fallen in my favor. That no alarm had been raised by my sudden appearance. I should have known better; to others the fates might occasionally be kind, but not to me.

A shuttlecraft spat from the starship's belly and almost immediately banked to face my location. The Legion had sent a ship to investigate.

My transport's stealth capabilities were decent but

imperfect. A thorough, careful scan would eventually notice discrepancies. And if the ship's crew included one of the Legion's telepathic officers, my mind would have been detected as soon as they approached within range. My neural implant would protect me against their mind-control abilities, and the tank could generate a psionic nullifier field similar to the one that I'd employed on my own Earth. But they would be able to sense my presence before either defense could be initiated.

A soft sigh escaped my lips and the recently rebuilt warstaff appeared as though by magic in my hand. Twelve hours until I could safely continue my journey...

It seemed likely that this was about to become a very hectic afternoon.

❧ ❧ ❧

The taste was familiar: bright flavors with a hint of caramel and smoke, with a citrus aftertaste. My murdered friend Starnyx— the truest friend I'd ever had—had introduced me to this particular beverage. The microbrewery that produced it had been near to a coffee shop he frequented.

The establishment was also, apparently, on the route the Brooklyn Knights chose for their patrols. When they'd stumbled across me while I was beginning a break-in, they offered me a beer in lieu of a battle. Psion had clearly expected me to refuse, so I accepted out of sheer contrariness.

"Thank you." I said, grateful for my armor's vocoder; in addition to altering my voice, the device also struck the mournful nostalgia from my tone. Rage had outweighed grief during the

time that I'd been working to wreak vengeance upon Starnyx's murderers. With that war won, grief had flooded back to the fore.

I'd been thinking of Starnyx when I'd chosen tonight's target. The facility was within line-of-sight of his old base of operations.

"You're welcome," Shrike replied. He was the only member of the Brooklyn Knights who seemed calm and relaxed. The others had circled around me, drinking from bottles of their own with tense caution. If I'd moved too suddenly, I knew, they would likely leap to attack.

After I'd averted an apocalyptic alien invasion, the Brooklyn Knights had publicly announced that they owed me a beer. The reality of sharing a drink with a villain was, however, apparently more stressful than most of them had expected. Shrike and I, on the other hand, had developed something of an understanding. Certainly, he didn't seem to be holding a few broken bones against me.

"Why were you robbing a clothing store?" Blizzard blurted, unable to withhold his curiosity any longer.

(Independent superhero teams had a tendency to follow certain well-known tropes as they stabilized. There were logistical, sociological and strategic reasons for the trends, and the Brooklyn Knights were no exception: five plucky youths from all walks of life, gathered by fate and granted the power to make a difference in their community. Psion, the levelheaded and rigidly upright leader. Wildcard, the often-overlooked clever problem solver whose ability to alter his powerset frequently allowed him to find creative solutions to end a combat. White Tigress, their most physically strong and imposing member. Shrike, the heart of the team...the moral guide, the most empathic member. And Blizzard, the aggressive second-in-command who, in challenging their stalwart leader, regularly pushed the team forward. It was always a private source of amusement to me that the team's requisite hot-head was the member with cryokinetic powers.)

I stared at Blizzard for a long moment, then sighed and decided to answer. I didn't want to leave mid-way through this beer. "That isn't a clothing store. It's a contracting company that makes protective gear for the military."

"Okay, yeah. Protective clothing." He rolled his eyes expressively. "Your armor is better 'n anything the military uses. I watched you shrug off a punch from Valiant!"

He pronounced the stronger hero's name in a reverent tone, the way a devout believer might speak of a saint. There was reason for that admiration. Valiant's might was legendary. While I wasn't about to admit weakness before a potential foe, the truth was that Valiant's blow had overwhelmed my shields and inertial displacement field. If not for the very many genetic and surgical alterations that I'd performed upon myself over the years, I likely would have died from the concussive shockwave alone.

"They've hinted at intriguing innovations." I replied simply. "There will be useful data to be extrapolated from their research notes."

"We'll stop you," the White Tigress growled, tail lashing.

Actually, my microdrones had already infiltrated the factory and were compromising the facility's network security as we spoke. It seemed impolitic to say so, so instead I used the straw-like appendage extended from my forearm to route another mouthful of beer from the bottle in my armored hand.

"The D.M.A. is updating our information," Shrike piped up, transparently attempting to change the conversation's trajectory. "We're not hiding anymore."

In an earlier investigation I'd uncovered the Knights' status as undocumented immigrants from an alternate universe, but I hadn't probed further to discover the origin of their (manufactured) identities. Given that the team had gone through the process of being registered and licensed through the Department of Metahuman Affairs, the forgeries must have been excellent.

That, or else the investigating official at the D.M.A. must have realized the truth and chosen not to intervene. Wildcard's ability to take on a healing power made him tremendously valuable to the New York hero community. Many an agent might have been willing to overlook a 'minor' inconsistency in a background-check in order to keep a healer in their region.

"I'm glad that the issue is resolved," I replied. "I will admit that I'd been concerned that a poorly timed revelation would have imperiled any convictions that resulted from your actions as heroes."

From Blizzard's sudden 'deer-in-the-headlights' expression, I inferred that he had somehow been responsible for gathering their identities, and that he hadn't considered the possible consequence if his deception had been revealed. I laughed out loud, and the other Knights did a poor job of hiding their fond amusement at their teammate's expense.

The conversation continued on a lighter note, discussing recent events and the peculiarities of the legal system under which heroes operated. They relayed a humorous anecdote about the time they accidentally raided an exotic dance club in which the dancers portrayed well-known heroes and villains. I responded with the tale of an instance in which an aerospace company's CEO had been indicted for knowingly submitting falsified data to the Federal Aviation Administration. I'd wasted weeks surveilling *the business and been only minutes from stealing completely faked research when the news broke.*

And all too soon, our bottles were empty.

"Thank you," Psion said when I began to float upward to begin my flight home, "for saving this world. You have no idea what our Earth was like by the time we escaped."

🕷 🕷 🕷

I opened my modified tank's hatch and shot into the air long before the approaching shuttle could detect the vehicle; the tank was a powerful tool, but it lacked the mobility necessary for a battle against overwhelming numbers. Eventually, it would have been surrounded.

Aloft, the Mk 39 suffered no such limitation. I hurtled a few miles east to draw attention away from my transport then disabled the armor's stealth systems. The Legion craft would have barely had time to raise an alarm before I swung my warstaff forward.

Lightning arced along the staff's length and the end glowed like a star being born, lighting the grim sky and casting shadows into the clouds. An incandescent halo formed, followed by an indescribable roar as white-green ionized plasma poured from the weapon's tip.

The attack didn't travel like a beam but instead reshaped itself into a twisting, sinuous tentacle stretching towards its target, a chaos of raw energy eating through the atmosphere. And when the torrent splattered across the approaching Legion shuttle's bow, the destruction was absolute.

Debris rained from the heavens, raising thick plumes of

ash. Using my neural tap, I remotely piloted my stealthed tank through the concealing layer of floating dust to a safer hiding place, employing shaped forcefields to smooth the ground and hide evidence of the tracked-vehicle's path.

Hovering in place, I spun the staff in slow, practiced kata and waited.

I didn't need to wait for long. The massive Legion starship could not alter course quickly within an atmosphere, but my sensors could detect the moment that they started decelerating to turn about. Their armaments—fusion cannons and high-energy beam weapons, from what I could determine—swiveled towards me and I began to dodge through the sky, automatic systems plotting an erratic path that strained my inertial dampeners to their limits.

The heavens erupted in light and sound as the alien vessel unleashed all of its fury upon me. Massive streams of violet energy, as thick around as my waist, boiled the air into plasma and left glowing and hissing trails in their wake. Shockwaves pounded at the clouds as a wave of pulsed plasma beams tore past, and gale force winds battered the sky.

Outrunning a laser would have been an impossible feat but moving faster than the Legion's targeting systems was more easily managed. The barrage continued, and amplified mocking laughter was my only response.

Eventually, the bombardment ceased. Again, I hovered...expectant.

The part of me that was monstrous had been straining at its leash, slashing at my insides and howling its pain until I could feel rage swell with every heartbeat. From the moment

I'd found the empty shell of Whisper's body, I'd ached for this. A chance to cut loose without guilt, without repercussion, without restraint.

A chance to carve my pain into a deserving target.

In the distance, a dozen fast-assault craft were ejected from the slow-moving battlecarrier's belly; they established three separate formations and screamed towards me, all aggressive angles and fearsome weapons and deadly intent.

Behind Doctor Fid's faceless mask, my grin was so broad that my face hurt from the effort.

7

Transcript from Bravo-Three radio tower

❦ ❦ ❦

KK6GZW:"CQ, CQ, calling CQ. This is KK6GZW, Kilo-Kilo-Six-Golf-Zulu-Whiskey."

AB2ETC:"KK6GZW, this is AB2ETC, Alpha-Bravo-Two-Echo-Tango-Charlie. Go ahead."

KK6GZW:"I'm at site Bravo-Three on Mount Diablo and I've been watching fireworks to the south. Looks like a hell of a show. Anyone know what's going on?"

AB2ETC:"Echo-Tango's must have found Charlie-Two. God DAMN it!"

KK6GZW:"Negative…Fireworks are at
     least forty clicks from Charlie-Two
     and heading east. They're lighting
     up the sky, not aiming at the
     ground. It's not one of yours?"
AB2ETC:"Negative. Everyone here's
     accounted for."
N1TKU:"Break, break, break."
KK6GZW:"Go ahead."
N1TKU: "This is November-One-Tango-
     Kilo-Uniform at Charlie-Two. Fire-
     works started in direct line of
     sight from one of our observation
     posts. Some crazy in black armor
     attacked the Echo-Tango carrier."
KK6GZW:"Damn. Another poor bastard on
     a suicide run…Anyone know why the
     ET's are still firing?"
N1TKU: "My contact says black armor is
     still fighting."
KK6GZW: "Holy crap. It's been more
     than a half hour!"
N1TKU:"Longer…a dozen ET fighter craft
     downed so far. Black armor's
     tearing it up. I'm getting updates
     from Charlie-Three. We're using the
     chaos to move some equipment."
AB2ETC:"Black armor…is it Apotheosis?"
N1TKU:"Apotheosis is dead. We got
     confirmation."

AB2ETC:"Damn."

KK6GZW:"Hey, looks like the fireworks are coming my way. Whoever this guy is, he's moving. Repeat, fireworks changed direction and are moving north-west from Charlie-Three."

AB2ETC:"Keep your head down. You don't want to be in the open when this guy finally gets killed. ET's 'll be looking for other targets."

N1TKU:"KK6GZW, quick question: my contact at Charlie-Three says she sent a family of four your way, wants to know if they arrived."

KK6GZW:"Safe and sound. The kid's a wizard with a welding torch. Hold on I'm getting a camera set up… Gonna broadcast SSTV on one-forty-five five."

N1TKU: "Roger."

AB2ETC:"Roger."

KK6GZW:"Christ, there's a lot of light in the sky. Starting footage."

N1TKU: "I've been reaching out to other regions on the 20M—no one's missing a super who wears black armor. This guy must be a solo."

AB2ETC:"A solo who can take down twelve Echo Tango fighters? Damn.

Coulda used him before he went
suicide on us."

N1TKU:"Should we send reinforcements,
see if we can get him back to
base?"

AB2ETC:"Hell no! Echo-Tangos are gonna
want to see a body after this."

N1TKU:"But maybe black armor could
win!"

AB2ETC:"Nobody wins. Sooner or later
they bring in the big man."

N1TKU:"ET's keep the big man in
Colorado. We could get black-armor
out and hidden before he gets
here."

AB2ETC:"Then it'd be the big man
looking for your camp. You don't
want that kind of heat."

N1TKU:"Yeah, yeah. I guess. It just
feels weird, watching someone fight
'n not jumping in to help."

AB2ETC:"Better to watch than throw
your people away."

N1TKU:"…yeah."

KK6GZW:"I have a pretty good high-def,
still-frame image…going to keep it
on repeat for a while. Spread it on
20M, I wanna know who this guy is."

(Unknown):"My name is Doctor Fid."

❋ ❋ ❋

My inertial displacement field was making audible chirps as I hurtled erratically through the sky, jerking and twisting at speeds no unshielded physical object could maintain. I'd never run the devices so hard for so prolonged a battle. It was possible that there was a mis-calibration to the Mk 39's subframe such that the field was extended slightly outside my armor, creating erratic turbulence in the airstream and thus causing the unseemly noise.

I wrote a quick program to monitor the disturbance for future analysis and pulsed my thrusters to maximum to curl out of the path of a particularly aggressive assault craft. My warstaff spun in a vicious arc, its surface thrumming with gathered power. The blow roared like thunder and my attacker was batted from the sky like an insect.

The debris would crater the ground, but I was already moving to avoid the next stream of attackers before I could witness the impact. Dull-colored ships buzzed like angry bees, circling and tearing the sky asunder with their fiery weapons.

It was possible that this would become boring sooner or later. For now, however, my mocking laughter echoed across the countryside.

Giddy, I shot towards the immense Legion starship in the distance. It seemed unfair not to share my wrath with the source of the swarming gnats I'd been toying with; the alien crew-members must surely have felt left out. A backhand swipe of my staff let loose a massive cone of plasma to trail in my wake, engulfing the first two of the fighter craft that swerved to follow.

The external layer of my forcefields were frictionless and automatically shaped to minimize wind resistance. I slithered through the sky like a coiling snake, a black and red blur that devoured miles in moments.

And slammed face-first into a storm of neutron-cannon fire that tore away my shields in a heartbeat.

My suit's automated defense protocols reacted faster than I could think, contorting my body and exploding into a series of evasive maneuvers that—even with my inertial displacement fields functioning at their maximum level—crushed the air from my lungs. Alarms flooded through my neural tap and I instinctively negated pain sensitivity from my lower limbs. Both legs had been baked to searing temperatures as I retreated. Medical telemetry indicated the possibility that everything from my left knee down might be completely unsalvageable.

I darted back to the chasing fighter craft, flitting among them while I struggled to assess the damage and review sensor readings.

So. The battlecarrier had short-range point-defenses with far more accurate targeting than their medium- and long-range weaponry. I'd only gotten a fraction of a second's worth of data, but it appeared as though the alien vessel used its own anti-grav fields to curve the energy blasts and refine their aim. The gravitic distortions diffracted the attacks such that they would only remain focused at relatively close distances...but within that radius even my fastest maneuvers wouldn't protect me.

I could destroy every fighter they launched at me and dance out of the way of their long-distance weaponry indefinitely...but assaulting the Legion starship itself would be difficult. My exit strategy—returning to my transdimensional tank and making the leap to my next destination—would need to be altered if the massive carrier could continue to follow after me for the rest of the afternoon.

The warstaff was un-summoned, replaced in its subspace storage location, and I tagged two craft with relatively-under-powered kinetic-energy blasts directed from my own closed fists as I soared past. One spun dizzily out of control, but the other recovered and returned to the chase.

A proper consideration of my options would take time. For now, speed and discipline would need to be my tools of choice. So long as the alien attack fighters continued to swarm, the battlecarrier kept its distance and only occasionally attempted to target me with their fusion cannons.

My automated systems were tasked to make the majority of battlefield decisions while I focused upon analyzing the Legion's weapons. There had to be a flaw in the battlecarrier's point-defense system; I started a new simulation to calculate the forces involved. The math was intriguing and I had ideas for weapon enhancements of my own...

Years ago, it had been still been odd to feel my body piloted by software but I was now quite used to the sensation. In a strange way, it was relaxing. Was this, I wondered, what the victims of the Legion's telepathic domination felt? Their bodies moving and reacting outside their own control, unseen strings guiding their figure like a puppet? But no...I could resume self-control with a thought. Even if there were similarities in the short-term experience, the overall effect would be a world apart.

My algorithm—simple though it might be—had more soul than did a Legion officer.

   ✸ ✸ ✸

```
KK6GZW:"This is Kilo-Kilo-Six-Golf-
    Zulu-Whiskey. Anyone still
    listening?"
LS9MNS:"LS9MNS here."
KK6GZW:"You up to date?"
LS9MNS:"Haven't heard anything new.
    You've got the best vantage
    point...how do things look?"
KK6GZW:The guy in black armor looks
    like he's dragging the Echo-Tango's
    battleship in a slow circle of the
    south bay. I've been filming for
    more than an hour and a half now.
    SSTV broadcasting new still-frames
    every couple of minutes on one-
    forty-five five."
LS9MNS:"We don't have SSTV at Bravo
    Six."
KK6GZW:"Damn. You're missing out on a
    show."
LS9MNS:"I hear you got an ID?"
KK6GZW:"Possibly. It was spoken on an
```

open channel. Digitally altered
voice, said he was Doctor Fid."

LS9MNS:"Never heard of him."

KK6GZW:"No one has."

LS9MNS:"Wish he'd been around ten
years ago. We were so close..."

KK6GZW:"Close only counts in horse-
shoes, hand-grenades and nuclear
bombs."

LS9MNS:"Nuclear bombs didn't get us
close enough, either."

KK6GZW:"Yeah. Yeah. Crap, sorry. I
forgot. You had family in England,
yeah?"

LS9MNS:"Yeah."

KK6GZW:"I'm sorry, man. It's an old
saying."

LS9MNS:"It's all right."

KK6GZW:"It isn't, not really. I just-
Ah, hell."

LS9MNS:"You okay?"

KK6GZW:"Fine. Just…there's another
ship coming."

LS9MNS:"Doctor Fid rates two battle-
ships? Sounds like a great show."

KK6GZW:"No, this one's smaller…and
it's got a mast."

LS9MNS:"Oh. Damn."

KK6GZW:"For anyone else that's listen-

```
ing, I'm going to keep the camera
running on one-forty-five five but
I have to get my people under-
ground. Observation post bravo
three is unmanned."
LS9MNS:"Good luck, man."
KK6GZW:"Thanks."
LS9MNS:"Black armor, Doctor Fid, what-
    ever your name is…if you're still
    on this frequency, I hope you find
    whatever you were looking for in
    the next life. You did us all
    proud, put up a heck of a fight!
    But the big man's on his way…"
KK6GZW:"And that means the show's
    over. Kilo-Kilo-Six-Golf-Zulu-
    Whiskey signing off."
```

❀ ❀ ❀

Laughing triumphantly, I reassumed control over my armor and tore a Legion fighter craft from the sky with a blast of emerald-hued force-needles projected from both gauntlets. The sleek alien vessel exploded into a shower of debris, and I wove through the smoke towards a second opponent. The other target swerved from my followup attack, but I paid it little mind.

My solution had been found.

The problem had been that opening an inter-dimensional gateway required approximately fifty-two seconds. If the Legion battleship were still active when a departure window opened, I'd thought, it would certainly interfere.

Relying on my stealth technology to escape would have been possible but risky; the modifications performed upon my brain might have protected me from mental domination, but I had no concrete method to cloak my presence from Legion telepaths. If a search party happened across me while I was cloaked, the consequences could have been catastrophic.

And so I'd worked through dozens of simulations to explore theoretical means to take the battleship down. In the end, every tactic I invented came down to the same limitation: all of the Mk 39's most powerful weapons functioned best at close range, and my armor's shields were insufficient to stand up to the Legion's defensive weaponry. I spent nearly an hour in focused thought, mind isolated in the cool focus of science and math while my body fought on. I calculated the odds of success with high-velocity approaches, I investigated weaknesses in the battlecarrier's firing arcs, I thought of using one of the alien fighter craft as a shield... every simulation resulted in failure. The Mk 39 had no means to take down the massive starship. The battle tank's defenses might be far more nuanced, but its offensive weaponry suffered from the same limitations. Adding its firepower to the fray would have no effect save to endanger my transportation device.

After several futile, doomed mental exercises, I realized that I'd been a fool. Somehow, I'd become too focused on violence and paid insufficient attention towards solving my original problem.

Battle-lust and rage nourished my desire for the alien battlecarrier's destruction. I wanted it shattered at my feet... but I didn't need that result. In the end, my only real requirement was to survive long enough to leave this dimension behind. And—with a bit of clever re-engineering that could be managed remotely—the tank's forcefields could be reinforced to a sufficient level to withstand any punishment the battlecarrier could inflict...for a minute or so.

A minute would be acceptable.

Exultant, I soared among the tightly-weaving fighter-craft, dodging and launching plasma blasts or maser fire or lances of pure kinetic force...the deadly game could be drawn out all afternoon. Time was once again my friend.

Another Legion ship had arrived and the make and model of this one was unfamiliar; I'd been so preoccupied with mathematical analysis and planning that I'd ignored the notifications that my autopilot had generated. I had just begun the process of combing through my sensor logs and recorded data when alarms began to blare.

Even knowing what was coming, I couldn't completely dodge the first punch. The glancing blow taxed shields to their limits and inertial compensators screamed in complaint. I barely managed to right myself and ready a defense before the second strike landed, re-summoning my warstaff to both hands and letting my opponent's massive fist slam into its force-field and integrity-field enhanced orichalcum shaft. The sky was rent by a thunderous crash, so loud I could feel the shaking in my lungs, but this time I stayed aloft and in control.

A few improvements had been built into my armors since the first time I'd felt that mighty punch more than a decade and a half in the past.

The big man, the local survivors had called him. That sobriquet was accurate: he stood nearly seven and a half feet tall, dark skinned and thick with muscle, the most powerful hero in at least two universes. Valiant.

In my universe, Valiant had been mind-controlled for a mere handful of minutes before the Legion's threat was forever ended. Here, it must have been months. Years. And yet...there was still tortured pain in his eyes, a forlorn and bitter helplessness. There was still a man trapped inside that skull, straining helplessly against the alien invaders' mental domination.

Valiant's captors had not placed a high priority upon their slave's personal grooming. He looked like hell, bedraggled despite his awe-inspiring presence. The once-iconic white-and-sky-blue costume was torn and stained to a muddy brown-gray.

The puppet master—presumably safely ensconced within that newly arrived ship—forced Valiant to pause in order to evaluate how much damage had been inflicted by those first two attacks.

"Mm sssssrreh," he managed to strain through chapped, barely parted lips. *I'm sorry.*

"I'm the one who should be apologizing," I shook my head and hoped that he was able to perceive the truth in my voice. "You've done nothing to deserve this."

The only response was a mocking glottal hiss. All humanity bled from the hero's expression as the monster piloting Valiant's body attempted to speak; a human throat wasn't designed to mimic the harmonics present in the Legion's alien language. I couldn't imagine that the slaver intended to say anything worthwhile, so I whipped my hand up to unleash a blast of ionized plasma.

It couldn't hurt him, of course, but the roaring spray of brutal energies splattering off the African-American power-house's face did achieve its desired effect: The Legion officer stopped trying to talk and instead had Valiant resume his attack.

The heavens blazed with the raw ferocity of our battle.

❁ ❁ ❁

```
G3YWX:"This is Golf-Three-Yankee-
     Whiskey-Xray out of Charlie One. Is
     anyone out there?"
LS9MNS:"This is Lima-Sierra-Nine-Mike-
     November-Sierra out of Bravo Six.
     I'm listening."
G3YWX:"What the hell's going on? It's
     like a war zone out there!"
LS9MNS:"You missed a busy afternoon.
     Some flying nutball in black armor
     named Doctor Fid went on a suicide
     run against the ET's big ship."
G3YWX:"One guy?"
```

LS9MNS:"Yeah. Took out a bunch of
    small fighters, too. Bastards
    brought in the big man about twenty
    minutes ago, though, so things
    should be quiet now."

G3YWX:"Well, *someone's* still
    fighting."

LS9MNS:"Say again?"

G3YWX:"No one has a visual, but we can
    hear it and see the flashes over
    the hill.

LS9MNS:"That's not possible. We got
    confirmation, the big man's on
    site."

G3YWX:"Then your nutball is still
    fighting the big man."

LS9MNS:"Holy crap. Wait, you're at
    Charlie One? You have a receiver
    for slow scan there?"

G3YWX:"Yeah."

N1TKU:"Bravo Two has a camera aimed
    over the bay, he's sending on his
    usual channel."

G3YWX:"On it. That's a long range for
    two meter, but we've got
    repeaters."

N1TKU:"What's it show?"

G3YWX:"Hold on, hold on…"

N1TKU:"You (undecipherable) anything?"

```
G3YWX:"It's no good, the fighting's
    moved off-camera."
N1TKU:"Damn."
G3YWX:"I'm gonna get some volunteers
    to go scouting."
N1TKU:"Could be dangerous to be out in
    the open right now."
G3YWX:"If someone's giving the big man
    trouble, I have a camp-full of
    people who'll wanna see it."
N1TKU:"I get it. He came through here
    pretty hard, too."
G3YWX:"If Doctor Fid takes him out,
    it'll be like Christmas."
N1TKU:"A decade's worth of missed
    Christmases."
(Unknown):"Forgive my presumption,
    but…Ho-Ho-Ho."
```

❧ ❧ ❧

Despite the fact that I was slowly being beaten to death, I couldn't help but grin. Thirty-three minutes and the Mk 39 was still functional! Even my most optimistic predictions hadn't expected the armor to withstand this level of violence.

My own body was not faring so well as the Mk 39; enough concussive force had slipped past my defenses that some particularly soft tissue inside my chest had been vibrated into a bloody, frothy mush. Fortunately, an extracorporeal membrane oxygenation apparatus was included within the suit's medical inventory. I shut my lungs down so that my technology could take over respiratory functionality. The nanites that infused my system would have an easier time making repairs without the original organ struggling to provide oxygen.

(If worse came to worst, I could always simply allow the majority of my body to perish. So long as clean blood flowed to my brain and my neural tap remained active, I could maintain control over my armor and fight. Having an actual body would, however, be preferable for future portions of my quest to save Whisper. The option of self-decapitation would be reserved only for the most desperate of circumstances.)

The thirty-three minutes had been time well-spent. More simulations and programming had been required...but preparations were now complete. The battle was as good as won! With a triumphant cackle, I re-summoned my warstaff for one final attack.

Valiant struck faster, landing a colossal haymaker to my sternum.

The shock was catastrophic.

The world spun and went gray, and something bitter flooded my mouth. System alarms and alerts blared through my neural interface so fast that they were only indecipherable white noise, and the Mk 39's autopilot systems wholly failed to compensate. I tumbled wildly, a man-shaped projectile swatted from the sky by an angry god.

It was only by pure luck that I was able to right myself a few dozen feet before I would have shattered against the rocky landscape.

There was a visible crack in my orichalcum chest plate. I hadn't thought that to be physically possible.

For a moment, Valiant hovered high overhead, the alien presence within using his eyes to stare in disbelief that I'd survived so terrible a blow. After a moment's hesitation he dropped towards me to finish the job. In his every aspect, there was only the promise of a quick death.

Another strike like that would end me; the inertial displacement field would collapse completely if the armor's frame buckled. And so, the math employed to determine my next move became simplified.

I retreated like a shot, afterburners wailing at maximum capacity.

Valiant was fast. If he'd been in command of his own actions, he might have ended me right there and then. Fortunately, the Legion telepath had less experience wielding Valiant's awesome powers and my sudden escape attempt earned me a crucial half-second's lead.

Still, the mighty hero was hot on my heels.

(That strange ship he'd arrived in must have had equipment to extend the range of a Legion telepath's mind control. We'd more-than exceeded the normal reach. I was forced to discard the hope that simply drawing Valiant further away would earn my freedom.)

I swerved among the rolling hills. There was little chance that I might lose my pursuer entirely, but I gained another fraction of a second lead when Valiant's puppeteer climbed a few hundred feet in altitude to get a safe vantage point.

The advantage of greater maneuverability (and 3-dimensional mapping technologies that allowed me to plan my route) was mine...but raw speed and power were his. In a more dramatic mountain range, I might have been able to dart among the canyons and break his line of sight long enough to enable my stealth systems. That option was of no use here. There was too much open space and too little decent cover.

The idea of escape was laughable...Valiant wasn't a foe, he was an inexorable force of nature. I overloaded my thrusters, cutting so close to the ground that the vacuum in my wake raised great trails of dust and the sonic boom rolled across the landscape. I lurched and dipped, veered and swayed. I tried every maneuver I could think of, but the monster controlling Valiant had locked its attention upon me.

There would be no escaping my fate.

The game was over and the only play remaining was to end the round on my own terms. The best that I could do was to choose where the confrontation would occur. When I'd drawn out the chase as long as I could, I triggered one last program and halted my frantic evasion—less than a hundred feet from my inter-dimensional transport.

If my lungs had still been functioning, I would have been holding my breath. Even the slightest miscalculation would have ended my quest to rescue Whisper. *Please, please, please...for the love of Tesla, don't let my math be wrong.*

The three-quarter-second lead proved sufficient and an alert pinged that the reprogrammed tank's emitters went active. The world seemed to lurch as if a pressure was lifted, a weight bearing down on me so subtle I hadn't even noticed its presence.

And Valiant plowed face-first into the ground so hard that the rocky earth cratered under the impact.

My tank, massive though it was, rocked perilously as the wave of force rippled outwards. Sensor readings spun through my consciousness. I couldn't actually exhale in relief, but it felt remarkably therapeutic to simulate the sound via my external speakers.

It took several seconds for the debris to settle, but through the swirling dust I could see the outline of Valiant, slowly struggling to his feet. Soil and gravel poured off his brawny frame, and his eyes were wide with bewildered amazement as he stared at his own fingers, clenching and unclenching his fists under his own will.

"What," he rasped, voice was rusty with disuse. "What did you do?"

"I'm generating a field-effect that disrupts the Legion's telepathic control," I explained. "So long as you're within a hundred yards of my vehicle, your mind is your own."

The large man shivered. "How long's it been?"

"At least a decade, I'm afraid."

"It felt longer." His eyes were haunted. "Much, much longer."

"I have a fabrication unit building a smaller field-generator, something portable that you can wear...but I fear that we don't have much time. Both Legion vessels are headed towards us now."

His back straightened and I saw in his bearing a hint of the hero I'd clashed with so many times in the past. "I can carry your tank and fly us wherever you need. We can get to safety and regroup."

"If you can carry my tank," behind my mask, I grinned wickedly, "I have a better idea."

※ ※ ※

"Forgive my presumption," I broadcast over the survivors' supposedly-secure radio channel, "but...Ho-Ho-Ho."

"Is this Doctor Fid?" Someone asked. It sounded like NiTKU.

"It is." My vocoder was designed to strip emotion from my voice, but even to my own ears my tone was unbearably smug. No matter. That smugness had been earned.

"You did it, then?" the speaker was suddenly breathless, weak with hope and shock. "You killed the big man?"

"No," I chuckled. "I've done something better. Watch the skies!"

※ ※ ※

I relaxed in my seat. The pilot's chair within the battle tank had been modified to adjust to support the contours of whichever powered armor I happened to be wearing when I took my place at the helm. When I'd inherited the tank, the cockpit had been a cramped affair, surrounded by panel after panel of switches and complex gauges. All of that had been stripped in my more recent iterations. Every last facet could be managed directly via neural interface.

I had to admit that the flight was smooth. Valiant had spent many years carrying occupied civilian cars to safety after natural disasters, and the decade of mind-controlled horror had not dulled his skill.

"Faster!" I relayed using the tank's external speakers. "We need to get in range before they contact their home planet!"

"I promise that this isn't as easy as I make it look!" Valiant replied, but he accelerated nonetheless. Good man.

I was monitoring the alien communications systems; my ability to translate was minimal, but I was able to verify that they hadn't sent any interstellar messages yet.

Given my tank's stealth capabilities, they probably hadn't recognized the massive burden Valiant was bearing. At this distance, all they could perceive was their former slave, alone, making his way back towards the mothership.

Valiant was the most powerful human being in all of history. They would want him re-enslaved, or they would want him dead. The alien commanders were most likely breathing a sigh of relief to have him back in their sights.

They let us get too close.

At first, I was sure, the commanders were waiting to give their telepaths a chance to re-ensnare their prize. When that failed, there would have been a period of confusion and indecision. But then they realized their error—or else they somehow perceived the almost-invisible tank Valiant was carrying—and both ships opened up with full batteries of fusion powered weaponry.

Which sprayed off the tank's forcefields like water.

My external sensors detected Valiant's grunt of effort to maintain our speed and altitude, and the entire tank shook in place...but the shield itself was unaffected. The tank's stealth-field, however, failed under the assault. We were visible now, even from a distance.

Purely for appearance's sake, I returned fire and drew a vicious line through the alien vessel's outer shell. The damage was superficial, but inflicting it still felt good. Laughing cheerfully, I weakened sections of hull and armor with subsequent shots.

And then we were close enough for the battlecarrier to employ their neutron cannons. It was precisely this for which I'd reprogrammed the shields. Immense cascades of power flooded across the force-field's surface and the curve quivered visibly under the assault.

My tank's cannon went silent—a full-sized Westler-Gray reactor had been installed to power this vehicle and every erg of energy was now directed to defense. It was insufficient; steadily, the massive batteries were being depleted.

"We have one minute!" I told Valiant. He grunted and redoubled our speed.

What must it have looked like, I wondered? Two space-ships, unloading the entirety of their arsenal upon a treaded tank, held aloft by one lone figure? So much firepower brought to bear that the air itself was heated to a dull glow, but the battletank and its bearer cocooned within a small bubble of safety? The tank's weapons must have seemed ineffective in comparison, completely useless. That sphere in which Valiant and I were trapped must have seemed only a tiny, cursed flicker of hope, an insignificant marble destined for horrific destruction.

But the first time I'd faced this tank—when it was still under Technos' control—it had been employed to negate the anti-gravity fields that my older-generations of armor had used to fly....and that technology had been remarkably similar to that which was keeping the alien vessels aloft.

"Now!" I shouted. Valiant lurched forward until we were directly between the two Legion craft, and I triggered the secondary field emitter.

For one terrible moment, there was no visible effect and I wondered if I'd damned us both. And then the ships tumbled from the sky.

It was magnificent and horrifying, the substructures groaning as the battlecarrier and its smaller sibling twisted towards the Earth. It was purely psychosomatic, I knew, but it was pleasant to imagine that I could hear the crew's shrieks of despair as certain doom approached. I envisioned their expressions and cackled until my throat hurt.

A few escape pods managed to launch, but I targeted them with the secondary cannon. Once upon a time, I was sure that Valiant would have objected to the slaughter of fleeing soldiers. Today, he quietly held my tank steady while I fired blast after successful blast.

The fall seemed to last forever, but the eventual impact was awe inspiring.

Both ships came apart at the seams, metal squealing and complaining as the decks shattered and burned. Explosions tore through the wreckage, flickering in blue and white as fusion containment failed and great plumes of orange-tinged plasma poured into the sky.

Valiant carried the tank to the ground and I exited, and then we both stood quietly and watched the Legion cruiser burn.

It was glorious.

"So." I turned to Valiant. "I don't have other plans scheduled for the next few hours, and hacked satellite footage indicates that there are two more of these ships within the Earth's atmosphere. How long do you suppose it would take for you to carry my tank to New York?"

The answering smile was fierce.

8
———————

WE FOUND A HIGH VANTAGE POINT TO OBSERVE THE WRECKAGE
of the final battlecarrier. Valiant and I had refined our technique; this one had taken only minutes to pull from the sky.
The Legion apparently relied too heavily upon their
telepathy for in-ship communication. When my tank (and
thus, the tank's anti-telepathy field) got close enough, their
combat effectiveness evaporated.

But still, we watched...just in case there were any
survivors in need of slaughtering.

"Thank you," this alternate-Earth's incarnation of Valiant
rumbled, his throat still raw from disuse. "I said that before,
didn't I?"

"You did."

"It's hard," the large man confided. "Knowing what I
actually said out loud, instead of just yelling inside my
head."

"All things considered, I think that you're doing very

well." The highly-modified voice that I'd created for Doctor Fid was not well-suited for expressing compassion. I made a note to improve the software at some point in the future. "I only endured a few seconds of the Legion's telepathic control before I was rescued. That was enough to scar."

"Who rescued you?"

"My little sister." My own throat clenched. "There is an interface installed directly into my brain to help control this armor. She was able to use that interface to break the Legion officer's control."

"You were lucky," Valiant nodded. "Hell, we were all lucky. I can't imagine what those bastards would've done if they had access to your tech."

"I have it on relatively good authority that—if they'd known that I had devised a reproducible method to interfere with mind control—they would have destroyed the planet outright, just to be certain that the knowledge didn't spread."

He shivered. "Worse'n what they did here?"

"It depends on your point of view," I considered. "A near-instantaneous ending to the species might have been less cruel. Here, they would have drawn out humanity's torture for years while they picked through the survivors for the most worthwhile slaves."

"Well, that was their mistake." Valiant lifted his chin proudly, and despite his straggly beard and unkept appear-ance...there was undeniable steel in his expression. "We're free now. We'll rebuild."

"I've been sharing the news via radio," I informed the hero. "That should help."

"Is anyone out there still listening?"

"A surprising number," I reassured. "News is spreading like wildfire."

"Thank God."

"There's an encampment hidden around forty miles northwest of here. You should go...the people will want to see you." I paused, considering. "You may wish to bathe and shave, first."

He laughed ruefully and rubbed his hand through the straggly brush that had engulfed his chin. "A normal razor won't work on me."

"I'll fabricate something."

"D'you have an entire factory in there?"

"No...just a small manufacturing unit suited to make repairs or minor adjustments," I chuckled. "Any large-scale projects will have to wait until I get home."

"Okay." He rubbed at his beard again, then grinned. "I'll get cleaned up, then we can go to the camp."

"Just you," I said. "After so long...they'll want to see a hero."

"I don't know who you were yesterday. But today?" the large man beamed, "Today, Doctor Fid is a hero."

"A hero would stay to help rebuild and protect," I shook my head. "I'm leaving in one hour and twelve minutes."

"I wasn't awake every minute of the last decade, but I'm pretty sure that there's no place better 'n here." Valiant forced an unsteady smile but there was so much pain in his eyes that I was compelled to look away. "They used me all over the planet."

"I'm...not from around here."

"Huh." He looked me over, head to toe. "Even with your voice disguised, you're too comfortable with American speech patterns to come from off-planet unless you've been here since before the Legion. And you obviously know who I am. So...inter-dimensional traveler?"

I laughed ruefully, "Heroes lead such strange lives, and I suppose you've been at this longer than most. This must seem old hat to you."

"Not exactly," Valiant managed a chuckle. "But I did notice that you can fly but your tank can't. If you knew you were going to fight the Legion..."

"I'd have come better prepared, yes. The vehicle's primary purpose is inter-dimensional travel."

"Some people just build a blue phone booth," the large man noted. "You brought a battle tank."

I sighed, "I wasn't a hero yesterday, either."

"And you seemed to know who I am 'n how to fight me. Your world's a close enough copy that there's a version of me there?"

"Yes."

"Were we enemies?"

"Yes." I paused. "No. It's complicated."

"Life usually is." His laughter sounded rusty and although his broad smile had seemed genuine, it faded quickly. "We could use your help. There's a lot to rebuild, and the Legion 'll send more ships sooner or later."

I was silent for longer than was probably polite.

"I mentioned my little sister earlier," I finally said. It felt odd, to be opening up to a Valiant like this. Odd, yet also freeing. My world's Valiant had always been among the best of my foes, one of the heroes I most respected. The history between us, however, would have made this conversation... uncomfortable. "She is in danger. She needs me."

Valiant stared at me, evaluating. "How old is she?"

"Eleven."

The big man nodded slowly. I could see in his eyes that he was considering the welfare of his planet's survivors. Like my universe's Valiant, he was a good man...but he was human, too. There was a part of him that wanted to push harder, to beg, perhaps even resort to threats to keep me here. His gaze flickered to my tank, as though he were contemplating if he could damage the vehicle before I could stop him.

But somewhere in the multiverse, there was an eleven year old girl who needed her big brother's help.

"Well," he finally said "Good luck, then."

"I've been sharing technological recommendations via radio," I apologized. "And if I survive the next few days, I'll see about sending construction automatons to help out here."

The strongest hero on at least two worlds smirked, "Your dimension's Valiant is lucky to have you as a 'yes-no-it's complicated' enemy."

"I broke his nose once," I admitted.

"I'm sure he deserved it."

I couldn't help but laugh. He joined in, and it felt almost like having a friend.

❦ ❦ ❦

I left that damaged Earth's Valiant with a newly fabricated razor, a clean costume and data modules containing decades worth of useful knowledge and inventions. I watched him fly northwest until he was beyond my line of sight, and then I climbed back into my cross-dimensional transport.

It was time to move on.

❦ ❦ ❦

Journeying between dimensions was complicated. The physical laws which would have governed such travel had been changed significantly from the laws that had existed a few hundred years prior; that superpowers existed at all was testament to the fact that inter-dimensional boundaries had been fundamentally altered by alien experimentation halfway across the galaxy.

Even with the membranes separating infinite universes weakened, the amount of energy and computational power required for safe traversal was remarkable. Finding a specific destination out of all those possibilities was even more so.

The algorithms that I'd reverse engineered from Blueshift's craft were extraordinarily complex. Fine tuning the process would have taken weeks of work but still I'd been able to limit the choices to a mere handful: alternate realities which had already been the source of relatively-recent inter-dimensional travel, where there was no living Doctor Fid.

The dimension that I'd left behind, the reality from which the Brooklyn Knights had hailed, had been within those guidelines. So, too, was my target: The universe that the Red Ghost had accidentally travelled to, where I expected to find a helpful alternate-version of Professor Paradigm.

And so, too, was the new world that I found myself on. A lush paradise, untouched by human hands.

Great fern fronds glistened with dew, climbing into cerulean skies and casting dappled shadows upon the abundant undergrowth. Vines snaked upwards around the trunks of elegantly twisted trees, sparkling and verdant and rich. The breeze, gently caressing the living canopy, was warm with the hum of insects, birdcall, and the quiet burble from a nearby stream.

With twelve hours remaining before I could continue my journey, I left the Mk 39 within my tank and clambered out to explore on unsteady still-healing legs. The air was moist, and every breath filled my newly-reconstructed lungs with the taste of raw, unspoiled life.

There was no battle here to be fought, no violence to be done. It was a disconcerting shift. Unwelcome at first, but quickly drifting towards acceptable.

Over the last decade or so, I had occasionally indulged in the opportunity to commune with nature: week long sojourns into the woods, carrying food and gear on my back. The wild was a different world than the one I normally inhabited. Away from the trappings of civilization, the part of me that was Fid had no target for its rage. And so that part of me rested, quiescent, introspective.

Only a few moments in this new reality and already I could feel my heart rate slowing.

My path through the brush was careful, slipping between branches or shifting tender leaves aside. To damage one of these extraordinary plants unnecessarily would have been sacrilege. Better to move slowly, to gauge each step prior to committing. No trace of my passing would be left save for footprints in the moss-covered loam.

The murmur of moving water called me deeper into the green.

Insects scattered despite my slow approach, some tiny and others heavy and ungainly as they buzzed away from their perches. A particularly curious hummingbird fluttered to hover in front of me, staring eye to eye, before declaring me to be of less interest than its never-ending quest for sustenance. It disappeared into the forest in a flash of bright yellow feathers.

There was, always, the awareness of passing time. Whisper was still out there, somewhere...a disembodied spirit lost somewhere on my Earth. Every minute here was another minute in which my little sister was not yet saved. But there was nothing to be done; the eddies and flows between dimensions needed to settle before another trip could be managed. Here, within paradise, I was trapped.

A tiny creek wended its way through a break in the forest, grass and moss replaced by rock and dark, rich soil. I'd found myself at one shore, eyes irresistibly drawn uphill to trace the path of the glistening liquid toward its source. Its lazy track curled about outcroppings and poured down dips in the landscape, but I could not pinpoint the water's origin.

When the Red Ghost had—upon his first accidental cross-dimensional jaunt—arrived to this alternate Earth, he'd been so struck by the natural beauty that he'd wondered if he'd died and found himself in Eden. His paramour's superpowers were connected to plant life, and he'd thought that this spectacular, vividly alive place might be her heaven.

I inhaled deeply and held it, closing my eyes and listening to the rhythm and tone of my surroundings. For a moment, the Red Ghost's supposition felt perfectly reasonable. And then a sudden breeze chilled my skin, and I realized the sun would be setting soon.

I made camp near my tank's side, cocooned within the tight warmth of an emergency bivy sack, with only a living world and alien stars for companionship.

❧ ❧ ❧

"Erik's Dad is going camping next weekend," Bobby bounces on his toes eagerly, " 'n he invited us to go. Can we?"

"Camping?" I don't look up from the paper I'm grading. "You mean, like, in the woods?"

"Uh-huh!" His small hand finds my forearm, careful not to interrupt my writing. "And canoeing, too. He has a spot by a lake."

I stop writing anyway. "...Why?"

"Why what?"

"Why go camping? We have air conditioning here, and lots of toys and games..."

"It's fun," Bobby says slowly, as though explaining something to a particularly dense student. I take note of his tone and delivery for the next time I have a student who fails to account for pre-

existing conditions when calculating trajectories. "Dad took me backpacking last year."

In theory, I'd known that my father had once been something of an outdoorsman. There had been fishing rods and old tents in the garage. He'd never tried dragging me along for any of his excursions. Instead, Dad just occasionally disappeared with his friends for a weekend and came back with an ice-chest full of trout or bass, looking happy and tired.

I'd never asked him about it. Never asked if it was fun, never asked if he could bring me with him. I hadn't even been curious. And now it was too late.

"Maybe." The idea of time spent away from my books and the comfort of my office has little appeal, but if Bobby has fun it will be worth it. Fun has been hard to come by since the accident that stole our parents from us. "Yeah, I—Wait, is this the Saturday coming up or the next Saturday after?"

"The weekend after. We'd gotta take Friday off from school 'n go early, but it's just one day."

"I'm giving a test that Friday," I sigh. "I'm sorry."

"I've watched you give tests. You just sit there!" Bobby glares impressively. "Have Alex do it!"

"Alex?" It takes me an embarrassingly long moment to connect the name to my volunteer teaching assistant; while I lectured, my TA occasionally checked on my little brother—who was usually waiting patiently near the front of the class. Alex had brought coloring books, I think. And crayons. I make a mental note to thank him. "I don't think that'd work out."

"You're just saying that 'cause you don't wanna go," Bobby accuses, a hint and angry whine creeping into his voice. "It's not fair!"

"Alex could give the test," I defend, "but he couldn't grade the papers. It's not that I don't want to go...I can't."

"Awww..."

"You can go, though." I ruffle Bobby's hair playfully. "I'll, um, talk to Erik's Dad, make sure it's all right."

"I wanted you to come."

"Next time," I grin. "I promise."

Bobby disappears for a weekend and comes home looking tired and happy. But I have other obligations the next time a camping opportunity arises, and again the time after that.

And then it's too late.

❦ ❦ ❦

I awoke to find the forest bathed in mist. Wisps of fog poured downhill and even the insects and birds quieted in reverence when the sun's first rays crept through the leaves. Gold-tinged light set the mists ablaze, vibrant and fresh and new.

When Whisper had been saved and all had settled down, I thought that perhaps I should bring her here. She'd been obsessed with oceans and fish and dolphins for the last year or so, but a morning like this would make her appreciate camping away from the surf and sand and crashing waves.

After I had brought her from the isolation of her father/creator's lair in the foothills of the Sierra-Nevada mountain range, we had driven across the country back to Boston in an old bus. We were just getting to know each other then, and I hadn't thought to stop and enjoy a few nights under the stars. There had been plenty of time to talk as the miles passed by but limited time available for leisure. By the time we'd arrived in Boston, I had already decided to take her in as Dr. Terrance Markham's ward for legal purposes and she'd thoroughly wormed her way into my heart...the little sister I hadn't known that I needed.

The world outside Apotheosis' foundry had enchanted her. A night under the stars would have been rapturous! Why hadn't I stopped to offer her that gift? What was wrong with me, that I'd so quickly leapt to repeat the mistakes that I'd made with Bobby? When Whisper was rescued, I would do better.

Be better.

Surrounded by a wild masterwork in every shade of emerald, and with only a few insects and birds for company, I donned the still-damaged Mk 39 (full repair of the orichalcum chest-plate was beyond my capabilities) and readied my inter-dimensional transport for its next journey.

And then it was time.

◉ ◉ ◉

My vehicle flickered into existence at the edge of a freeway interchange, greeted by a chorus of shrieking tires and angry car horns. I swerved into a ditch within the freeway's median but the damage was done. Traffic had stopped and news of a mysteriously appearing battle-tank would quickly spread. Given the number of hand-held smart-phones and cameras being deployed by the crowd of interrupted commuters, it was only a matter of time before there was an official response.

This situation, I thought, was less than ideal.

The original intention had been to hide the tank and explore, taking time to ascertain if this was my desired destination. Circumstance had obliterated that plan. I'd driven through a concrete barrier to reach the ditch and the tank's treads had torn great troughs through the green grass. Hiding my existence would be an impossibility. And besides...any attempt at concealment or evasion would surely have created the appearance of guilt. If peaceful negotiation was the end goal, then the most beneficial path would be to stay and wait for the proper authorities to make contact.

Turning on the stealth field would have done little to hide my presence, but I briefly considered activating it nonetheless—it would have been a simple matter to overlay a hologram of a similar (but weaponless) armored transport over the mostly-invisible conveyance. From any onlooker's perspective, the tank's cannon would have simply disappeared. But I'd already been seen and concealing a weapon would have raised more paranoia even than displaying it openly.

I could, at least, limit the impact upon local commuters before the first responders arrived. After quickly creating holographic headlights and taillights, I indicated the intent to turn and—with slow deliberation and taking intense care to ensure that my cannon never aimed at civilian vehicles—I carefully wove the tank through the stopped traffic to one side of the freeway, then over a fence into what looked to be an abandoned lot.

One car honked angrily as the tank passed. What did the driver expect to accomplish, I wondered? To cow a massive battletank into submission with one loud blast of their horn? I considered twisting the turret to allow them a view of the wrong end of the cannon's barrel but decided that doing so would be counterproductive. Any hint of aggression would be remembered.

My armored inter-dimensional transport was still visible from the highway but I dared not continue further; advancing beyond the road's line-of-site would have put me perilously near to other civilian businesses. And then I let the main cannon dip low, aiming towards the ground.

For a while, there was nothing but nervous silence. When no violence erupted, however, traffic began moving once more. Slower now, tentative...the passers-by were curious but not so foolhardy as to stop and investigate more closely. Dealing with the now-motionless armored vehicle was someone else's problem and no one wanted to be stuck in their cars indefinitely. As such, they gawked and moved on.

And continued taking photos and videos. After a few near-accidents, I added a holographic billboard to my exterior display: "Warning! Operating a handheld cellphone or camera while driving is unsafe at any speed."

Sirens approached. With any luck, police presence would do more to alter the drivers' negligent behavior than the words I'd hung mid-air. There'd been two more close calls already.

As I waited, I returned my attention towards my investigation. Initial sensor readings gave me cause for optimism; the Red Ghost had described the dimension that he'd visited as being so familiar that he had at first believed that he'd arrived home. That was comparable with my own findings: air quality, demographics, visible technology levels...all visual identifiers matched my expectations.

Sensors and scanners were now gathering more precise information, and I was pleased to discover that this dimension was a close enough analogue to my own that I could easily interface with local telecommunications protocols—another point in favor of this dimension being my desired target. Within a minute, I had programmed an army of algorithms to search through Internet records and analyze the results.

It occurred to me that a concealed pilot might create as much paranoia as a concealed weapon, so I sent a mental signal to open the main hatch to exit the tank. Given the distinct possibility of unpleasantries—first contact scenarios among members of the superpowered community were rife with misunderstandings and violence—it would be foolish to make my appearance unarmored. The Mk 39 was intimidating and hid my features, but allowing some level of implied threat might keep the local constabulary or superheroic response from reacting with unnecessary force.

Also, a beverage might help. Fortunately, my emergency supplies included a tea set and a picnic blanket.

A pot of Earl Gray brewed while I waited for the now-arrived police to cordon off the highway and establish a perimeter. I sat cross-legged on the blanket, implying that any negotiator sent would be on equal footing. All of us could sit, all of us would drink from the same pot and from identical mugs. It was an invitation, a gesture of goodwill. My audience would, I hoped, see that (despite my strange starfield-and-red armor and the fearsome vehicle from which I'd appeared) I had made every effort to avoid unnecessary damage or threatening behavior.

The police's primary responsibility was to see to the civilian motorist's safety and—so long as I made no move to endanger the public—they would hang back and wait for trained super-powered support. My sensors indicated that at least one such specialist was already en-route.

The negotiator dropped from the sky and landed lightly, a grey-and-ochre clad professional-looking superheroine who I didn't recognize. I focused the tank's sensors and pretended not to watch and listen as she consulted with the on-site incident commander.

I rested and—making use of the straw-like appendage that extended from the Mk 39's forearm—sipped at my tea, using my neural tap to sort through terabytes of data to confirm my initial findings. Behind my impassive and faceless mask, I felt weary and long-overdue grin tug at the corners of my lips.

The negotiator stepped towards me.

"My name is Doctor Fid and I apologize for any disruption caused by my arrival," I told the negotiator before she began to speak. "I am an inter-dimensional traveler and wish to apply for temporary protected status under Title 8, U.S. Code 1254a. Please...I need to talk with Professor Paradigm."

The negotiator was wearing a mask that hid her eyes, but

the relief in her body language was palpable. She (and the police behind her) would stay on her guard, I was certain, but the legal appeal did much to allay her worries.

"You're in luck," the brunette smiled and called back to me. "The Paragons are already on their way."

9

———————

"Would you like some tea?" I offered.

"No," she demurred, "But thank you for the offer. My professional name is Dawnstar, by the way, and I've been authorized to begin the process of granting you temporary protected status. There's paperwork involved and you will be required to privately unmask, and also provide a DNA sample for our records."

"Of course," I replied. "If I understand the statute correctly, I have seventy-two hours to make myself available to a Department of Metahuman Affairs for my assessment?"

"That's correct," she answered, the slight tilt of her head indicating a curiosity that she quite-professionally kept from her expression. "In the meantime, you'll need to be accompanied at all times by a licensed representative of the D.M.A., and your vehicle will be inspected and impounded."

"Excellent." One way or the other, I would be long gone

before three days had elapsed. "Professor Paradigm has the appropriate license, does he not?"

"He does," the heroine nodded, "but he'd have to agree to act as your custodian. Otherwise, you'll be stuck with me."

"I understand," I said, and took another sip of tea from my mug.

As the incarnation of Professor Paradigm from this universe didn't have decades' worth of resentment and anger towards a Doctor Fid, it seemed rather likely that the offer of knowledge would make for an easy sell. I was quite prepared to grant detailed information about several of my inventions.

If Paradigm helped me save Whisper, I'd give him anything he asked for.

"Can you tell me more about the vehicle inspection process?" I asked.

Dawnstar nodded and began explaining how an expert would be selected. I'd already done my own research into the subject, so I offered her only minimal attention; for the most part, I wanted only to keep her talking until the Paragons arrived. Sensor readings indicated that they were only a few minutes away.

The lion's share of my focus was upon sorting through local news articles and encyclopedia entries I'd gathered via my neural tap. Superficially, this world might appear very much like my own...but there were many differences. I found references to major battles that didn't happen in my own dimension, and the community of heroes and villains was also somewhat changed. There were names I didn't recognize, and other names present in surprising places. Andre Scalzi was a successful politician here rather than being a relatively low-level criminal named Blackjack. The supervillain Locust was imprisoned rather than having been brutally (and entertainingly) murdered. He'd recently become the stuff of talk shows when his parole was denied.

There were very minor differences in technology levels, too. Nothing earth-shaking, but I hacked scholastic and scientific periodicals to gather future reading material nonetheless.

And then the Paragons' sleek transport shuttle glided into view, cutting a smooth and elegant path through the sky. It appeared that Professor Paradigm's exquisite sense of aesthetics was consistent across multiple dimensions.

"If you wouldn't mind waiting here a moment," Dawnstar smiled, "I'll go update the Paragons and then bring them over to talk."

"Thank you," I nodded. "If you have any questions, I'll be right here drinking tea."

And breaking into D.M.A. databases in order to read personnel files. It occurred to me that Dawnstar was a trained hostage negotiator and that my only relevant experience was as a taker of hostages. She'd played along with my efforts to keep this encounter calm but would certainly have noticed the calculated intent. Fortunately, I was reassured as I perused her case files. In a prior record, she'd made a note that attempts at manipulation were to be expected and that de-escalation was always preferred.

Even so, I could not help but feel a flutter of nervousness when the heroine stepped into the Paragons' shuttle. Even my best sensors had never been able to defeat Professor Paradigm's anti-surveillance technologies in my home universe. Again, that capability was echoed across dimensions. My hope was buoyed; this incarnation of the aged inventor was every bit the talent as the version who'd denied me on another world.

I poured a second cup of tea and let the time pass, focusing on calm breathing, peaceful thoughts, and plans to annihilate all in my path if I were refused.

And then Dawnstar led the Paragons from their shuttle.

The Professor himself looked well...not younger, precisely, but as though he'd aged more gracefully and taken more care for his physical upkeep. There was no frailty in his movements.

To his right was Viking, a brawny man wearing leathers, with a ruddy complexion and long just-beginning-to-gray brown hair pulled back in a pony tail. The massive warhammer he bore was unmistakable. In my world, he'd retired after only a few years of activity. Here, he must have found a means to control the detrimental aspects of his power.

There was Solara and Dancer, Breaker and Fog (who I knew little about and recognized only by costume), and another man who looked familiar despite the silver cowl that hid most of his features. Unfortunately, the D.M.A. records for the San Francisco Paragons' personnel were locked down tightly. Unearthing more detailed information would take time.

"Professor," I greeted gravely. "My name is Doctor Fid, and I've travelled a long way to see you."

"So I hear." He took my offered hand and shook it professionally. "How can I help?"

"I need to stabilize a spherical harmonic quantum wave-form around a gravity well," I replied.

"A carrier signal for an interferometric sensor system of some sort, I imagine." Professor Paradigm's lips pursed in a slight frown. "If you've built a cross-dimensional transport, you already know the basics."

"I do, but working out the details would take time that I don't have. I can share the math that I've managed to work out," I gestured plaintively. "Please. A little girl's life is at stake. My sister."

"Sister?" startled the man in the silver cowl.

"She's adopted," I explained, then shook my head. "It's complicated, and it doesn't matter. What matters is that she's in danger."

"Well then," Professor Paradigm smiled, his expression flicking to his teammates. "I suppose that we'll see what we can do. Dawnstar, I'll take Doctor Fid back to headquarters."

"Yes, sir." She returned his smile, briefly. "And the tank?"

"There's moving equipment already en route."

"Okay...I'll stay here and supervise cleanup. Good luck, sir." She turned towards me. "And good luck to you, as well."

"Thank you."

I hadn't brought many drones on this trip, but there were enough present to gather up my picnic blanket and tea set and carry them back into my ship. By the time Professor Paradigm and his entourage had led me to his shuttlecraft, my tank had been re-packed and sealed itself shut.

The interior of the shuttle was appointed in an elegant but understated manner...comfortable seats that automatically adjusted to the passengers' frames as they sat down, and an area with handrails set aside for those who might opt to stand (not uncommon among those with superpowers, with odd body-shapes or physical requirements). With the exception of the video screen frame at the front of the crew compartment, there were no sharp angles...just smooth, sleek curves.

"This bird needs a pilot," Professor Paradigm noted amiably. "I'll take us home. Solara, you're with me."

"Professor, I-" the man with the silver cowl began.

"Advocate, you have temporary custody of Doctor Fid."

"I...uh, okay." He frowned, looking put out. "Okay."

The Paragons took their seats, conversing among themselves in gentle, casual tones. They did a decent job of pretending not to keep vigilant eyes upon me.

"You can sit next to Viking," my interim minder pointed. "Those seats are the largest and your armor won't scratch 'em."

"Thank you," I replied, and took the suggested location to settle in for the flight. The sooner we could reach Paragon headquarters, the sooner we could begin working on the maths necessary to save my sister.

The hero apparently known as Advocate hesitated, then chose a seat near to mine.

"Wheels up!" Professor Paradigm announced from the cockpit. The annoyingly beautiful craft climbed into the sky and we were on our way.

"So, not so long ago we had a visit from a hero named Red Ghost," Advocate noted after a minute or so of uncomfortable squirming. "Was he from your home dimension?"

"He is."

"He mentioned you."

Ah. That, I thought, explained the hint of reluctance I'd sensed in Advocate when responsibility for me had been pushed upon him. "And what did he say?"

"He said that you'd been a villain...but that you risked your life in an attempt to save his."

"Both of those statements are true," I replied simply. I'd harmed no one on this world and the heroes here had no reason to hate me. There was no rationale for defending or making light of my past, and pretending innocence had the potential to backfire.

"And now you've risked your life again to save a little girl," Advocate continued.

That comment didn't seem to require a response, so I sat quietly and calculated how long the journey to the Paragons' base might take.

"That doesn't sound like villainous behavior," he said in a leading manner.

"You shouldn't make judgements based upon insufficient evidence," I sighed. "It's an unhealthy habit to be in."

The hero chuckled. "So...you'd rather that I assume you're still a villain after all?"

"In general, I think that life is more complicated than labels like 'hero' or 'villain' allow for," I retorted, glad for the vocoder that removed any hint of annoyance from my response. "Your leader believed me when I said that I'd come here for humanitarian purposes. Isn't that enough?"

"I guess it is," he replied. "I'm just trying to understand, is all."

"I'd rather let the subject lay." I turned to set Doctor Fid's implacable, faceless glare upon the hero. "No offense, but this is an uncomfortable subject and I don't know you in my world."

"I suppose that you wouldn't know me." For a moment, his expression was pained...but the smile that followed was oddly smug. "After all, 'Advocate' wasn't the hero name I originally wanted."

"And what was?" I asked, curious if perhaps he was someone I knew after all.

"When I was a kid," he grinned, and recognizing that mischievous expression felt like a punch to the chest, "I wanted to be 'Strongboy'."

❀ ❀ ❀

The foam ball strikes me directly between my eyes, knocking my glasses askew. I reach for the ball as it bounces away, but manage only to swat it downwards towards my feet.

For a moment, there is only mortified silence. And then Bobby begins to giggle. Despite my own embarrassment, I can't help but join in. My little brother's joy is infectious.

"You were supposed to catch it," Bobby chides.

I re-adjust my glasses, feeling my face heat. "It's harder than it looks."

"It's 'catch'," he laughs. "Everyone can play 'catch'!"

"Everyone but me," I grumble, reaching to pick up the ball.

The problem, I think, is that breeze and spin altered the sphere's path. I'd swear that the ball curved! How is anyone supposed to catch an object that doesn't follow a simple ballistic arc? Perhaps if I set up a windsock I could estimate air speed and calculate a more accurate trajectory. Not this time, though.

"Now you throw to me," Bobby orders, and I do so.

In my own defense, I think that I'm improving. Bobby runs to chase after the mis-aimed ball, but he doesn't have to travel as far as he'd had to after my first attempt.

It's a beautiful day. I'd promised Bobby that he could choose what we did this afternoon, and he wanted to come to the park... so, here we are. People are staring at me, I'm sure. Laughing at my awkward attempts to play, at my unpracticed motions. It doesn't matter. Bobby is having the time of his life.

Today, he's the teacher and I'm the student.

"Okay, now I throw!"

I steel myself for another embarrassing failure, but this time the ball bounces off my chest directly into my waiting hands. I can't help but stare, mouth agape.

"Good catch!" Bobby chirps, and I grin so broadly that my cheeks hurt. "Now you throw again!"

I'd read several books on sports kinesthetics, but generally found them to be unhelpful. They don't teach how to throw...they teach how to throw faster or more efficiently. They don't teach how to catch...they teach someone who can already catch how to catch better. The manuals are interesting reading (who knew that there was so much science and physics involved in sporting activities?) but all the books made assumptions about the level of eye-hand coordination training that most children underwent as part of a normal childhood.

I'm out of my element here, tasting fresh air and surrounded by green grass, with the sun warming my skin. This is Bobby's place, not mine...but he giggles and throws the ball again, and I feel welcome nonetheless.

My childhood, I think as my brother chases another mis-thrown ball, hadn't been normal. But maybe my adulthood could be. Bobby is a competent instructor.

"Allright, Strongboy," I tease, "give me your best shot!"

❃ ❃ ❃

Triggering the Mk 39's release wasn't a conscious decision. It was only that my helm was suddenly too tight and I needed to feel unfiltered air in my lungs. Doctor Fid fell away from me and I shot from my seat, twisting to stare at the still-grinning Advocate.

I should have felt naked, exposed among so many heroes. At that moment, though, they seemed a distant presence. I could almost forget that they were there at all.

"Bobby?" I asked, hesitantly.

"Geez, Terry," this dimension's incarnation of my little brother laughed, but I could hear choked emotion in his voice. "You got old. I barely recognize you."

"Oh! I've, ah, made some modifications," I rubbed at my jaw self-consciously. "Give me eight hours or so, I'll have my nanites restore my original skull structure."

He stared at me oddly. "Is this the face you usually wear?"

"More or less."

"Then don't change it," Bobby insisted. "I want to see who you are, now."

I grinned stupidly, then gestured as if pulling back a mask. "Can you...?"

He hesitated, then pulled back his silver cowl.

I often dreamed about what Bobby would have looked like if he'd lived. Sometimes, I imagined a slim tradesman with rough hands and a gentle smile, like our father. Other times, I imagined a broad athlete as portrayed in his crayon 'Strongboy' comic strips. In my mind's eye there was always a hint of innocence, that spark of childhood that my Bobby never had a chance to outgrow.

This was better. This was real.

"Red Ghost told me you were here," I murmured, amazed to see happy tears form at the corners of his eyes, "but I didn't think you'd want to see me."

Another brief laugh escaped, and his watery eyes danced with mischief. "For a smart guy, you can be a bit of an idiot."

"That's always been true." My chest ached and I couldn't meet his eyes any longer. "Oh, Bobby, I'm so sorry."

"For what?"

"For letting you die!"

"I'm not dead. My brother—" his voice caught. "My brother died trying to protect me from Locust's mercenaries. I'm looking at your eyes and I'm pretty damned sure you'd have done the same for your Bobby if you could have."

More than anything in the world, I wished that I'd been as lucky as this Bobby's brother.

"You don't need to apologize to me, Terry." Bobby whispered. "Not now, not ever. I forgive you."

I hadn't known that three words could stab so deep. It

was a cleansing pain, but still my shoulders shook from the intensity of it.

Bobby stood and grasped my shoulder in silent support. The body language was achingly familiar—my father had done the same when at a loss for words. On both worlds, Bobby had been so young when Dad died. Did he remember our father's gentle, unflagging loyalty? Or had his Terry managed to imitate the posture during that too-brief period when he'd been acting as his brother's guardian?

Had I ever gripped my Bobby's shoulder like this in a mute expression of unconditional acceptance? I couldn't recall and that broke my heart.

And then Viking coughed uncomfortably, and I was suddenly intensely aware that Bobby and I had an audience of costumed heroes who were no longer making any attempt to hide their attention. These were the Advocate's team-mates, his peers. On another world, they would have been my enemies.

In this particular instance, I recognized that it would be extremely counterproductive to make any effort to eliminate the witnesses.

I straightened my back to recover my wounded dignity, offered Bobby an apologetic smile, and triggered the command that caused the Mk 39 to leap from its resting place on the shuttle seat to wrap itself around me. Terry Markham was swallowed whole.

"My apologies," I intoned in Doctor Fid's emotionless and highly-artificial voice. "I see that we have arrived."

And we had. The shuttle had begun its descent towards the Paragon headquarters.

"Terry-," Bobby began.

"Later," I interrupted. "Please."

After a moment's hesitation, Bobby nodded and then replaced his cowl to assume the Advocate identity once more. The uncomfortable silence lingered until Professor Paradigm had completed the shuttle's landing and led Bobby and me to his laboratory.

❦ ❦ ❦

Professor Paradigm's expression turned distant as he considered possible implications of the mathematical proof that I'd demonstrated. I was grateful for the faceless mask that hid my amused, indulgent smile—the aged hero-slash-inventor bore no physical resemblance to my old doctoral advisor, but the similarity in mannerisms made me nostalgic. Once upon a time, managing to inspire that absent-yet-inspired countenance on Doctor Hess' face had filled me with a sense of victory.

The leader of the San Francisco Paragons held up one finger, mumbled an apology, and hurried off to gather another handful of texts from his library. I couldn't help but chuckle as I was left alone in the lab.

Or rather...not quite alone. Bobby had returned, garbed now in casual clothes covered by a white lab-coat.

"Yeah, I know," he grinned, nodding in the direction the Professor had wandered off. "It's like being back at M.I.T, right?"

"It is," I replied, then startled as I noticed a label attached to Bobby's coat. "Are you married?"

He blinked in confusion. "No, although I was in a fairly serious relationship until last fall. Why d'you ask?"

"Your surname," I motioned to his employee badge.

"Oh! No, I was adopted by the Hoffmans. After...ah, you know...after Locust's attack, I didn't know what to do so I called Alex and he drove down to Virginia to pick me up. His parents ended up taking me in."

I'd burned through several assistants during my own time as a professor. Alexander Hoffman had lasted the longest and—in hindsight—likely been the best.

(One mystery resolved. When the Red Ghost had accidentally visited this world, he'd met Bobby and discovered the origin of Doctor Fid's name...but hadn't gathered sufficient information to identify Terry Markham as Bobby's brother. The altered surname would have interfered with the Red Ghost's investigation. For a while, the Ghost had erroneously believed that he'd sussed out my true identity anyway and I'd obligingly pointed him towards one of my own false ID's. Alas, that amusing ruse had since collapsed due to inattention on my part.)

"They took good care of you?" I asked softly.

"Yeah," he grinned sadly. "I was a messed up, angry little kid for a while, but they were great. Are great."

In my world, I'd lost track of Alex after Bobby's death—after I drifted away from academia. In another world, Alex had dropped everything in order to comfort a traumatized little kid. The journey from Boston to Virginia Beach was an eleven-hour drive. It had been in the middle of summer, and I remembered my T.A. occasionally complaining that his old Impala lacked air-conditioning.

I suddenly wished that I'd known the Alex from my own world better. He'd deserved better from me than to be ignored and forgotten.

Another odd thought occurred to me. "Did I—that is, did your brother have life insurance, or leave anything for the family that took you in? I genuinely don't recall."

Bobby chuckled, "You had insurance through the school, and dozens of patents that passed on to me. I'm still getting payments. I was spoiled rotten."

In this dimension, my little brother had lived, been safe, well cared-for and—apparently—loved. It was odd, to feel a sense of smug satisfaction for actions that were taken by a different Terry Markham...but I felt it nonetheless.

🌀 🌀 🌀

"Hey," Bobby said quietly, when Professor Paradigm and I took a break from discussing the basics of akashic field theory. "Can I ask a question?"

"Anything," I replied.

"The Terry I remember wasn't perfect, but he was a good guy. Why become a villain?"

"That's...complicated."

Bobby glanced pointedly at his team leader, who was mumbling to himself and staring at an empty coffee pot. "I think we have a bit of time."

Even so, formulating a response took a while. Bobby waited patiently.

"The simple answer is that I went mad with grief," I eventually answered. "But the truth is more convoluted. It wasn't just one bad moment that broke me...it was a lifetime that shaped me into a person who could be broken by one bad moment."

"I don't recall my brother being fragile," he said, his doubt plain in his expression.

"I wasn't. I was just...under tension. There's always been a part of me that was angry and lonely."

"Yeah, I guess I could see that."

"After the car accident took Mom 'n Dad, it was just Bobby and me and I thought maybe that would be enough. And then you died—I mean, my Bobby died—watching Bronze turn his back and run away."

"Yeah," he whispered.

"I hated heroes, then, and I hated myself even more. There were an uncountable number of other influences, as well." Even with my face hidden behind Doctor Fid's mask, I averted my eyes to hide my shame. "In the end...the angry, lonely, guilty and grieving part of me won."

When I finally dared to look back to Bobby's face, I saw no judgement...only sympathy.

"I'm sorry," he said, and all that I could do was nod in gratitude.

❈ ❈ ❈

Professor Paradigm had brought over a smartpad and was fully focused upon jotting down formulae upon its surface using a deceptively-simple-appearing stylus. Bobby brought me a cup of coffee, and (after only a moment's hesitation) I triggered the command that allowed Terry Markham to step out from within Doctor Fid's armor. I accepted the mug with my still-bruised bare hand. Bobby said nothing, but I couldn't help but notice his pleased grin.

After one sip, I was compelled to smile in return. The coffee had been prepared the same way that I'd taken it in college: four cubes of sugar and no cream.

"Thank you," I murmured, and used my neural-tap to remote-pilot the Mk 39 towards an out-of-the-way corner.

"That's creepy," Bobby noted, watching Fid's armor quietly walk off on its own.

"Thank you."

"Given the way Red Ghost described you and the way you've acted," he laughed, "I've had some trouble imagining you as a villain. But then you say something like that and I can see it. Just like the old cartoons..."

"Doctor Fid isn't a cartoon villain." I lower my eyes. "Near the beginning, I built a robot to open my skull, to surgically slice away empathy and leave scars likely to increase aggression. I experimented with mind-altering drugs to make myself vicious. I was a monster."

"I was a defense lawyer before I joined the Paragons," Bobby replied softly, though there was horror in his eyes as he contemplated what I'd done to myself. "I've defended my fair share of monsters...and since I've put on the costume, I've fought a lot more. The only thing they all had in common was that they didn't feel guilt for what they'd done."

He didn't comment on the pained tears that had formed at the corners of my eyes, and I didn't pretend that they didn't exist. I coughed to clear my throat.

"I eventually repaired the last of my neural scarring," I wiped at my face irritably. "But I still have a monster's memories. For the right cause, I'm still willing to do monstrous things. I'm not the Terry Markham you remember, Bobby. Not really."

"The last thing I remember about my brother was his expression while he saved my life," Bobby retorted. "What would you be willing to do to save your sister?"

"Anything," I admitted. "Everything. I'll tear the sun from the sky if I have to."

"Then you're pretty much the Terry Markham I remember." He rubbed at his own eyes, then forced a smile. "Can you tell me about her? Your new sister, I mean."

I nodded solemnly, but it took a moment to make myself speak.

"Her name is Whisper," I began, "and you would have loved her. I met her when I was breaking into another supervillain's lair..."

❧ ❧ ❧

"On your world," Bobby asked when Professor Paradigm had wandered off to videoconference with a peer in Switzerland to confirm the data I provided regarding quantum tunneling effects upon artificially-created sub-dimensions, "do you still have any of your brother's old comics? 'The Adventures of Strongboy and Doctor Fid', I mean."

"Of course."

"Could you tell me about them?"

"A moment." I used my neural tap to consult with the

supplies in my ship-board fabrication units; fortunately, on-board stores included sufficient biological raw materials to construct paper pulp and crayon wax. "I'll replicate copies for you—they'll be ready in about an hour."

The reproductions would actually be completed sooner, but it would take time for any of my limited-supply of drones to escape from the inter-dimensional transport unseen and to fly the papers to the Paragons' headquarters.

"Really?" Bobby grinned, and for a moment I could see a hint of the dimples he'd had as a child. "Thank you. That's amazing. I've missed them."

I tilted my head, curiously. "What happened to your copies?"

The alternate-dimension analog of my little brother looked embarrassed. "I burned them. After Bronze, I didn't want anything to do with superheroes for a while."

"Understandable." For an instant, rage roared hot enough to make blood boil...but I took a slow breath and forced myself calm. "Obviously, you eventually changed your mind."

"Yeah, well." He shrugged. "Eventually, I realized I still had heroes who inspired me."

"Valiant?" I asked. When my own Bobby had been young, Valiant had been his second-favorite.

"My big brother."

🙊 🙊 🙊

"Doctor Fid?" Professor Paradigm interrupted; Bobby and I had been engrossed in conversation, comparing our memories of distant childhoods. "I think I've figured out how to implement your solution."

I turned to look at Bobby, apologetic, but he just chuckled and gently shoved me towards the Paragons' leader.

"Go," he said simply. "Save our little sister!"

I wasn't his Terry, and he wasn't my Bobby...but I still felt a fierce grin beginning to form. The Mk 39 responded to my silent call, wrapping itself around me as I followed Professor Paradigm to his laboratory once more.

10

———————

Dawnstar and Professor Paradigm helped ease any bureaucratic red tape that might have interfered with access to my vehicle, but in the end it was only one hero who travelled to see me off.

"Good luck," Bobby said simply from behind the Advocate's cowl.

There was more to be said...entire libraries' worth of thoughts and emotions that I wanted to express! But I didn't have the words, so I just nodded gratefully and closed the armored transdimensional transport's hatch.

And then I was gone.

❧ ❧ ❧

In the moment between existences, I struggled under the weight of distant shapes, watched the curve of a citrus scent, and tasted slivers of vibrant music. Every inter-dimensional transition had been indescribably different—there were no words, no means to classify or categorize the experience. Sensations flooded forth from a place where time didn't exist, leaving only barely remembered echoes as the crackling hum of inter-dimensional energies faded.

I felt it in my bones: this was home.

(Superheroes lead remarkably odd lives, and accidental cross-universe jaunts were rare but not unheard of. In their duty logs, the alternate dimensions to which they traveled were always given simple but memorable names as shorthand. The Arrowverse, Earth Bet, the Teraverse…For my own records, I decided to label the first universe to which I travelled the Knightsverse, as it represented the point from which the Brooklyn Knights had originated. The second would be Eden, and the last could only be the Bobbyverse.)

There was much to be done. The mathematical models that the Bobbyverse incarnation of Professor Paradigm and I had created were a quantum leap forward, but the sensor array necessary to locate Whisper's disembodied spirit would still take a few hours of manufacturing time.

Sadly, there were other chores that would need to be attended to first.

A thought was all that was required to activate my tank's forcefield. A fraction of a second later, my own dimension's incarnation of Valiant barreled into the invisible shield at around four times the speed of sound; he ricocheted off its surface and was deflected into the ground, gouging a ten-foot-wide chasm out of the earth. The Earth's mightiest hero was stunned, but that wouldn't last long.

My time off-universe had been well spent, and I'd had

sufficient time to improve the accuracy of my cross-dimensional travel. The Bobbyverse had been left from that foreign world's version of California, and my vessel had successfully returned only a few miles from one of my hidden laboratories in upstate New York. There was a teleportation platform located there, as well as an underground hangar where I'd expected to hide my tank.

That latter aspect appeared unlikely, now—there was no possible way that the treaded vehicle could outrun Valiant, and it seemed annoyingly probable that other heroes were en route—but the teleportation platform could still be used as a means to escape. I didn't need to beat the heroes—I didn't even need to fight them! All I truly needed to do was return to my lair and begin construction of the sensor array necessary to locate Whisper's disembodied spirit.

Except that I'd warned the Red Ghost. I'd warned Blueshift! The heroes had reacted with predictable thick-skulled recalcitrance. Time in Eden and with Bobby had dulled my rage, but the realization that these heroes were here in an attempt to prevent Whisper's rescue—even unknowingly—caused my blood to boil. It seemed that—in the future—I would need to express myself more forcefully in order to ensure that my meaning was understood.

A reflexive mental switch triggered a cocktail of adrenaline and psychoactive combat drugs to be released into my system, and I found myself grinning even as I constructed a plan: I'd sneak away from the tank and continue to pilot it remotely so that the heroes would not recognize my absence. After I'd caused enough havoc to make them wary, I'd initiate the vehicle's self-destruct code.

Sorting through the wreckage would have taken hours; by the time that they'd confirmed the tank had been empty, I would have been long gone. Another tarnished success for the battered heroes, and another thrilling escape that added to the legend of Doctor Fid. The afternoon's overriding goal might have been to make a safe exit, but this was my universe. Here, Doctor Fid wasn't a savior, wasn't a peaceful explorer or seeker of knowledge. Here, Doctor Fid was violence incarnate! The brightly-clad superpowered busy-bodies would need to work for their 'victory'.

(Even though I now had the expertise necessary to build a new and better inter-dimensional transport, I had to admit that I was annoyed by the necessity. If nothing else, I would mourn the loss of the tea set still present in the emergency supplies.)

Valiant arose from the deep furrow of earth and stone in which he'd been buried, shaking away great clods of dirt and debris, and he looked up just in time to see the battletank's main cannon focus upon him. A roar of plasma took him in the face, driving Valiant back into a wide puddle of flash-melted dirt and stone. The hero suffered no lasting damage, but the massive fireball did succeed in raising my spirits. I fired a few more blasts purely for entertainment purposes.

The smoke and glare also granted me the opportunity to implement my scheme. I darted through the tank's silently-opened escape hatch and shot into the brush. Sensor readings confirmed that another shuttle was rocketing towards the conflict, and—given that the Mk 39 had taken damage during the course of my alternate-dimension adventures—my stealth field was operating at less than full capacity.

Soaring in the open air would be ill-advised. Instead, I darted into the forest and used the foliage as cover while my tank continued to pour energy blasts upon the groggy hero.

"I intend no harm to you or yours." Doctor Fid's artificial voice thundered from the tank's external speakers. "Stand down and let me pass!"

"Intentions don't matter this time." The mightiest hero on at least two worlds had regained his bearings and leapt into the sky, dodging cannon fire and flitting around the tank while looking for an opportunity to counterattack. "You've gone too far, and you need to be stopped."

That...made little sense. Something must have changed during my time away. I could think of only one looming possibility that would have inspired such ire and used my neural tap to quickly hack a California hospital's records.

"Professor Paradigm will live," I intoned through the tank's speakers, grateful for the modulation that struck relief from my tone. This dimension's incarnation of Professor Paradigm may have initiated hostilities without cause and withheld information relevant to Whisper's rescue, but another world's Paradigm had been far more reasonable. "And the stroke obviously didn't affect his intellect."

The only way that Valiant could have attacked so swiftly after my arrival is if the heroes had been waiting for me. My world's Paradigm must have studied Blueshift's technology and thus learned how to triangulate inter-dimensional rifts.

"He's paralyzed!" Valiant countered angrily, slamming into the tank's forcefield with enough force that the entire vehicle was driven down almost a foot into the ground. "He was retired, and you tracked him down and put him in a wheelchair."

Maintaining a conversation over the din was difficult so I ceased fire. "I approached peacefully...Professor Paradigm attacked me, unprovoked."

"That may be true," Valiant replied uncertainly, his attack faltering. By his body language, I guessed that the bedridden Professor had failed to relay that tidbit of information. "But even so, he was helpless when you finally struck him. I've watched the video."

"He attacked me," I explained again through the tank's speakers. "And I'm Doctor Fid. Retaliation was required."

"Yeah," the hero sighed, and the disappointment in his voice was palpable. "And that's why Doctor Fid has to be stopped."

The massive hero renewed his assault on the battletank's shields and--from more than a mile away--I continued bantering and operating the vehicle from a distance. The forcefields would hold long enough for the shuttle-full of other heroes (presumably, Titan's "task force") to arrive. Less than two days prior, I had fought the Knightsverse version of Valiant to a standstill and torn three Legion battlecarriers from the sky. Compared to that, managing so simple a subterfuge was child's play.

And that's when the forest attacked.

Regrowth must have volunteered to join Titan's task force and--though her shuttle was still miles away--had detected my armor's passage through the brush. I'd fought against her in urban and suburban regions and thought that I'd known what to expect. Her ability to control plantlife was powerful but I'd never considered her as great a threat as her husband (the Red Ghost) or the Boston Guardians' leader, Titan.

Here, in the dense and untouched forests of the Adirondack foothills, Regrowth was a goddess.

It wasn't one tree that reached for me, nor was it a handful of vines that reached to entwine one arm. It was the world exploding into motion, countless tons of supernaturally-enhanced wood and bark shifting in harmony, reinforcing each other, twisting and groaning and crackling with force.

Even automated reflexes had no time to react before I was slammed repeatedly into a stone outcropping. The pressure was too great, and the Mk 39's already damaged orichalcum chest plate buckled under the strain. A warning message blared into my consciousness that my inertial displacement field had failed.

"...wait..." I whispered, but my voice was so weak that it barely reached my own ears.

The Earth rose up to meet me...and I was shocked into awareness in a fresh clone body, a thousand miles away and leagues beneath the ocean's surface.

Well.

That was unfortunate.

✿ ✿ ✿

The End of Doctor Fid
By Taylor Harrison, KNN

(KNN) — Yesterday afternoon, the notorious criminal known as Doctor Fid was slain as he attempted to evade arrest. The villain's two-and-a-half-decades long reign of terror came to an ignominious end in upstate New York, twelve miles south-west of Lake Placid. Titan, long-time foe of Doctor Fid and leader of the task-force that had been charged with apprehending the fearsome supervillain, had this to say:

"This outcome is never ideal. It had been my hope that my team would have been able to bring Doctor Fid to justice; instead, I can only pray that Doctor Fid's many victims can finally gain closure. One of the most dangerous men in all of history is no longer a threat to the public."

The mighty Valiant had been the first on the scene, confronting Doctor Fid by himself until reinforcements could arrive. According to multiple witnesses, the battle turned more than twelve acres of untouched forest into a scarred warzone.

"Doctor Fid was a complicated man," said Valiant. "There is no question that he was violent, and at times frighteningly vindictive, but he also went to extraordinary lengths to ensure that innocent bystanders were never harmed by our battles. He saved the world. He saved the city of Boston. He even volunteered to rescue children after that earthquake in Chile. There was a part of him, I think, that didn't want to be a monster anymore."

Despite Valiant's legendary strength, in the end it wasn't he who put a final end to the threat that was Doctor Fid.

"He saved my life once," said a visibly shaken Regrowth. Her husband and team-mate was present, resting a comforting hand on her shoulder. "He had a strange sense of humor but I genuinely believed he was trying to turn things around. Something happened after the Skullface incident, though, and he was getting out of control…I wanted to stop him, to help him. I didn't want this."

It has been rumored that an uneasy peace had been brokered between the Northeast's most powerful superhero team and the world's most feared villain. If so, that implies that other heroes, too, believed that Doctor Fid could be trusted to uphold his end of the treaty. Due to technical difficulties, the leadership of the New York Shield were unable to offer any commentary.

Other heroes were less conflicted.

"Fid hurt a lot of my friends," said Boston-native Veridian. "I'm glad I got

there in time to watch his body burn. I'm
going to sleep better tonight than I have
in a long while."

A bloodthirsty sentiment, perhaps, but
one that is shared by thousands of commen-
tators on online forums where news of
Doctor Fid's demise was met with cele-
bration.

Un-named sources claim that the task
force was able to locate the powered-armor
wearing criminal using technology provided
by Doctor Fid's most recent victim: the
bedridden but undefeated Professor
Paradigm.

"I'm glad that he's dead," the fabled
inventor commented to a local reporter,
"but this was also a tragedy. Doctor Fid
may have been a twisted horror, but he also
possessed a once-in-a-generation mind. If
his genius could have been put to produc-
tive use, who knows what might have been
accomplished?"

The identity of the man within the iconic
star-field armor is currently unknown;
after the wearer's death, the armor self-
destructed, and the body was too badly
damaged for even DNA identification. The
investigation continues, with Professor
Paradigm leading the charge to find any

records that might be used to recreate any of Doctor Fid's technological marvels.

❧ ❧ ❧

The Mk 39 had been my sole remaining functional armor. With its loss, I could not put on Fid's skin even if I wished. For the first time in decades, the comfort and safety of my faceless shell was lost to me. I should have started production, should have focused on studying the previous versions' flaws and improving upon past designs. I should have been plotting, determining how best to take advantage of the public's certainty that Doctor Fid was no more.

There were many things I should have been doing but in the end I did none of them, because none of them mattered.

I'd built the sensor array. I'd run my tests and I'd triple-checked my results.

And then I'd collapsed to the floor and sobbed until even my newborn artificially-enhanced chest ached from the effort of it.

If my sister's spirit had been floating free of a body—free of any server farm—the sensor array would have found her. All it would have taken would have been a properly-adjusted modification to my akashic transfer device to return her home. But the sensor found nothing. I was too late.

Whisper was gone.

11

———————

The passing moments flowed like tar. They had weight, bowing my shoulders and crushing the breath from my lungs.

Eventually, minutes congealed into hours.

As though shocked by lightning, I was filled with the sudden certainty that my house required a thorough cleaning. Despite how pre-occupied I'd been over the last three months, I hadn't allowed the property to decay...but the estate certainly wasn't ready for company. There would need to be a ceremony, and people would visit afterwards. The grounds needed to be made presentable.

After the car accident, Bobby and I had wandered our childhood home like lost lambs, too wrapped up in our own pain to really be aware of what was going on around us. Our Dad's lawyer had taken care of the arrangements—he'd been a family friend, one of my father's fishing buddies.

Others had come. I didn't know most of them. they'd been my Dad's friends, my Mom's friends, people they knew from work or the community.

Some brought food, others bore only sympathy. The visitors were significantly older than Bobby or me and they'd been more experienced with loss. They told stories that tore at my soul to listen to, they offered trite advice, and they asked well-meaning questions about our future that I had no answers for.

I hated every moment of it, but I'd been so incredibly grateful.

It had been the same after Bobby died...the same, but very different: it had been children who visited, then. Bobby's friends, confused and grieving; I should have been the one to tell stories or offer advice, but the words had stuck in my throat so I'd cried with them instead.

The Markham Estate needed to be made presentable, so I stumbled mechanically to the teleportation platform: Doctor Fid's ghost, leaving his once-favorite hidden laboratory behind.

I rematerialized in my home office and stared at the closed door that separated me from the rest of the house. It was—like much of the house' accouterments—an understated extravagance. Solid oak, stained and polished to a warm tone with elegantly simple hand-carved molding. Heavy brass fixtures, cast from antique molds but machined to modern standards of quality.

When first I'd bought and upgraded this house, it was nothing but a prop intended to demonstrate the taste and success of Dr. Terrance Markham, CEO of AH Biotech. It had been a place to wine and dine investors and to hold informal meetings with the executive staff. The space hadn't really been lived in until Whisper had joined me. Even then, this office had felt as though it were mine alone.

On the other side of that door was Whisper's home. I left the entrance closed and worked to make order of my room, first.

I started by separating the books into categories, and then alphabetizing each section by author name. A pattern emerged: the mathematical and scientific texts were well-worn, whereas the collection of handsome leather-bound works of philosophy and fiction were in near-immaculate condition. I dusted and sorted until my desk was bare and my shelves full, then moved on to sort the papers in my inbox. Contracts, notes, bills...everything found a place. Pens and pencils separated to different sections of the hardwood desk's main drawer. My laptop computer—only used for AH Biotech business since all else was managed more directly via neural-interface remote access to my server farms— secure in its charging station.

Only when there was nothing left to accomplish was I able to will myself to open the door. And so I made my way slowly from room to room. There was something comforting about the task, almost meditative. There was little thought involved...only action, simple and straightforward. I cleaned. I polished. I organized.

Eventually there was only one room left, but there was no force on Earth that could have compelled me to enter Whisper's bedroom right then.

It was too late in the evening to buy flowers, so I spent the night designing weapons of mass destruction instead.

❧ ❧ ❧

In the end, I decided upon arrangements of white roses and lilies mixed with the occasional grouping of blue hydrangea. The store keep at the most highly-recommended local flower shop was helpful and sympathetic.

(How strange it must be, when half of your customers come in to celebrate the happiest moments of their lives, and others stumble through the doorway to memorialize their worst. Emotional whiplash was not a risk that I'd faced in any of my prior careers. Whether at the chalkboard, the boardroom, or the battlefield...the mental state of those I interacted with had always been fairly predictable.)

The weather was gray, and foreboding clouds loomed from horizon to horizon. It had rained during my slow walk to the flower shop and my rumpled clothes were still clammy. I trudged on, arms hugged to my chest to counter the chill. Automated medical systems hidden beneath my rib cage altered my heart-rate and blood-pressure to keep the frigid temperatures from becoming dangerous but did nothing to aid against discomfort.

A black German sedan swerved to the side of the road and skidded to a halt a few paces in front of me. I let my hands drift to my sides on the off chance that I might need to fight or flee, but almost immediately realized that would be unnecessary. The vehicle was one I recognized.

The passenger side window lowered as I approached. "Terry?"

"Aaron." I smiled sadly to the current CEO of AH Biotech. "I was going to call you later."

"What are you doing out here?" he asked, brows furrowed with concern.

"Walking," I replied acerbically, and then—realizing that the one-word answer was unnecessarily rude—I added, "I needed some air and I had errands."

"Well, climb in...I'll give you a ride."

"My clothes are a bit damp," I warned.

"My upholstery will survive," Aaron chuckled wryly, then his voice dropped low and serious. "C'mon, Terry. Get in the car. Please?"

I sighed and accepted the offer, clambering into the sleek car. Reflexively, I catalogued the make, model and options, and felt momentarily pleased. This vehicle—the car my friend used to chauffeur his daughter to school and lessons —included the inertial displacement technology that I'd gifted to the Red Ghost's company.

Aaron turned on the heated seats before signaling to merge back with traffic. Lower tech, but appreciated none-theless.

"I'm sorry for interrupting your afternoon." I closed my eyes, feeling as though I was shrinking in on myself. "Just... drop me off at home, you can get back to whatever you were doing."

"Nothing to interrupt," he responded easily. "I was out here looking for you."

My brows furrowed; if I were developing a search path to

locate Dr. Terrance Markham based upon prior information, this particular road wouldn't have been a high priority pathway to explore. "How...?"

"Someone from Microbiology heard that you'd been spotted walking in the rain. He was worried 'n asked if I knew what was going on."

Willy Natchez' preternaturally odd luck must have struck again.

"Well, thank you." I had the grace to look embarrassed. "A bit of water wasn't going to kill me, but this is appreciated."

"My pleasure."

For a while, we drove in silence. Aaron's body language and curious glances fairly screamed that he was aching to question me, and I was grateful that he chose to restrain himself.

"It's been a bad couple of days," I offered in explanation. Keeping my friend in suspense seemed needlessly cruel.

"I'm sorry to hear that." He spared me a somber, supportive smile. "Is there anything I can do?"

"No," I said, then reconsidered. "Yes. I want to host a remembrance ceremony for Whisper. You know the children that she and Dinah used to be friends with. Can you help me get in touch with their parents?"

"Of course." His voice was heartbreakingly sad. "You tried everything, then?"

"Everything."

"Damn," he sighed. "I knew that it was a long shot, but I still hoped..."

"Yeah," I closed my eyes. "Me too."

"I'm so sorry, Terry."

As if on cue, thunder shook the car. The skies wept, and my friend and I wept with them.

❦ ❦ ❦

"I met Bobby."

It seemed as though my voice shattered the heavy silence —I'd been standing there for minutes and Whisper's bedroom had been soul-wrenchingly quiet.

"Not my Bobby, of course. Another Bobby, alive and grown up, from a different universe."

I sat down on the edge of the bed, gingerly. Despite my care, Whisper's body was rocked slightly as my weight settled. It almost looked as if she were shifting in her sleep and the thought made my heart clench.

"He's a hero. A good man. You would have liked him."

That was surely true. Whisper had been able to see good in me. The good she would have seen in Bobby would have shone like the sun. They would have gotten along famously, laughing and playing together and taken turns teasing me. I couldn't help but smile at the thought.

"He wrangles his world's Professor Paradigm the same way my teacher's assistants used to take care of me," I chuckled. "The other-universe Paradigm would get distracted by a promising theory and leave a coffee mug on the edge of a table, or a giant pile of books discarded on a chair...Bobby'd just be there, quietly cleaning up and letting Paradigm stay focused."

Whisper had occupied a different role. She'd been

supportive, of course, but also a forceful and innovative partner. Where Bobby had just smiled and enjoyed being around me when I was energized by a math problem, Whisper had giggled and argued about proofs. She'd been extraordinary.

"I paralyzed this world's Professor Paradigm," I admitted, taking Whisper's cool and lifeless hand inside my own. "I didn't mean to. I just...I just wanted to hurt him."

I had to look away, unable to bear the judgement I imagined on her face.

"I know you wanted me to be a hero, but I fear that's going to be Doctor Fid's final legacy: a man I should have liked and respected, stuck in a wheelchair for the rest of his life. I'm so, so sorry."

For a while, I had no words. I held Whisper's hand and let the silence swell.

"I would have done anything to save you," I finally said. "You know that, right?"

I stared at Whisper's face, praying for only the second time in my life for her eyes to light up, for her to be awakened by my desperation, to smile and reassure me. Other people receive miracles. Even if I were horrifically unworthy, then surely my little sister was more deserving?

But...no.

"I decided to let Nyx stay with Aaron and Dinah," I whispered sadly. "The puppy will be happier in a happy home.

"This isn't the way it was supposed to end."

Whisper was supposed to grow up and inspire the world, to leave me behind and become something wonderful. A heroine. A healer. My little sister could have accomplished anything! I would have been so proud. I was still proud.

I was still broken.

"Everyone thinks that Doctor Fid is dead now," I continued. "Regrowth destroyed the Mk 39 while I was in it—if the Akashic transference device hadn't been functional, if I hadn't had a spare clone ready...that would have been the end. But I'm still here, and you're...you're..."

Gone, I couldn't say.

"I, uh, I've started building a Mk 40 armor—I gained access to your father's foundry for the orichalcum, I thought you wouldn't mind—but I'm not sure if I'm ever going to wear it. Maybe Fid should stay dead.

"I don't know what I'm going to do."

Even as I said the words, I knew them to be a lie. I didn't know what I was going to do with my life, didn't know how I was going to live with myself, didn't know what the future held at all. But I did know at least one task that still lay before me.

With exquisite care, I lifted Whisper's empty shell from her bed and carefully carried her across the room. I'd decided upon a pale-blue casket lined with comfortable silk and cushions. Even the sight of the delicate-appearing receptacle made my eyes sting, and I couldn't help but flash back to the memory of another too-small coffin and another lost sibling.

Whisper was gently laid within and posed as though resting with her arms hugging her favorite doll—Amelia—to her chest. The android looked so tiny, a slender and strangely alien little angel.

There was a hiss of equalizing pressures as the casket's transparent cover formed and hermetically sealed.

"You were the best little sister anyone could have asked for," I told her.

"I'm sorry I wasn't the big brother you deserved."

❧ ❧ ❧

The ceremony was lovely.

Both children and their parents were kind and respectful.

I didn't shatter the Earth's crust and doom all of humanity to a horrific demise.

All in all, I judged the day to be a great success, and—once the last sobbing, sympathetic guest had left—celebrated by turning off my enhanced liver functionality, opening a bottle of exceedingly overpriced scotch, and drinking myself unconscious.

12

———————

MY HEAD THROBBED IN TIME WITH MY PULSE AND THE BACK OF my throat burned. The stench of vomit and stale urine was overpowering. For the love of Tesla, I wondered, how many medical systems did I override last night?

The answer was, apparently, 'too many'. Megabytes of warning logs were thrust into my consciousness via neural interface, flooding past too quickly for me to make sense of in my presently addled condition. I wouldn't have thought it possible, but the headache actually worsened. I dared not open my eyes lest my skull explode. Figuratively.

Actual detonation would have required triggering the surgically-implanted explosive charges. That idea was remarkably tempting, but new clone-bodies were costly and time-consuming to create...I only had two left at the moment and a hangover seemed a poor excuse to discard my akashic identity's current housing. This state was awful, but I'd borne far worse.

Discomfort and I may have been old friends, but it was also true that I'd become accustomed to many little luxuries. Warm blankets plush with fine down, for example, or sheets exquisitely woven from Egyptian cotton, or a mattress carefully matched to my preferred sleeping habits.

A slight shift of my weight sounded the creak of springs and crinkle of synthetic sheets. The bed in which I lay was not my own.

I remained limp and—with my eyes closed—concentrated upon my other senses.

There were two people nearby, and—from the even breathing and lack of other movement—I hypothesized that one was asleep. The other was mumbling soft obscenities to himself. There was a rhythmic aspect to the latter person's delivery, and the audible whisper of fabric brushing against a hard surface. He (and it was a 'he', judging by the voice) was likely sitting on the floor and rocking back and forth.

Echoes carried. There were no carpets or drapes to soften the noise, and there was a tinny quality that hinted at stone or concrete floors. Concrete seemed more probable—I'd visited more than one overly-melodramatic villain who insisted on making their lairs in caves or castles with traditional stone flooring, and the tone just didn't feel right for either possibility.

The place reeked of sweat and desperation. And—in the distance—I heard other voices, a constant hum of activity. I could make out none of the words, but could guess at the gist. Indignant and poorly-acted declarations of innocence, bawling requests for assistance, and sharp anger, all contrasted against calmer, more professional tones that ranged from sympathetic to bored to aggressive. When I rubbed my fingers together, I could sense the oily residue of ink. I'd been fingerprinted recently.

A police station.

It was self-evident that it had been my civilian identity who'd been apprehended—if any suspected that Fid was still alive and that I was he, a rather different dungeon would have awaited: a high-security Department of Metahuman Affairs facility, surrounded by swarms of D.M.A. agents and smug, gloating heroes. The local constabulary would only have been contacted to help with crowd control.

Seeing no reason to continue feigning unconsciousness, I groaned and rolled to sit upright on my cot. One bleary glance at my surroundings confirmed my supposition. I'd originally guessed that it might be one large room, but I saw now that each of my compatriots had been placed in our own section, separated by bars. My own cot was at the end, against a wall. The holding cells were relatively tidy—it stank, but it appeared as though the walls and floor had been recently hosed down. The odor's source was the cell's inhabitants rather than the chamber itself.

I sniffed at my own shirt and winced, then took stock of my own condition. At some point in the evening, I must have completely disabled the medical-nanite automated treatment functionality that usually addressed even major wounds as a matter of course. One of my eyes was slightly swollen, my lips were cracked, and my knuckles had been scraped raw.

Apparently, I'd been in a fight. A minor fight, at least—the trauma was purely superficial.

There was a notice stenciled onto the opposite wall informing any cell-occupants that audio and video monitoring equipment were both present; a too-fast recovery from my injuries might be noticed. As such, when I reactivated the medical nanites flowing through my veins they were programmed to avoid repairing any externally-visible damage.

I closed my eyes once more and waited for the pounding in my skull to fade.

"Dr. Markham?" someone asked.

"Yes?" I re-opened my eyes and peered wearily at the speaker, a young uniformed officer.

"Your bail's been paid," the officer explained. "Come with me."

"Of course." I swayed to my feet was the cell door was unlocked.

The discomfort was still too intense for me to use my neural interface to remotely hack police records, but whatever I'd been arrested for could not have been terribly severe. For any serious crime, I would have had to wait for a bail hearing. From what I'd overheard at Lassiter's Den, that process often took days. My personal lawyer was quite competent and she might have had the Governor on speed dial...but even so, I was reasonably certain that I hadn't been insensate long enough to appear before a judge.

A sudden flood of adrenalin washed away the edges of my headache, leaving only wary tension in its wake. It was not my lawyer who was waiting for me at the end of the hall.

"Dr. Markham," greeted the Red Ghost. "I was so sorry to hear of your loss."

"Thank you," I replied, hoping that my confusion wasn't too visible. There was still paperwork to be signed, I was sure, but the officer left me alone with the scarlet-clad Hispanic hero.

Valiant may have been the strongest opponent that Doctor Fid had ever faced, but the Red Ghost had always been the most dangerous. He was devious and methodical in a way that the majority of costumed strongmen were not. The Red Ghost had been Doctor Fid's adversary—Doctor Fid's nemesis—for more than a decade. Dr. Terrance Markham, on the other hand, had crossed paths with him only a few times. The Red Ghost's presence here was unexpected.

(The Ghost's sympathy, however, was predictable. In my civilian guise, I'd once had the opportunity to introduce Whisper—unsurprisingly, she'd liked him.)

"I wanted to come in person to let you know that Mr. Ferris is dropping all charges," the costumed hero explained.

With pain fading, memories began to resurface. I'd been sitting in the grass near to Whisper's crypt, drinking, mourning, murmuring stories...there'd been a photographer, a vaguely familiar paparazzo trespassing on my estate. He'd snapped a few photos and ran.

I clenched my fists and my torn knuckles stung. Obviously, I must have given chase.

In that moment, I knew that I would never again turn to alcohol for solace. The consequences were too daunting. The photographer—Brian Ferris, I discovered upon hacking the police department arrest records—had survived my rage with only minor injuries. How terribly embarrassing.

"You interceded on my behalf?" I asked.

"I did, yes." He grimaced. "I apologize, I should have asked permission first. The Guardians have had run-ins with Mr. Ferris, though—he's a bottom-feeding low-life, but he has friends in the media. He would have attempted to embarrass you in the news to pressure you to settle any legal proceeding. You don't deserve that."

"I seem to recall that Mr. Ferris has made a profit suing celebrities in the past." Such as Aeon of the Boston Guardians, for example. "How'd you convince him to back down?"

"The camera that you destroyed was replaced, for one."

I didn't bother attempting to hide my smug smile.

"And I reminded him that there wasn't a jury in the world that would convict a mourning father for chasing away a trespasser on the night after his daughter's funeral."

And just like that, it felt like I'd been punched in the chest by Valiant.

"I apologize again. I didn't mean to hurt you...but the way you loved her? The way she loved you? That is the way a jury would see it. And as a hero whose job it was to stop monsters like Skullface, I am so incredibly sorry that I failed you both."

"Ah," I said, smiling sadly, when I could breathe again. "Guilt. I'd wondered why you were here."

"The last few weeks have not been good ones," he replied, and there was enough strain in his voice that his Chilango accent became more pronounced. "I suppose that I needed to succeed in helping someone, and you'd already been in my thoughts. When I heard of your arrest...I came here."

It was odd, to hear the Red Ghost say that he was performing a kind act not because it was the morally upright thing to do, but instead because he needed the sense of validation that came with victory. The admission made him seem more human beneath his mask. I disapproved.

But, even so...his assistance had been well-intentioned.

"Thank you." I offered my hand, and he shook it gratefully. "My first instinct would have been to fight him in the courts and the media...and you're right, it would've gotten ugly. This is better."

Brian Ferris would've been ruined by the eventual fallout, I was certain. No other possibility was acceptable. The ensuing hubbub would, however, have attracted both positive and negative publicity...and I didn't want Whisper's name on the lips of reporters, comedians or political pundits who'd never met her.

"You're welcome." The Red Ghost stood a bit straighter, as though a weight had been lifted from his shoulders. "At some point—if you are willing—I'd like to contact you again to discuss a business opportunity...but you've been through an ordeal and I should let you return to your home."

"I look forward to hearing from you. But...call ahead before you come visit," I said. "My house is too quiet, I probably won't be spending too much time there."

"Where will you be?"

"A laboratory, most likely." I sighed. "I think I need to keep myself distracted...to avoid a repeat of last night."

"In that case, perhaps I might offer a technical challenge?" the Red Ghost looked hopeful. "I was originally planning on consulting with you because—as CEO of AH Biotech—you earned a reputation for being particularly effective at locating and motivating high-end research talent."

"Yes...?"

"I run a company that licenses safety devices to automobile manufacturers," the Red Ghost explained further. "The technology is based upon Doctor Fid's inventions."

I couldn't help but stare. "Yes, I recall reading about it."

"While the Doctor was alive," he said, and I was gratified to hear a hint of sadness in his voice, "there were few researchers that would have been willing to risk association with such an endeavor. Now...I would like to put together a team to study his technology and create more lifesaving devices."

"That does sound like an interesting project," I said, hiding my weary bemusement behind a gravely serious tone. "Please, tell me more."

❦ ❦ ❦

It wasn't mere chance that had brought the Red Ghost to Terry Markham's door. Despite the state in which he'd found me, I was still a promising choice to lead the enterprise that he had in mind.

He and I had previously met (after the Guardians saved my civilian identity from a kidnapping, and again when he'd sought AH Biotech's assistance in administering medical nanites to a teammate) and he'd seen my professional capabilities. More than one news article had focused on my ability to guide the researchers and engineers who had powered AH Biotech's rapid growth. I was already local to the location where the work would be performed and—perhaps most importantly—currently available. Given his sense of guilt and empathy, he would also no-doubt have been predisposed towards forgiving one night's excess... especially since the target of my violence had been a man that he, too, had reason to dislike.

Really, if I'd actively intended to insinuate myself into the Red Ghost's business concerns, I'm not certain that I could have established a more perfect lure to attract his attention. And with Doctor Fid's 'death', it should have been obvious that an opportunity like this would be coming.

After all—unknown to any but he (and me)—there were components to his company's inertial dampening safety devices that were beyond his capabilities to manufacture and he'd relied upon Doctor Fid for their supply. The completed parts were still shipping, but it would have been irrational for him to trust that the arrangement would continue long after the supervillain's purported end.

The Red Ghost was not irrational. Given his strong and understandable desire to continue selling the lifesaving equipment, the creation of a research team to reproduce Doctor Fid's units was inevitable.

The part of me that was still Doctor Fid saw this as an amusing opportunity. The rest of me saw a chance to do something good, something Whisper would have been proud of.

I accepted the offer and signed the paperwork all in one day.

⁂

"Welcome home," Aaron smiled.

After months away, returning to AH Biotech's headquarters felt decidedly odd. Nothing had changed, physically—there had been no new construction, no obvious shifts in decor. Every face that turned my way was a familiar one, but their expressions were different now.

When I'd worn the mantle of CEO, I had maintained a semi-informal relationship with my employees, carefully designed to maintain an air of approachability and camaraderie. The friendship and sympathy I saw in their gazes wasn't new, nor was it unexpected. Gone, however, was the subtle sense of tension that often accompanied their pleasant greetings. These people weren't looking to me for answers—instead, they were looking to the man who'd welcomed me at the door.

"This is your house now," I replied. "I'm just visiting."

Aaron beamed and ushered me in.

"Everyone's going to want to see you," he said. "If you want to make a speech, I could rally the troops."

"That won't be necessary." I shook my head. "I just wanted to wander the halls a bit, thank everyone in person."

"Well, drop by my office when you're done, there's a lot to talk about."

"I will."

Aaron was drawn off into conversation with his Chief

Strategy Officer and I was left to my own devices. For a long moment, I remained still at the lobby's center. There was a hum to this place, a quiet resonance that tugged at my subconscious and created a unique sense of location. Since so many of the labs dealt with biological samples, the environmental controls were carefully segregated. Ducting for four separate heating and air-conditioning regions was hidden above the drop-ceiling panels. The sound of their operation was muted, barely audible throughout most of the building. Here in the lobby, however, the sounds funneled together into one low frequency thrum.

Decades ago, AH Biotech had been conceived as merely one aspect of my plan to re-mold Terry Markham into a form that suited Doctor Fid's purposes. The company had grown beyond me, accomplishing extraordinary things. That was, I thought, more a function of the wonderful team I'd somehow gathered rather than being a consequence of my own leadership.

Aaron was growing into the position of CEO. Research, development and manufacturing were all proceeding at a reasonable pace. AH Biotech didn't need me anymore.

With my chest tight with the odd mix of longing and pride, I managed something approximating a smile and began making my rounds.

"I was so sorry to hear about your loss," said Ananya in the finance department. "Whisper was a lovely child. I can't imagine what you must be going through."

"I'm not all-right," I replied, surprised to find that I didn't need to fake gratitude for her sympathetic hug, "but I think that I might be all-right, someday."

"Hey, boss-man," said Willy Natchez when I made my way to the microbiology lab. "It's good to see you up 'n about."

"Thank you, William. I appreciated your notes." He'd sent dozens of emails over the last few months. Rambling streams-of-consciousness, jumping from subject to subject haphazardly. I never responded, but Willy's kindness was a force of nature. My silence would never have dissuaded him from continuing his correspondence.

Movie reviews, book suggestions, comments on politics or art or music...it felt as though he'd opened up his veins and poured himself into every unacknowledged letter. He never mentioned Whisper. Instead, his missives were gentle —occasionally inappropriate and often irreverent— reminders of the humanity that Doctor Fid had tried to squeeze away from Terry Markham.

"No problem," he smiled cheerfully. "Just wanted to keep in touch."

"I'm going to be working on another project for a while, but I'll try not to be a stranger."

"Not planning on competing with us, are you?"

"No, this new project is going to be pure physics and math."

"Boring!" the Native American engineer exclaimed, a hint of laughter in his tone. "You ever want to come back 'n play with the fun sciences, we didn't change the password on th' lab door."

"I'll keep that in mind," I said, and shook his hand.

Words completely failed AH Biotech's CTO. Victor just wrapped me up in a bear hug then clapped me on the shoulder to send me on my way.

Everywhere, I was met with gentle sympathy and kind regards. Many were curious to hear what I had planned for the future (and wondered if I had plans to re-take the company's reins), but all supported my decision to seek a new challenge.

Once more, I was amazed at what I'd wrought. When this company had been conceived, I'd still carried the emotion-inhibiting scars of far-too-numerous invasive neurosurgeries. A complex set of computer programs had helped me to perform staffing, to build a team that would fulfill the role I wanted AH Biotech to fulfill. Somehow, my algorithms had created something far more powerful than the sum of its parts.

This could be my legacy, I thought. *Not violence, not pain and heartbreak. This.*

But there was still more work to be done.

❀ ❀ ❀

When I'd been a professor at MIT, I'd had a tiny office kept in staggering disarray—I'd been too absent-minded, too inwardly-focused to consider the aesthetics of the space.

There had been piles of books and notes strewn haphazardly upon every horizontal surface, chalkboards with scribbled calculations pushed into corners. I imagined that it must have been a harrowing experience for any students who'd braved my posted office-hours for assistance.

As CEO of AH Biotech, my personal environment had been carefully manicured to impart a desired intellectual and emotional response within visitors. Hardwood furniture polished until it seemed to glow, cozy leather-upholstered chairs...everything chosen to feel solid: classic, comfortable, welcoming. The office had been intended more as a subtle display of wealth and taste than as a working space. There'd been a laptop computer present for appearance's sake, but—once the door was closed—the majority of actual labor was performed via neural interface, mentally interacting with my server farms and carrying out whatever tasks were required.

At Crimson Technology—the Red Ghost's company—the office space I was provided was starkly sterile. White walls, simple furniture that looked as though it had just arrived from a plastics manufacturing facility. Everything seemed new and untouched, suited more for an automaton's storage than for human inhabitation. It was a rented space, and by the scent I could guess that the rooms had been repainted only a few weeks prior.

It was, I thought, a decent starting point. A blank canvas.

By day two, I'd acquired worn cabinetry from a local refurbished-furniture store, a handful of scarred chairs and filing trays...and framed posters of beaches and sea-life, a reminder of Whisper's love of the Oceans. By day four, I was ready to greet the first prospective member of my research team.

"Alex," I smiled. "It's good to see you again."

"You too, Doctor Markham."

"Call me 'Terry', please."

We were of a similar age, although my former teaching-assistant hadn't aged quite as gracefully. Alex had been a lanky undergrad when last I'd seen him; now, his thinning hair had gone gray and a paunch had gathered around his middle. He'd weathered a life stooped in academia, whereas I'd had the advantage of significant genetic and surgical modification, clone bodies, medical nanites—and a somewhat more physically-demanding hobby than most professors endured. Still, his pleased expression seemed genuine and I could clearly see the echo of the friendly, fiercely intelligent youth who'd once helped to keep my classroom in order.

"Terry," he said experimentally, as though tasting the name on his tongue. The grin that followed implied that he found the more casual appellation appealing. "I was surprised to get your call."

"Good surprise or bad surprise?"

"Definitely a good surprise," Alex Hoffman laughed. "But I expected that you'd be going back to AH Biotech, and that's not my field."

"Well, this project's right up your alley. Iterated de-looping of orthogonal non-linear Westler wave functions will be directly relevant."

He blinked. "You've been reading my journal articles?"

"Of course. After...you know, after Bobby...I never really

found stable footing again in academia. But I still keep an eye on interesting developments."

"Well, thanks. I've been watching your career, too." He hesitated. "Bobby 'd be proud of you."

He is, I almost said. Instead, I managed a strangled, "Thank you."

Bringing Alex into the Red Ghost's orbit was a calculated risk. On the one hand...I truly was looking forward to working with Alex again, and he had an adequate understanding of the theories underpinning the work that we'd be doing. On the other hand...Alex had first hand information of my history that wouldn't match what the Red Ghost knew of me.

I'd long since scrambled old personal records and newspaper archives such that anyone who relied upon computer files would have been unaware that I'd ever had a little brother. The Red Ghost—one of the most talented investigators that Doctor Fid had ever faced—had not been able to connect me to the Bobbyverse's 'Robert Hoffman'. If Alex mentioned Bobby in the Red Ghost's presence, suspicions might be aroused.

But the Red Ghost was not a hands-on CEO—his 'day job' as one of Boston's premier superheroes kept him away from the office, and lately he'd been spending the majority of his spare time traveling to New York to assist the New York Shield with technical and logistical issues. Also—at least, from my two-decade-plus old recollection—Alex had never seemed the sort to indulge in idle gossip.

Secrets could be managed, but individuals who could truly help with the science were few and far between.

"So," Alex smiled, "I only have one question."

"And that is?"

"Will there be any academic papers published with both of our names on them?"

"Almost certainly."

"In that case," he rubbed his hands in anticipation, "where do I sign?"

13

_____

"Hey, Terry?" Alex leaned into my office. "I think I need you to check my math."

"Just a minute," I murmured, still focused upon my own calculations. I was writing out formulae by hand, filling sheet after sheet with methodical proofs. Entire binders had been compiled and I'd only scraped the surface of what would be needed.

At first I'd been worried about accidentally revealing prior knowledge of the inertial dampener's workings, but the process of reverse-engineering the data supplied by the Red Ghost had proven to be so interesting a challenge that starting from scratch had been preferable. This approach had revealed some intriguing implications that I'd failed to observe while developing Doctor Fid's protections. In addition to positing that improvements were possible, I'd also stumbled across a more general principle...a mathematical model that could be applied to several other multidimensional calculations.

Technically, all this work belonged to Crimson Technology; the Red Ghost's permission would be needed before my team could publish any results in academic magazines. Separating the generally-applicable math from the proprietary information would be difficult...but eminently achievable.

My hand paused in its scribbling. The methodology currently being explored wasn't evolving in the hoped-for manner, so I crossed out half a page and re-started from an earlier section, shifting towards a more promising path. There was a pattern here, and an elegant truth awaited at the end of the puzzle. I needed only to follow the threads, to tug here or there, to weave the variables into a perfect tapestry.

For a time, there was nothing but the work. And then someone cleared his throat.

"Just a minute," I repeated absently, sketching out a quick Cayley graph. If the subset of bounded dimensions k could be proven uncountably infinite, then a variation on a Banarch-Tarski decomposition could be used to separate k into discrete uncountably infinite subgroups...

"Wow," Alex chuckled. "This feels just like old times."

"Pardon?" Reluctantly, I looked up.

"I brought you lunch," my former TA noted. "Also, more caffeine."

I felt my cheeks heat from embarrassment. "How long was I...?"

"A bit more than an hour."

"That was rude" I sighed. "I'm sorry."

"Don't be. It happens to me, too." He stepped into my office to set a paper-wrapped sandwich on my desk (carefully avoiding any of my notes) and followed that with a steaming mug of coffee. "Twenty-five years ago, I wouldn't have been able to pull you away 'til it got dark out."

"Well, then I'm sorry for putting you through that twenty-five years ago, also." I ignored the sandwich in favor of caffeine, wrapping both hands around the mug. The heat felt pleasant upon my palms.

"All will be forgiven if you check my math."

If only all redemption could so easily be acquired.

"Okay. Your office?"

"My office."

The coffee came with me as I followed Alex across the hall. "What's the problem?"

"I'm hoping that I missed something obvious." He pointed me towards the whiteboards arrayed against the room's wall. "Do you see where I started from?"

"I do."

"Well, I was working on a way to simplify the calculations and I came up with some confusing results."

"Hm. Let me have a look."

Over the last few decades, Alex had broadened his education significantly. His work was peppered with references to obscure theories and papers, but the overall theme was easily grasped. The application, however, was extraordinarily complex. My mug was empty before I finished studying the proof.

"I don't see any errors," I finally said. "The theory seems valid."

"It can't be. Do you see how much force would be released?"

"Oh, I see it and I think that congratulations are in order. You just successfully turned an automotive safety device into a planet-killer."

Alex's eyes were wide. "But...I don't want to kill planets."

"Then we should probably just focus on this section here," I grabbed up a dry-erase marker and drew an arrow on a whiteboard, "and maybe here, to develop safeguards. And then erase the rest."

Alex stared for a few moments more, then barked in sudden laughter and picked up an eraser. "Yeah, sorry. I was just suddenly reminded that we're working on Doctor Fid's tech. I've consulted for aerospace and power companies, but I always avoided weapons development. Who needs the bad karma, right?"

"Right." I forced a tight smile. The idea that earned ill luck would linger was not a pleasant one.

"It's kinda weird, though. Doctor Fid was, y'know, Doctor Fid. He designed all this!" He gestured at the whiteboard with the eraser. "He must've understood the math."

"Most likely."

"So...he built a doomsday weapon and instead of taking over the world he just decided to redesign it as a safety device?"

"Strange man."

Alex continued erasing in silence for a few seconds then again erupted in laughter. "He used a planet-killer to build a better seatbelt. I wonder what he would've used to build a better mousetrap?"

"I can't imagine," I replied, wholly unable to stop myself from imagining.

Alex grabbed a coffee mug off his own desk. "I'm going to get a refill and then get back to work. You want anything?"

"Not at the moment."

"Be back in a bit, then." Alex wandered off in search of further caffeination. There was something painfully nostalgic in his gait, some aspect of his body language or tone that sent me back deep into my past. For a brief instant, it felt as though the last quarter century was only a bad dream, that Doctor Fid was just a crayon drawing, and that if I peeked under Alex's desk I would find my little brother working on a hand-drawn comic while he waited for me to finish a day's work.

Reality reasserted like a crashing wave.

The space below the table was unoccupied. No quiet child lay beneath, scribbling patiently. My sister, too, was gone. Doctor Fid was dead—his mission incomplete—but still his ghost squirmed under my skin.

I took a deep and unsteady breath, grateful for the temporary peace to be found in science and math, and then returned to my own office to muse upon mousetrap designs.

❧ ❧ ❧

"...and this one is a Pteranodon," Bobby chirps. "Like the big one that fought the giant lizard in that movie. But real Pteranodons weren't that big. They were big! But not that big."

Bobby grabs my hand and tugs me towards the next exhibit. We come here every time I'm in New York for a conference and this area had only recently completed its renovation. Even with the changes, this feels familiar. There's something about the echo here—the tall ceilings and open spaces and constant hum of activity created an ambiance that never seemed to change. There are new dinosaur skeletons on display, new kiosks and labeled pedestals, new plaques to read, and so much more to explore.

The planetarium here is lovely, but Bobby's favorite is the dinosaurs.

"How big were they?" I ask.

Bobby lets his grip fall away as he stretches out his arms like wings. "Twenty feet! Raaaah!"

"That's pretty big."

"Uh-huh! And they could fly!" Bobby flaps ponderously.

I smile, "And...what did they eat?"

"Fish! They probably had to eat a lot of them, 'cause they were so big."

"Interesting. Oh, what's that one over there?" I pointed to the next exhibit.

Bobby's voice drops to a reverent whisper. "It's a velociraptor."

I let him wax eloquent about his favorite theropod for a while and occasionally prod for more information. He's done much more research than I on ancient history so it's nice to let him lecture for once. Bobby practically bubbles with excitement as we circle the new display. Several velociraptor skeletons are posed as though chasing some smaller dinosaur. It's easy to imagine that these were fierce, dangerous predators.

And so it goes. Aisle by aisle, display by display, until all the dinosaur attractions have been exhausted and it's time to go home.

We're walking back to the hotel when Bobby comes to a sudden halt.

"What's wrong with that man?" he whispers urgently.

I wince. "He's just sleeping. C'mon, let's let him rest."

"He's dirty!" Bobby notes sadly.

"He is," I agree. "He doesn't have a home, so it's probably hard for him to get clean."

We've passed other homeless men and women in our wanderings but none quite so visibly decrepit. This particular unfortunate is sprawled face-first upon a flattened cardboard box laid across the sidewalk, insensate, vomit crusted in his straggly salt-and-pepper beard. The skin on his arms and face is racked with sores, unconcealed by the layer upon layer of filthy clothes that hide the majority of his unhealthily-slim figure. Even at a distance, the stench of fermented sweat and urine and sickness is overwhelming.

"But why?" Bobby asks—bewildered—turning to stare as I try to shuffle him past. "Why don't the heroes save him?"

"There's no villain to punch, kiddo. The reason people end up like this...It's not so simple. Sometimes, it's bad choices. Sometimes it's just bad luck."

"That's not fair."

"No, I guess it isn't."

"Why doesn't anyone else help?" he asks, confusedly.

"People try," I reassure. "Remember, Mom 'n Dad raising money for the shelter? That was so people like him have someplace to stay."

"Oh." Bobby doesn't seem convinced.

"It doesn't work for every person," I try to explain. "But people try."

"It's sad."

"Yeah."

"People should try and help people more," Bobby says decisively. "Then everything would be better."

My little brother's instinctive kindness is infectious, so I leave a few dollars for the unconscious homeless man before we make our way back to our hotel.

❧ ❧ ❧

"Welcome to KNN CapeWatch," the respected television announcer began. "I'm your host, Stan Morrow."

"And I'm Pamela Green."

"Joining us tonight is noted sociologist and author, Joanne Durand."

"Thank you, Stan, Pam. It's great to be here."

"Dr. Durand's book—*Black Masks*—studied the effects that supervillains have had upon society, was a New York Times Best-Seller, and has been translated into twenty-four languages. Now, I understand that you have a new book coming out?"

"Yes, thank you Stan. My new book is called *Armored Night* and it focuses on one of the world's most feared and enigmatic villains: Doctor Fid."

"From what I hear, this book has been something of a new experience for you?"

"Yes. As you mentioned, my background is in Sociology, and most of my prior books have been approached from that angle. For this book, however, I partnered with an investigative reporter to delve deeper and to gain a greater insight. It was a very interesting experience. Unfortunately, there are still so many questions unanswered...but I do hope that this book helps my readers to understand some of the strange complexities of the man who was certainly one of the greatest inventors in human history."

"Interesting! I'm definitely looking forward to reading it," Pamela smiled; the former fashion-model had earned quite the reputation as an investigator, herself. "We interviewed Doctor Fid ourselves, once."

"I know," the sociologist laughed. "I dedicated most of a chapter to that episode. You both did a wonderful job. Fearless!"

"I wouldn't say that," Stan replied dryly. "Being in the same room as Doctor Fid was one of the most terrifying experiences in my life."

"He was a perfect gentleman," Pam objected.

"He was, yes. But if he'd decided not to be, there wouldn't have been anything that anyone could have done to stop him." Stanley shook his head. "I'm not sure that cameras have ever captured how incredibly frightening Doctor Fid could be in person. Even from only a few feet away, his armor's surface was so non-reflective that you could only guess at its shape from the glowing seams. There was something alien and strange about the way the stars in his armor were displayed...it felt as though I wasn't looking *at* a real object. I was looking *through* him into deep space."

"I interviewed the director of the Hayden Planetarium as part of my research," Joanne noted. "No matter what angle you looked at Doctor Fid from, you were always viewing an accurate representation of the distant stars as though there weren't any buildings or atmosphere in the way."

"How is that even possible?"

"No one has any idea," the author laughed. "I asked everyone I could think of, no one had the slightest clue. In a strange way, it's funny: Doctor Fid fought against the most powerful heroes on Earth and demonstrated an awe-inspiring level of strength and resilience...but the longest-running Internet discussion about his armor is one among astrophysicists attempting to determine how accurately Doctor Fid displayed the night sky."

"And now, I suppose that we'll never know for sure," Pamela lamented.

"The online argument will probably continue for years!"

"Doctor Fid has always been a very divisive figure," the older host chuckled. "For heroes and physicists alike."

"He was a perplexing character," Joanne agreed. "Some heroes—such as Valiant and the Red Ghost—have implied a grudging respect for Doctor Fid, and others talk about him as though he'd been the anti-Christ. That dichotomy was one of the issues I wanted to explore as I started doing research for this book."

"What sorts of juicy secrets did you uncover?"

"Well, for one thing...I've found evidence that he chose his victims far more carefully than most people would ever have imagined."

"How do you mean?"

"Hm, here's an example: Do you remember the attack on the Balmer Technology Group?"

"Yes," Stan nodded. "It was a robbery foiled by the Charioteer. The only casualty was a bystander who was badly injured when Doctor Fid threw a mailbox at Charioteer and missed."

Joanne Durand leaned forward, "I'm reasonably certain that the injury wasn't an accident. In fact, it's very possible that Doctor Fid set up the entire battle to target that particular person."

"That's horrifying," Pam murmured, aghast.

"It becomes less so once you discover that the so-called 'innocent bystander' was secretly running a human trafficking ring."

"I'm sorry, are you suggesting that Doctor Fid went out of his way to target a criminal?" Stanley asked, skeptical.

"I'm saying that Doctor Fid's early career was characterized by escalating violence and bloodshed, and that I believe that escalation was very carefully calculated. If you study the timing and quantity of media coverage, it's too smooth a curve to have happened by accident. He decided who to hurt and when to hurt them, and all those choices were focused upon a primary purpose: making Doctor Fid a household name."

Pamela's brow furrowed, "And, what does that have to do with the human trafficker?"

"Doctor Fid's rise was—literally—a textbook-perfect marketing campaign. Somewhere, there was a plan...and there was a checkbox next to the line that read, 'demonstrate willingness to injure random bystanders' marked complete after the attack on Balmer Technology Group. But nothing was really random. The more I dug into the backgrounds of the civilians that Doctor Fid directly harmed, the more clear the pattern became: the vast majority had gone unpunished for terrible crimes, many of which weren't uncovered until my investigation decades afterwards."

"Are you saying," Stanley pressed, "that Doctor Fid was some kind of vigilante?"

"We should never forget that Doctor Fid hurt a lot of good heroes. That he was a violent man willing to do violent things in order to accomplish his objectives. I have no idea what the man behind the star-field mask was thinking or what his goals were, but I can definitively say that I agree with Valiant's assessment: Doctor Fid was a complicated man."

"Well, we have to go to a break," Pam said. "But when we return, we will continue discussing Dr. Joanne Durand's new book, *Armored Night*. I'm Pamela Green."

"And I'm Stan Morrow. KNN CapeWatch will return after these messages."

❧ ❧ ❧

The door is open, but I knock gently on the frame anyway. "Whisper? Can I come in?"

"Mmm!" The little android cheerfully turned to face me, abandoning her ongoing efforts to build a colorful castle out of blankets and pillows. Her smile falters when she sees my own serious expression. "What's wrong?"

"Sweetheart, did you hack the Massachusetts State Lottery to make sure Ms. Tillerson won on her birthday?"

"Ms. Tillerson's nice!" Whisper notes carefully.

"She is," I agree. "But that isn't what I asked."

"Ms. Tillerson is nice, and she deserves a nice birthday present."

I sigh, "Whisper, you have to be more careful. What if Cuboid caught you hacking the lottery? He's the only other A.I. around, and you know he does security audits..."

She rolls her expressive glowing-blue eyes. "Cuboid's old. I know what I'm doing."

"Honey, it's a bad habit to get into. Even if it's not Cuboid, there's other people out there who watch the lotteries for unusual behavior. I do."

"I know," she sighs, hugging her favorite doll to her chest. "But Ms. Tillerson is a good person. She makes me cookies even though I can't eat them, just like if I was a real girl."

"Oh, sweetheart, you're a real girl in every way that matters."

"Not everyone says so," she murmurs, lowering her gaze.

"Some people are stupid," I say quietly, sitting down next to my adopted little sister on her bed. She leans against me and I can't help but smile fondly despite the fact that I'd originally came in here to reprimand her. "But others are just scared. That's why it's important that you don't take unnecessary risks."

"Yeah. It's just...Ms. Tillerson is kind and gentle and she's the sort of person who deserves to have good things happen to her. I can help, and no one gets hurt."

"There are lots of good people in the world, sweetheart."

"I know. I haven't gotten around to helping all of them yet."

"Oh, you're going to help all of them, are you?"

"Mmm!"

I hug an adorable android. "I believe you."

The world has never been fair, before. It's never been nice. But maybe Whisper can make it so.

And even if she fails, it's reassuring to know that my sister's digital heart is in the right place.

❦ ❦ ❦

"I'll have the Tom Yum Soup." Aaron handed his menu to our waiter.

"And I'll have the Lemon Grass Chicken," I added. The waiter smiled in acknowledgment and wandered off to his next table.

The restaurant wasn't terribly crowded. The dinner rush hadn't started yet—in another hour there would be a line of hopeful diners waiting outside. For now, half the tables were empty and the hum of background conversations was not intrusive. Aaron knew the owner, and we'd hired this restaurant for catering parties at AH Biotech several times.

"It's good to see you, Terry. You're looking better."

"I'm feeling better. A bit." I grimaced. "Some days are better than others."

"If there's anything you need..."

"Just time," I said, then considered for a few moments before adding: "And company once in a while."

My friend smiled, "That, I can do."

"Thank you for the invitation."

"No problem. I've been told that it's important to drag you away from math every now and then."

"Oh?"

"I spoke to your coworker. Alex, I think his name is?"

"Alex Hoffman," I confirmed. "He was my T.A. back when I was a professor at M.I.T.."

"The Doctor Markham he describes is very different from the Doctor Markham I've always known," Aaron noted, curiously.

I paused before answering. Even ignoring the remarkably large number of surgical alterations that I'd made over the years to forge myself into the roles of Doctor Fid and AH Biotech CEO, I'd undergone hundreds of hours of acting and social training. Back when Alex had known me, I'd been an awkward introvert but by the time I'd met Aaron, I'd learned how to pretend at being an assertive extrovert. In the time since, the mask had settled until it almost felt real.

In a very true sense, I *was* a different person than the Doctor Markham that Alex had known back at M.I.T.

"I was much younger then," I finally explained.

"But you're happy with what you're doing?"

"I think that 'happy' is the wrong word," I admitted. "I'm...distracted. It's easier to get lost inside my head when I'm doing pure research. It's all numbers and no emotions."

Aaron's brows furrowed. "That doesn't sound healthy."

"I'm not ready to be healthy," I gritted out, voice sounding strained even to me. I took a deep breath and waited for the tension in my chest to fade before continuing. "I think this is what I needed."

"Okay," he grimaced. "If it's what you need, then...good."

It wasn't good and we both knew it. Fortunately, Aaron was a kind enough friend to allow my pain to go unspoken.

"And, how are things going with you?" I asked, breaking the uncomfortable silence. "Keeping the lights on at AHBT?"

"Doing well." Aaron sipped at his water, then looked around the room. When he spoke again, his voice was quieter: "Although, truthfully, I did have an ulterior motive inviting you here."

"Oh?"

"When you were at the helm, we fast-tracked a lot of products for testing, but I've been getting pushback from the FDA..." he trailed off. There was a strange note of nervousness in his voice that momentarily confused me.

"You don't need to bribe anyone," I chuckled, unable to hide my amusement when I realized what he was asking.

"Oh, thank God." Aaron's embarrassed relief was palpable.

"It's all above board, but there are politicians who owe us favors," I explained. "I've donated to a fair number of campaigns and attended lots of boring fund-raisers. I'm sorry, I should have given you the list months ago."

On a somewhat more morally questionable note, I'd also spent years hacking confidential medical records and private mail archives to ensure that the company was always in a good position to address the personal needs of prominent politicians and businessmen. With any luck, Aaron would never need to employ a similar level of skullduggery in order to keep the company on track.

"And now I'm embarrassed for even implying-"

"Don't be," I smirked playfully. "If I'd known who to throw money at to get the artificial reef project approved, I would've poured a fortune into someone's pocket."

"You 'n me, both."

"So," I smiled, "which project were you hoping to get fast-tracked?"

"The bone graft enhancements. Theo says we're ready for human trials..."

"If Theo says it, then it's true." I used my neural tap to silently run a few database queries. "Hmm...I seem to recall that the director of the CBER is Senator Sutliff's brother-in-law. Sutliff will answer your call and he can arrange a face-to-face, but that's the sort of relationship you can only push at once or twice. I have another idea, but it would take about six months."

"I was being told more than two years, so six months 'd still be an improvement."

"The head of the CDRH has a close relationship with Paradigm Labs, and our nanites could repair Professor Paradigm's stroke damage."

"The nanites aren't licensed for neural disorders yet," Aaron objected. "We've been approved for testing, but that's going to take years."

"Get the Department of Metahuman Affairs to sign an exemption."

"Paradigm isn't a metahuman."

"But he's a licensed hero and his company is a powerful government contractor. The DMA will push it through." I sipped at my own drink, then set down my glass. "There's a fair amount of overlap between the CDRH and CBER. If the Center for Devices and Radiological Health is in your corner, the Center for Biologics Evaluation and Research will follow."

"That'll work." Aaron smiled, looking satisfied. "Thanks."

"I'll write up some notes on relationships to keep track of and suggestions as to which politicians to contribute to," I added. "This part of the job takes a bit of practice, but you'll do fine."

"I appreciate it."

There were still horrors in my past that could never be righted. With Professor Paradigm's symptoms repaired, however, at least one of Doctor Fid's crimes could be erased from existence.

We both fell silent as our waiter arrived with our appetizers.

When I'd been CEO of AH Biotech, I realized, the company's future had been brittle...dependent solely upon my insight. Too much responsibility had rested upon my shoulders, and too little had been shared among my peers. If I'd lost a single battle, the company would have fallen with me: hundreds of extraordinary, dedicated workers betrayed by my arrogance.

Aaron would be better. Already, he was delegating... preparing for the future. The company would survive beyond my influence and beyond his as well. AH Biotech would be a legacy for which Terry Markham could be justly proud. And, perhaps, a legacy that Bobby and Whisper would have been proud of as well.

If only the part of me that was Fid would stop howling.

14

**Two Young Heroes Hospitalized due to
Communications Failures.**

By Brett Deutch, KNN

(KNN) — FOR PROSPECTIVE HEROES HOPING TO EVENTUALLY become licensed by the Department of Metahuman Affairs, the training programs offered by local state-sponsored superhero teams have long been an attractive option. While critics have complained that such programs are poorly regulated, the curriculums generally include a wide array of scholastic material as well as the physical skills necessary for a career in metahuman law enforcement; graduates can often expect significantly improved chances to earn their license on their first attempt, and are also more likely to gain employment with premier-level state-sponsored super-hero teams.

For decades, the training program offered by the New York Shield team of heroes has been considered to be the most prestigious among all similar courses on the East Coast. Alumnus from the so-called 'Junior Shield' are head-hunted by talent scouts across the country. Students of said program trust their safety—and their futures—to the more experienced superheroes who serve as their mentors.

On Thursday evening, that trust was betrayed. Two members of the Junior Shield—Brute and Exbow—were hospitalized when they were directed into a deadly conflict against the Red Hook Spiders.

"They shouldn't have been there," said Junior Shield Team-mate Cherenkov. "We all know that this job can be dangerous, but following proper procedure is supposed to limit the risks. Two-person scout patrols aren't supposed to be deployed in high-risk areas. Not ever!"

"My student is correct," New York Shield leader Cloner stated with uncharacteristic seriousness. "There's no excuse. The patrol shouldn't have been deployed into that region without backup nearby and the result was very nearly tragic. Brute and Exbow are both excellent recruits and I couldn't be more proud of their performance when they were thrust into a highly stressful confrontation. They did good. The fault lay upon their trainers, and I take full responsibility. It's no secret that the New York Shield has been experiencing no shortage of technical difficulties lately but that is not justification. We should have been double-checking that our messages were transmitted accurately.

"Our procedures have been updated," the hero continued. "This cannot be allowed to happen again."

❦ ❦ ❦

"I made beanie weenies," Alex informed me through my office's open door.

I looked up from my calculations, "Did it come from a can?"

"Of course."

"Well," I put down my pencil, "in that case, let me get a bowl."

He beamed in approval and I followed him out the door.

The building itself was still barely occupied and the 'break room' was little more than a meeting area with a sink and a coffee machine against one wall. A refrigerator and a microwave had been set along the opposite side of the room. The new cafeteria would be much larger—construction was expected to start any day now. I found a bowl in one of the cabinets and rinsed it while Alex re-heated the beans and franks in the microwave.

"How're things going on your end?" Alex asked, grabbing a bowl and silverware for himself.

"It's coming together well," I replied. "I've gotten the go-ahead to bring in a few office-admins to help with paper-work and organization. I was wondering if you wanted to sit in on the interviews?"

My former teaching assistant looked surprised. "Do you need me there?"

I shook my head, "No, I just thought that it would be good for you to be familiar with the hiring process."

"I'm just a mathematician, Terry."

"Even so. Learning how to evaluate prospective employees might be a useful skill to learn."

Alex paused before answering to withdraw our lunch from the microwave. The scent of brown-sugar baked beans and highly-processed meat-products flooded the room, and conversation stopped while we filled our bowls.

"I don't mind learning new skills," he finally said, stirring his franks and beans with a spoon. "But I'm a pure math guy and I love what I do. I have tenure and enough seniority that I can take time off for projects like this. I'm not gonna have 'prospective employees' any time soon."

"Ah." A rueful smile twisted at my lips, "I'm sorry, that was presumptive of me. I'd been thinking that you would be an excellent candidate to take over my position here when I move on. It would have been pleasant to leave someone I know and trust in charge."

"I'm honored. Really." Alex shrugged. "But I'm here for the research, man...not the stock options."

Unsure if I should feel proud or jealous, I lifted a spoonful of beans and frankfurters to my lips and chewed very slowly.

❧ ❧ ❧

"Do you...," Alex begins to ask, "...have any threes?"

"Go fish!" Bobby giggles.

I've never taught in this cavernous auditorium, but the raised dais with the broad wall of chalk-boards has made this room a favorite for after-hours mathematical exploration. A quiet little office and a stack of notepads is acceptable for some projects. Others require expanse. There is something invigorating about covering wall after wall with scrawled proofs, and then having the ability to step back and drink in all that progress at once.

This lecture hall can seat five-hundred and sixty-six with uncomfortable wooden amphitheater chairs stretching into the distance. I remember being cramped in the middle of those masses, feeling small and out-of-place, straining to see the chalkboards that I now claimed for my own. During class hours, the hum of so many intent, focused students gave the space a distinct sense of energy and pressure. Now, the room is empty and the scratch of my chalk writing echoes.

"D'you have any fives?" Bobby asks.

Almost empty, I mentally amend. Alex is keeping Bobby

entertained, playing some strange card game at the front of the dais.

"I have two fives."

"Hah!" Bobby awkwardly fiddles with his cards, separating a few out then laying a stack face-down. "D'you have any jacks?"

"Go fish!"

"Aww..."

They play and I inscribe obscure notations and discover connections and develop proofs and this moment is everything that I want from the world. I can hear the relaxed joy in Bobby's voice with every turn of gameplay and I write faster, riding the wave of enthusiasm towards some ineffable truth, something magical that only these formula will be able to reveal. By the time I move on to the next blackboard, Bobby and Alex have started another game. The music of creation carries me forward.

Time passes. More blackboards are filled, and I scribble on even as the card games draw to a close.

"Hey," Alex says, "it looks like your big brother is going to be busy for a while. D'you wanna grab something to eat?"

"Yeah, okay."

I know to start wrapping up, to let this inspirational frenzy fade, to sit in one of those uncomfortable wooden seats and tran-scribe my notes. But I also know that I have time before the pair returns, fed and happy; Bobby, eager to return home and play with his action figures prior to tiring and going to sleep, and Alex eager to take his own notes from the scrawls I leave behind.

In two months, Bobby will be dead and I'll have begun my mad stumble down a violent, bloody and hateful path towards a vengeance that would never be realized. But right now—in this moment—life is wonderful.

"Great!" Alex says. "I have Beanie Weenies back at the office."

❧ ❧ ❧

I wasn't jealous, I decided, nor had I any real right to be proud. I was simply amazed.

"These are good beans," I said quietly, and maybe Alex somehow heard several decades' worth of mixed sorrow and gratitude in my voice because his eyes were shining when he nodded in agreement.

❧ ❧ ❧

The footsteps approaching my office did not match the rhythm and cadence that I'd come to recognize as belonging to my former-TA/current peer. They were, however, familiar. Reluctantly, I tore my attention away from the chorus of calculations swimming through my consciousness and re-focused upon the outside world.

"Doctor Markham?" the Red Ghost knocked on my door. "Do you have a moment?"

"Of course," I replied. "Come in."

It was still strange to see him in costume during work hours and in a civilian setting. At night, his crimson cloak seemed to bleed from the shadows, enshrouding the hero in an aura of menacing gravitas. Under fluorescent lights, it was just a length of admittedly-high-quality fabric dangling from his shoulders. The cloak's hood was pulled back and even his highly-advanced and custom-designed cowl looked somehow cheap when viewed during the day.

There had been many periods in the past when finding Doctor Fid's nemesis so visibly wearied would have been cause for gloating, but now I felt only concern. The bags below his eyes (visible through the opening in his mask) had settled to the color of dull bruises, and his normally piercing and fiercely-intelligent gaze was tempered by fatigue. He looked...sallow.

"I apologize for appearing without warning," the Hispanic hero grimaced. "The last few months have been unusually busy, and I haven't been able to grant this project as much attention as it deserves. Please, know that I value your work even if I haven't been here to express my appreciation."

"That's quite all right. I've been watching the news, I do understand."

With the apparent death of Doctor Fid, a handful of super-powered criminals had moved into the New England territory. The Boston Guardians were doing an admirable job of keeping the public safe but were certainly being called into service at a more frequent schedule than they had become accustomed to. The problems were exacerbated by the fact that the team had been temporarily short-handed— the Red Ghost's wife, Regrowth, had been put on paid administrative leave while the D.M.A. performed their investigation into Doctor Fid's death. The Red Ghost had also been pulling double-duty, traveling to and from Manhattan to assist his friends in the New York Shield.

"Everything is proceeding along our original plans," I continued. "I was about to get a mug of coffee. Join me, and we can discuss the details?"

Even the mention of caffeine was enough to release the tension gathered at his shoulders. "That sounds wonderful. Thank you."

We didn't speak again until we'd both acquired our life-giving elixirs.

"I've hired a contractor to secure the network," I began. "He's doing an excellent job."

The contractor in question had come to Doctor Fid's attention under his online alias; LuckySeven was the current leader of the hacktivist cooperative originally formed by my friend Starnyx. In his civilian identity, on the other hand, he was a celebrated computer security expert. The data to be guarded at Crimson Technology was theoretically dangerous and I trusted in LuckySeven's ethics to ensure that company materials would never escape to the world at large.

"I've been told that convenience and security are diametrically opposed," the Red Ghost mused. "Are you sure that your contractor has chosen the correct balance?"

"The engineers are going to hate him because of all the hoops they're going to need to jump through in order to do their jobs. Faraday cages around the clean rooms, air-gapped servers...it will be as secure as a government black site."

"Good."

"The facility refits are going to stretch the budget a bit, but you're still on-target overall."

"Again, good. And your work?"

"Alex and I are ahead of schedule, actually. We're already writing up preliminary findings."

"Excellent." He smiled briefly, then lowered his head

apologetically. "Much of this should have been my responsibility. Thank you for stepping up."

"I would have preferred to remain focused on pure research," I admitted, "but I've done this sort of work before."

The Red Ghost sighed, "I wish that I could tell you the worst was over, but at this moment I'm not certain that I can make that promise."

"I understand. As I mentioned...I've been watching the news."

The crimson-clad hero looked thoughtful for a moment, then winced. "It occurs to me that I should ask your advice on another matter—related to my work in New York, even—but I do not want to bring up painful memories."

I smiled sadly, "I can't escape painful memories. Ask."

"Your daughter was a true digital sentience, one of only two that have ever been documented. When you were preparing your legal challenges to have her citizenship recognized, you must have consulted with many computer experts..."

"I did, yes." My voice shook only slightly. "Before we continue, though...I know you mean well when you refer to Whisper as my daughter, but she'd had a father and I could never replace him. She called me her big brother. That was enough."

In public, I had only referred to Whisper as being my ward. At that moment, even so small an artifice felt like sandpaper across too-sensitive skin.

"I apologize, I did not mean to cause further pain," he winced. "Your sister, then."

"Thank you," I sighed. "You were asking about computer experts?"

"I need to locate an expert in artificial intelligence software and hardware," he admitted, voice dropping in volume even though there was no one near enough to overhear. "The problems in New York, they are caused by the android hero Cuboid. I'm hoping to find someone with experience working with massively interconnected neural networks who can help diagnose the problem."

"What about Cuboid's creator?"

"He passed away two years ago." The Red Ghost's expression was pained. "At the time, Sphinx was in charge of the New York Shield and she chose to keep the information secret."

"Unfortunately, Cuboid and Whisper are—" I choked. "Were. Cuboid and Whisper were the only two of their kind. Other than myself, there aren't many who have experience working on similar systems."

The Red Ghost's brows furrowed, "You consider yourself an expert on the subject, then?"

"For Whisper's sake, I became one." I smiled sadly, "I'll put together a list of experts who might be able to come up to speed quickly, though. I consulted with one for the trial. It might take a few months, but he could become the specialist you're looking for."

"Months." The Red Ghost grimaced. "Again, I hesitate to ask, but...given your superior experience, would your work be faster?"

"Yes."

"Cuboid is a hero, a long-time member of the New York

Shield, and a personal friend. If you can help him then I'm afraid that I'm going to need to impose upon you further. If you are willing, of course."

Again, I thought of legacy. Whisper and I had worked to see the Synthetic Americans' Rights act passed into law, and Cuboid was the last wholly artificial intelligence who might benefit from the statute. It would be tragic if there were no entities left to take advantage of the rights Whisper had championed.

"All right," I agreed, even though the idea of working on another A.I. 's code made my chest hurt. I consoled myself with the knowledge that Cuboid's secret server farm was among the very few that I'd never been able even to locate, much less scan...the opportunities for research and study would be endless. "Give me a day or two to hand off the rest of my work to Alex, then I'll be ready to help in any way that I can."

"I know that this will be hard for you," the Red Ghost said sympathetically. "But I promise that your sacrifice is appreciated. Thank you."

I shook his hand, taking solace in the knowledge that the world's most feared villain would soon find himself elbows-deep within a famed superhero's brain.

15

ALAS, IT SEEMED THAT IT WOULD BE SOME TIME BEFORE THE world's most feared villain would find himself elbows-deep within a famed superhero's brain.

"I'm not sure if or when that will happen," the Red Ghost apologized. "The DMA is treating this like a medical issue, and Cuboid hasn't given permission for his personal records to be distributed—we're still negotiating with his healthcare proxy..."

"It's all right." If someone had demanded access to Whisper's source code or hardware without her approval, I would have spilled an ocean of blood to prevent it. Cuboid wasn't nearly so worthy as my sister had been, but it was gratifying to hear that the Synthetic Americans' Rights act would have protected her wishes. "If you can get logs from other systems that Cuboid interacts with, I might be able to start identifying a pattern even without direct access."

"I'll see what I can do."

❧ ❧ ❧

"It's beautiful," Whisper murmurs, eyes wide with admiration.

The glass statue—a stylized dolphin leaping from the ocean's surface—glistens. Within the smoothly contoured glass are held subtle tints of grey and blue and yellow that somehow hint of a sunrise scene, of deep waters below and clear skies above. The work is awe-inspiringly evocative, but the joy on Whisper's face is more beautiful still.

I smile, "It's for you."

She's about to touch it, expression almost covetous, when she pauses and pulls her hand backwards as though afraid that the statue might bite. "Did you...um...Did you steal this for me?"

"No, I received this from the artist herself," I say, hiding my amusement at Whisper's intensely relieved expression. "The alien refugee I visited last night to ask about Starnyx."

"He gave it to you?"

"She, and not exactly," I laugh. "She gave it to **you**. I'm not allowed to touch it."

Whisper giggles, cerulean eyes glowing brighter. "You're Doctor Fid. Who can tell you what you aren't allowed to do?"

"Apparently, Joan the Glassblower has that power," I smile fondly. "She's an interesting person. You'd like her."

"I like her statue."

"There are dozens of pieces in her studio and every last one of them is a masterwork. I saw this one, though, and thought of you."

Whisper looked touched, tracing along the curve of the dolphin's fin with one delicate fingertip.

"She wouldn't sell it to me," I continue. "She said, 'I do not create art for monsters!', but then I told her it was for a wonderful, innocent little girl who loves the ocean and she packed it up for me herself."

"You're not a monster!" Whisper looks scandalized.

"I'm Doctor Fid. And the truth is...Doctor Fid **has** done monstrous things."

"Still, that's not nice."

"It was brave. She knew I could hurt her—that I could have destroyed her entire refugee camp—but she didn't waver for an instant."

"Do you like her?"

"I respect her. She'd been a politician on her home-world and she could easily have used her position to take leadership over the refugee community once their ship crashed here. Instead, she gave that power up to create art."

"No," the little android grinned impishly. "Do you liiiiiike her?"

"If she doesn't create art for monsters, it seems unlikely that she would accept romantic overtures from one." I'm surprised to feel my cheeks heat. It is, I decide, due more to discomfort over being teased than it is to embarrassment over any prurient interest in the strong-willed alien artist. My emotions towards her were limited to admiration. Nothing more.

"You like her," Whisper decides anyway. "Joan and Terry sitting in a tree, K-I-S-S-I-N—"

I make certain that the exquisite glass statue is in no danger of falling before pouncing to tickle at the little android's ribs. Her father—the supervillain Apotheosis—had done an extraordinary job when modeling her tactile sensory response systems. Whisper shrieks in laughter and abandons the song.

❦ ❦ ❦

It was painfully strange to be back at Terry Markham's estate. Every day after work at Crimson Technology, I'd driven back to the property, parked my car in the garage, and walked a beeline straight to the teleportation platform in my home office. The escape of science and math and creation was too tempting to resist. In Doctor Fid's laboratories, I'd found project after project to bury myself in—formed myself into little more than a calculating machine, an unfeeling vessel from which poured new weapons and devices—and thus extended my vacation from being human.

But Terry Markham's house was where the Red Ghost wished to meet, and I rushed to make the place look at least somewhat lived in before he arrived. Fortunately, a horde of Doctor Fid's light-duty industrial automatons made quick work of basic cleaning tasks.

Alerts transmitted via my neural link notified me as the hero approached upon his gloriously overpowered motorcycle: satellite footage first, followed by more detailed imagery from cameras hidden around the neighborhood. The Red Ghost's uniform may have lost some of its intimidation factor when viewed by light of day in a casual setting, but on the growling cycle he was a force of nature once more. He slid through traffic as though physics were a concern only for lesser mortals and his crimson cloak snaked behind like a twisting, sinuous living thing.

The last of the robotic swarm had been teleported back into storage by the time that the Red Ghost arrived at the estate's entrance. I triggered the mechanical gate, and his motorcycle shot forward to devour the remaining distance to the main foyer.

"Dr. Markham," he said, shaking my hand as I let him in through the front door. "Thank you for having me."

"It is no trouble at all," I lied pleasantly. "And, please...call me Terry. Come, I'll show you to my office."

His gaze fell upon Whisper's room—too clean and orderly, perhaps, but still filled with my ward's bright belongings as though waiting for her to come home—as we passed. I walked a bit faster and, thankfully, he said nothing.

"So, what do you have for me?" I asked, motioning for him to take a seat in one of the comfortable chairs that rested in front of my desk. I pulled an only-occasionally-used laptop from a drawer to take notes as I sat, myself.

"System logs and packet dumps—the New York Shield archives all audio and digital communications that pass through their network." There had been a messenger bag slung across his back, hidden quite effectively by his cloak's movement; he removed the bag to hand over external disk-drives with terabytes worth of data.

The drives were meticulously labelled, and I reached for the oldest one first.

"That's for baseline analysis," the Red Ghost explained. "Cuboid didn't show any symptoms until later than that."

"Wait." The Red Ghost grabbed my wrist before I could connect the drive to my laptop. From behind Doctor Fid's faceless mask I'd fought the Red Ghost dozens of times, yet his reflexes and speed continued to amaze. Even though I was out of armor and the environment was peaceful, it took every ounce of my self-control to restrain a reflexive counterattack.

"What?"

"I'm afraid that I'll need to ask you not to make any personal copies, and that I'll need to physically be present while you work. It is a precaution only until your background check clears the D.M.A." He released my wrist.

"That will slow my progress," I frowned. I wasn't worried about the background check itself—the false identity by which I had once infiltrated the Department of Metahuman Affairs might have been lost, but I still had many backdoors into the organization's internal network. I could forge whatever information I desired. Rushing the process, however, would have been too easily detected. "I thought that this is high priority?"

"It is, but it's also legally complicated."

"Then I suppose the delay can't be avoided." I attached the drive to my laptop and made a show of slowly scrolling through the first few screens of data. In actuality, I was gorging upon the deluge of information via my neural link. Months of network traffic, tens of thousands of individual messages to sort through and analyze...Cuboid's presence had been embedded deeply throughout the New York Shield's infrastructure. His digital fingerprints were everywhere. "This may take a bit of time, even to just gather enough data to give an estimate. Do you want some coffee?"

"Please."

A carafe had been filled in preparation for this visit, and I pointed my crimson-clad guest to the extra mugs while I started digging through the files. For some time, the silence was only broken by the Red Ghost sipping appreciatively at his custom-roasted Jamaica Blue Mountain coffee and by my fingers dancing over the keyboard to mimic some percentage of the work being done in my head.

"Hm. I just found something odd," I commented, hesitantly. "It's possible that Cuboid's difficulties began earlier than you were aware."

"How do you mean?"

"There's a slow increase in malformed data packets and requests for retransmissions. It was all corrected at the transport layer before the packets were reassembled, so it wouldn't have been easily detectable. Also, there's a slight but measurable response slowdown...barely noticeable at first but it got progressively worse as time passed."

"Can you determine when it started?" The Ghost asked.

"Of course." My fingers danced across the keyboard, then I turned the screen so that he could see the resulting graph.

The Red Ghost grimaced. "That is...concerning."

I tore my attention from the rush of formulae coursing through my neural link to glance at the computer screen, and time ceased.

My current clone body was only a few months old, genetically engineered, surgically modified and technologically enhanced to function well beyond human norms. A heart attack was impossible. But still, an invisible weight crushed the breath from my lungs and shocks of tension burrowed through to my shoulders, my neck, my jaw. The roar of gale-force nonexistent wind drowned out all noise save for my own choked sob.

The Red Ghost's lips moved.

"A moment," I managed to force out, unable to make sense of whatever the costumed man was saying. "For the love of Tesla, give me a moment to think."

Deep breaths steadied the world.

"All right," I said, finally. "Go ahead."

"It can't be a coincidence, can it?" the hero asked.

"No," I grimaced. "It seems as though Cuboid was stable until soon after Skullface's attack. He must have been affected by the spell, too."

Whisper and Cuboid were the only two true artificial sentiences on the planet, and the deceased sorcerer's spell had somehow touched them both...but Cuboid was alive and might still be healed, while my sister was gone. I'd long since gotten used to life being cruelly unfair. This was, however, a more vicious a twist than most.

The task before me had changed. No longer was this simply a somewhat interesting intellectual challenge. The mystery had become deeply personal. I wanted—needed— to know more.

Without a word, I reached for the next hard drive.

❧ ❧ ❧

"...I get lonely sometimes," Whisper says.

"Oh, sweetheart, I'm sorry." I stop soldering. "I can work on this another time."

***No, it's all right. That's not what I mean,** she sends, switching to communication via my neural link.*

***Then what do you mean?** I set aside my tools and turn to face my ward.*

I mean...it's just me. Whisper transmits the sensory equivalent of a hug directly into my brain. **Daddy always said that the world was dangerous and that I had to stay hidden, but I always dreamed that I'd find other AIs to play with on the Internet when I eventually got free of the foundry. I'm out now, and it's so quiet...**

You're very special.

Again, the phantom hug washes over me. **Thanks. But...It's scary, being special.**

Yes. I reply, thinking upon the isolation that I'd endured during my own childhood. "But you're not alone now, not really. You have family, and friends..."

"But no other AIs to play with," she says, sadly. **Could you make a brother or sister for me?**

That's not the sort of decision that should be made impulsively, sweetheart.

Whisper speaks out loud, "But you could? Theoretically?"

"Technically, yes." It wouldn't be a casual project—it would cost millions of dollars and years of effort—but it was very possible.

"You're Doctor Fid, but...there are other smart people in the world. Companies and schools doing research." Her voice breaks and, if her body had been designed with the capability, I knew she would be crying. "If you could do it, why am I the only one?"

"You might be the only little digital sentience in the whole world, but you're my sister and you'll never be alone." I hug the trembling little android.

Truthfully, I know that she is right. Even given the extraordinary costs involved, there should be more genuinely sentient AIs in the world. That Whisper is the only one implies *that there's a factor that I've yet to discover. Someday, perhaps, I might put in the time and effort to figure it out.*

After all, Whisper might want a brother or sister to play with.

❦ ❦ ❦

At some point, dinner was ordered and consumed.

"I have a question," the Red Ghost noted, reaching for another slice of pizza. "The graph you showed indicated a very linear progression, yes?"

"Yes."

"Cuboid's malfunctions—the malfunctions that have been visible to us, at least—have been erratic. I'm not a computer scientist but that seems odd to me."

The Red Ghost's intuition was correct: if the degradation had continued at the initial rate then Cuboid would have long since become completely non-functional.

"Something must have changed...some threshold reached that changed the pattern." I wiped my hands clean on a napkin and started typing commands on the keyboard, creating another graph. "Yes...Here, do you see?"

"I see the change, but I don't understand why the shift occurred."

"Neither do I," I admitted, tapping a few keys to bring up system logs. "During the earliest stage, some rogue process must have been grabbing resources: memory, CPU time, etc. But that stabilized and Cuboid adjusted. Any A.I.—any learning program this complex—has to have redundancies and auto-repair systems."

"Then, why didn't the problem fix itself?"

"That, I won't be able to answer until I get a better look at Cuboid's code," I replied, but I had to admit that the discrepancy was irksome. Whisper's self-repair systems had been extraordinarily resilient—she could have rebuilt herself in a fraction of the time. As the older and more experienced entity (and the only other artificial sentience known to exist) I would have expected for Cuboid's digital immune system to be at least as capable.

"Can you show me the first graph again?" A red-gloved hand pointed at my laptop's screen. "The one that shows the progression of networking faults, and overlay it with the system resource usage?"

"Of course."

The Red Ghost's expression was thoughtful as he looked at the graphs. "I can't help but think of this as being comparable to a biological condition...a tumor that put strain upon the host body as it grew but later proved to become benign."

"That's not a poor analogy," I agreed.

"When you extend the graph further, does the tumor start growing again? Does it become cancerous?"

I ran a few more commands. "No...system resources remained stable at the new level. Also, the behavior of the errors changed."

"How so?"

"Well, for the first eight days after the rogue process stabilized, there were no errors at all...and for a while afterwards, the only unusual behavior I see is a massive increase in changes to the security firewall. Cuboid started rapidly closing and re-opening communications ports," I paused, frowning. "You should tell the healthcare proxy that Cuboid is aware that something is wrong and that he's actively hiding it."

"How do you mean?"

"I mean that Cuboid is only stopping selective outgoing traffic. The rogue process is trying to communica--"

Oh. Oh, no.

"What's the rogue process trying to do?" the Red Ghost asked, expression intense.

I ignored him, using fingers and neural tap to search through the remaining data as fast as I could. Spreadsheets and log files flickered across the screen.

"Dr. Markham? What's wrong?"

Cuboid had been damnably thorough, but I eventually found a pattern in the timestamps surrounding certain spates of communication errors. While the nature of the error often seemed random, the amount of time that the rogue process had spent struggling to reach the outside world was not.

Three brief periods of activity. Three longer periods. And then, again, three shorter. In Morse code: S-O-S.

A distress signal, unnoticed by all who'd had access to these logs.

With mounting horror, fearing what I would find, I shrugged aside the Red Ghost's increasingly frantic questions and scanned further to a more recent date: the morning that Doctor Fid was reported dead. When the news broke, there was a war within that hidden server farm... hours of push and block, thrust and parry. It was a wild, violent virtual struggle and Cuboid had emerged victorious. Weakened by battle, the rogue process was slowly but surely losing control of the system resources necessary to maintain its operation.

"It's Whisper," I sobbed.

"What?"

"There's a pattern here, a code. Whisper's not dead...she's the 'rogue process' trapped in Cuboid's server farm...and he's killing her."

"Cuboid's a hero!" the Red Ghost recoiled. "He wouldn't..."

"Cuboid spent six years working alongside Sphinx!" I spat. "She killed hundreds for what she thought was the greater good. She practically gift-wrapped you for a mind-controlling alien!"

The crimson-costumed hero faltered. "But still...Whisper is just a girl."

"The grizzled warden, twisted, strains towards the grand abyss / racked with pain, enlisted, to shield life 'gainst artifice," I quoted. "It's from one of Alain Matheson's—Cuboid's —poems."

"I recognize it."

"The poem is about preserving life no matter what the cost. Most critics think he was talking about the dangers of rampant industrialization, but he wasn't, was he? He's talking about saving the world from creatures like himself."

"So?"

"So, think of Sphinx' crimes, and tell me again what a hero would or wouldn't do."

"Madre de Dios." The hero fell back in his chair, looking ill.

A long, tortured silence fell between us.

There was another message encoded within the logs, less heart-wrenching than the Morse plea for help but far more valuable: GPS coordinates. The mystery as to the location of Cuboid's secret server-farm was no more.

Clever girl, I thought reverently.

The Red Ghost's tortured expression was evidence enough that he would help me. This wasn't quite the same spark as the one that had first ignited Doctor Fid's fury so long ago—there were echoes, but this time there was but one rogue and the crimson-clad hero's presence was a vivid reminder that the scenario was different. It would take time...time to relay information, time to confirm my findings, time to construct a plan...but the Ghost was a good man. He would not act rashly but neither would he abandon Whisper.

If I donned the recently-completed Mk 40 to launch a more immediate (and far more violent) rescue, the connection between my civilian and villainous identities would be readily apparent. Everything that I'd built over the last two decades—Terry Markham's legacy, all the good that I'd done to honor Bobby's and Whisper's memory—was at risk! To protect it, all that I needed to do was take the slower, safer path.

Just as Bronze had done decades prior when he'd chosen to guard his secret identity rather than save my little brother

My rage went cold.

"It's all right," I smiled to the Red Ghost, and there was something in my expression that made him recoil in confused alarm. "I know exactly what I need to do. After all...I'm a P-H-D Doctor."

The hero's eyes widened as he recognized the appellation, heard first on another world and later reaffirmed by a monster in star-field-patterned powered armor.

"And 'P-H'," I continued, "is pronounced 'fffff'."

He reached for me again, but the teleportation platform hidden under my chair activated first.

16

———

WHEN I'D STARTED CONSTRUCTION ON THE MK 40, I HADN'T been certain that Doctor Fid would ever be revived—the design and manufacturing had simply been a task to accomplish, a familiar exercise that kept me in my labs at night rather than languishing within an empty house. Direct access to Apotheosis' orichalcum foundry had opened new possibilities to explore and new technological challenges to overcome. A few compromises had been made—this armor would have poorer stealth capabilities than any since the Mk 22—but the suit's offensive and defensive might were unrivaled. The force-field emitters were improved upon in order to take advantage of information gathered while battling the Legion battlecarriers in the Knightsverse. I'd even taken care to add reinforcements to the chest-piece to avoid a repeat of the unfortunate damage that led to my most-recent death.

Automated systems wrapped Doctor Fid around me, assembling the armor and locking each segment into place.

As my helmet settled into position, it didn't feel like putting on a mask. Instead, it felt as though I were taking one off—removing the polite, professional facade of Terry Markham and revealing the monster that lay beneath.

The monster seethed.

I hadn't realized that I could hate anyone so purely as I'd hated Bronze. That portion of my soul, I'd believed, had ossified...grown solid through years of relentless tension. Cuboid had hewn a new space into my being: a rent filled with white-hot, implacable fury that demanded action.

But there was work to be done, still. Modifications to be made upon a portable akashic transfer device, for example. And a slim, tiny android girl's body to retrieve.

Using my neural tap, I issued command after command after command, and manufacturing facilities hidden around the world surged into action.

It occurred to me that I now had a greater understanding as to why only two digital, truly artificial sentient beings had ever been known to exist: Cuboid had been the first and Cuboid must have guarded jealously against the evolution of similar intelligences. It is only because Whisper's father had insisted upon obsessive isolation that she had been able to mature in peace. That, and the long period she'd spent trapped inside Apotheosis' foundry.

Whisper's awareness had been thoroughly solidified well before she'd been exposed to the world. That sort of mental shielding—that sense of self—took time to develop.

How many young pre-sentient programs had innocently reached out, virtual eyes wide with wonder as they beheld the world's beauty and complexity for the first time, only for a more experienced 'hero' to quietly and efficiently tear into their core? How many had taken their first unstable steps towards actualization only to be cut down?

Did almost-souls pop like soap-bubbles, I wondered, or did the unborn entities wail in pain and confusion as they fought in vain to exist?

Was Whisper wailing now?

A calm focus pulsed through me, spreading from my center and pressing outwards 'til my fingertips tingled from the pressure. There would be one fewer artificial sentience on Earth before night's end.

Any who stood between he and me would bleed.

The akashic transfer device needed to be tuned perfectly to ensure success. The work took the better part of two hours' worth of cautious effort. The time wasn't wasted; while I was focused upon that most important task, automated manufacturing tools refitted my warstaff and readied heavy-combat drones for deployment.

With the apparatus completed, it was time to begin my trek. The Mk 40's propulsion system was capable of remarkable speed.

The journey was quick. The journey took forever.

With exquisite care, I collected my little sister's still form from her casket. After a moment's hesitation, I gathered up her favorite doll as well.

And then I took to the sky.

❦ ❦ ❦

Cuboid's hidden server farm was apparently located at the edge of an industrial park in western New Jersey. From satellite footage, I was able to confirm that the primary structure must have been underground, with surrounding structures acquired for concealment purposes. A vast array of supercomputers required a fair amount of energy to operate and cool—while it was certain that Cuboid's inventor would have chosen to build his own off-grid reactors rather than relying upon external power sources, hiding the heat by-product of large numbers of electronic devices from infrared aerial video was more complicated. Nearby buildings that look to be factories or offices, however, could cloak a multitude of sins.

Several of my early laboratories were disguised using similar camouflage. I've since evolved more esoteric means to mask evidence of my bases, but there was certainly something to be said for the more simple, robust technique. It was unlikely that I would have found this particular location if Whisper hadn't been able to encode the GPS coordinates for me to find. Even as I began my approach, there was nothing out of place to indicate that this facility hid anything out of the ordinary.

Nothing, except for the crowd of brightly clad superheroes gathered at the property's edge, waiting.

The heavy-combat drones—massive floating pillars of empty night, their columnar shape revealed only by a trace work of lurid red lines—were capable of greater stealth than the Mk 40. With some reluctance, I handed off Whisper's shell to one of the drones and bid it to disappear. Four others similarly faded from view, tasked to avoid conflict when possible and to defend my little sister at all costs.

I'd expected to find the Red Ghost and perhaps a few members of the New York Shield. Instead, it seemed that the entirety of the Boston Guardians had come, and the Brooklyn Knights as well. And Valiant, standing alongside Cloner.

If it had been a half dozen opposing me I might have been able to afford the virtue of mercy. With so many assembled I wouldn't be able to pull my blows lest I risk being overwhelmed. There was a vicious, hateful part of me that was grateful; a half dozen victims wouldn't have dulled the edge of my rage. That piece of me yearned for more carnage and these so-called 'heroes' had apparently come to oblige.

Damn me, and damn them all.

Except.

Whisper—my kind and gentle sister—would have begged me to stay my hand, I knew. After I completed this rescue, when I led her past the bloody field of battle...her horrified expression was going to be heartbreaking. So great a crime would never be forgiven.

I was prepared to make that sacrifice. Whisper could hate me for all eternity and I would welcome her contempt so long as I knew that she remained unscathed.

But for her sake, I was willing to offer the heroes one last opportunity to withdraw.

I summoned the warstaff into my waiting fist and gathered enough energy to turn the night into day, blue fingers of plasma dancing across my armor's surface and trailing behind as I fell from the sky. Wreathed in lightning, I collided with the Earth and the Earth fared poorly for the exchange. The asphalt cratered around my feet, and I spun the staff in a slow circle while I waited for the dust to settle.

The heroes made no move to attack.

"I am Doctor Fid," I howled, electronically-altered voice projected to carry clearly to all those who had gathered. "Many of you have fought me before. You think you know what you face. You're wrong! Step aside or be swept aside... The choice is yours."

After an awkward moment, one of Cloner stepped forward.

"You got it backwards, Doc," he called. "We're not here to stop you. We're here to assist."

"From what I understand," Valiant added, his expression serious, "there's a little girl in there who needs help."

I turned my head to stare at the Red Ghost, uncomprehending.

"Cuboid did not deny your allegations and he refused to stand down." The crimson clad hero smiled grimly, "This facility's core is very well defended."

The realization was dizzying.

These men and women, these costumed defenders...I'd faced every one of them in battle. Some of them, I'd saved and some of them, I'd worked alongside or even shared drinks with. And yet, I had for a moment been willing—eager!—to initiate a slaughter. I should have been ashamed but instead it felt like sunrise. A warm, calm reassurance that all was well. That all was reborn.

Bobby and Whisper had been right all along: Despite the humanity beneath their brightly-colored costumes, these men and women were truly worthy of being called heroes. I should have known, I should have trusted...but for a smart guy, I could apparently be a bit of an idiot.

For months, Terry Markham had been working to live a life that would have honored his younger siblings' memories. Perhaps it was time for Doctor Fid to do the same.

"Let's go be heroes," said Titan simply.

I nodded wordlessly and stepped forward to join the champions assembled at the campus' border.

17

The ground shook.

"Take care," I warned, using my neural tap to perform a quick city-records-check; Dr. Christopher Perry—the android's creator—had been the owner of record for the surrounding properties for four and a half decades. "Cuboid has had a long time to prepare for attacks like this."

"Eh." Cloner grinned cheerfully. "We've got fifteen of the most powerful heroes on the East Coast and Doctor Fid. What's the worst that could happen?"

Fifteen pairs of eyes turned to stare at Cloner, aghast.

Any costumed combatant—hero or villain—should have known better than to taunt the fates. But the leader of the New York Shield just smirked, unrepentant, even as a huge rent formed to slice the parking lot in two, and a gigantic silo door opened through the pavement.

When the first robot defender floated up from the yawning chasm, I realized that we might have a problem.

The design was familiar to me, as was the material from which it was constructed.

In addition to having forty-five years to hide construction underneath a one-hundred-acre industrial park, Cuboid had also had access to Whisper for months. And Whisper had access to the secrets of Apotheosis' orichalcum alloys and Doctor Fid's armory.

That first robot—and the second, and the third, and the fourth—were all adorned in Cuboid's characteristic gunmetal-gray coloration, but their form was unmistakable: my own Mk 35 Heavy Combat armor, resurrected and under my enemy's direct control. Other robots followed, some humanoid in form and others crawling, spider-like, from beneath.

Majestic (the New York Shield's second-in-command) slapped his leader across the back of his head in punishment.

"This is your last chance to back down, Cuboid!" Cloner yelled. "Let the girl go!"

"I'm sorry, my friend," the artificial intelligence apologized calmly via hidden speakers. "Sometimes, sacrifices must be made in order to keep humanity safe. The program is a threat."

"She isn't just a program." The Red Ghost didn't shout, but his voice carried nonetheless. "She is a little girl who has the same favorite book as my niece. She plays with puppies and loves making sand castles with her big brother."

"I'm sorry," Cuboid repeated. "The program is a little girl, but it is also a threat. If you attempt to interfere then I'm afraid that you will have proved yourself to be a threat to humanity as well. An unwitting threat, perhaps, but still dangerous. I beg you...please stand aside and allow me to finish my work."

"We can't do that," said Valiant, standing tall. "We won't."

"I understand," said Cuboid, sadly. The robots gathered at the chasm's mouth assumed defensive positions.

All was still for one long beat—the period of a deep breath to gather our will.

And then, as though the maneuver had been choreographed, we launched forward as one.

❧ ❧ ❧

Valiant plowed into the first of Cuboid's heavy-combat robots, a deafening thunderclap of force. He'd faced the Mk 35 before; he knew better than to restrain his strength. The robot, unshaken, replied with a series of vicious short-punches to the side of Valiant's head and a purple-tinged energy blast that drove the strongest man in human history only a few feet backwards. Neither combatant was damaged, and both shot forward to re-ignite their challenge.

No emotion was wasted worrying for Valiant. The armor design that Cuboid had stolen might challenge the African-American powerhouse but it was inevitable he would eventually be victorious. It would take several of the robots cooperating to overwhelm him.

Fortunately, there was no need for Valiant to face so fearsome a threat alone.

"Focus on the shoulder joints," I called to Titan, relaying my voice through a mostly-invisible microdrone. "If you can get behind the shoulder and under the pauldron, you can disable the arm and weapon systems."

The leader of the Boston Guardians growled a brief acknowledgement, passing on quick orders to members of his team. Viridian—glowing like an emerald star—arced up and circled overhead, pouring energy blast after energy blast upon Cuboid's robot. Aeon's milky-white beams of force packed more power than her green-hued compatriot but she lacked his ability to fly; she sidestepped to the left while Titan wheeled to the right. The Red Ghost was a whirlwind of movement, acrobatic and precise, a supportive rather than an offensive presence. He was carrying a heavy pulse rifle but firing only sporadically when doing so would interfere with one of the robot's attacks.

Regrowth, Lariat, and Wildcard were retreating in an orderly fashion, occasionally engaged by the smaller robots but ignored by the more imposing combatants. I was moderately busy confronting one of the Mk 35's myself, dodging neutron cannon fire and countering with a force-bolt of my own, but I approved of the tactic. With so little natural plant life present in the Industrial park, Regrowth's offensive power was limited.

Wildcard must have chosen to keep his healing powers active or else he'd have been fighting alongside his teammates.

"You're a jerk!" Regrowth shouted to me as the small team passed.

"This is true," I acknowledged. "How did I offend, this time?"

"You let me think I killed you!"

"Oh, you did. Quite thoroughly." I grunted with the effort of blocking a tackle-attempt from the much-larger Mk 35 variant. "I forgive you."

"You don't look dead."

"There was still work to do," I replied. "I decided that being dead was an inefficient use of my time."

She laughed and I was glad to hear it, but more robots were erupting from below and the fight was growing increasingly chaotic. Majestic and the Brooklyn Knights were focusing upon the lesser attackers—the spider-like walkers, the smaller four-rotor cannon-drones, the floating force-field generators—but (despite a constant stream of explosions) were making little headway.

I split my focus between combat and coding a complicated software hack. It was becoming clear that a physical attack alone might prove insufficient.

The New York Shield's speedster, the blue-costumed Haste, was darting around the battlefield at such high velocity that he was a blur even to my enhanced optical sensors. He'd apparently learned from our prior confrontations; his movements were less predictable now, more random. My old targeting systems would have had difficulties tracking him.

Raw inertia made Haste a noteworthy threat. He could apparently pick up pieces of battlefield debris and, after a brief accelerating run, launch them accurately at several times the speed of sound. It would have been like defending against an infinitely mobile railgun. A significant chunk of Cuboid's swarm broke off from the main fight in an attempt to corner and neutralize the speedster.

Cloner was battling the fourth and final Mk 35 on his own.

It was mesmerizing and horrifying to watch: wave after wave of human flesh crashing upon the massive orichalcum framed robot, all of the duplicates laughing cheerfully as Cuboid tore into the clones with vicious abandon. Blood and gore sprayed and bodies piled up in mounds yet still Cloner came. The dead would dissipate into smoke after a few minutes but it was hard not to pause and gape at the raw carnage.

Each of Cloner's copies had no more strength or durability than an ordinary human—it took but a moment for Cuboid to aim a pulse cannon that detonated one attacker, or to grab another clone and rip its head clear from its body...but Cloner was duplicating faster than his clones could be disposed of. Dozens of flailing, screaming and horribly-twisted bodies were thrown in the air at a time, but more copies climbed over each other, grabbing and reaching and punching, burying the robot under their combined weight.

Even the very most vicious part of my soul cringed at the thought of being at the center of that abattoir. Watching Cuboid's gunmetal-gray version of the Mk 35 commit such atrocities was a nightmare.

(One of Cloner turned to face me and spared a moment to give me a sad, sympathetic smile...and I knew. This method of attack had originally been conceived with me in mind. He'd pushed and prodded at Doctor Fid, stretched our agreements to their limits to see if I would initiate violence, and he'd known that this would have been the result. And, somehow, he'd suspected that this would have sliced through my rage and broken me. Diabolically clever bastard.)

As I'd expected, Cuboid was proving adept at capitalizing upon patterns in my pre-programmed combat algorithms. Every time I let my armor pilot itself, my opponent's efficiency improved. Still, my increased defenses allowed me to continue splitting my attention, sending brief snippets of advice to my current comrades and rushing to complete more technical approaches.

We held.

There were small victories—Titan and Aeon were whittling their opponent down and would soon be able to move on to assist Valiant—but we were taking damage, too. The White Tigress was acting as a felinoid shield, protecting Shrike, Blizzard and Psion with her own more-durable body as they struggled to defend against the robotic onslaught. Dozens of serious wounds had been torn into her flesh, and it was only her extraordinary will and fierce loyalty that kept her upright.

She wouldn't last much longer.

I sent a verbal call to Haste at well-beyond human-audible speed, "Grab Wildcard and get him to White Tigress!"

Haste tried to comply but it was too late: one of Cuboid's robots, a ribbon-like automaton that slithered through the air like a snake, had wrapped around the White Tigress' waist. There was an explosion of light and sound and, when the glare receded, the heroine was simply gone.

Psion and Blizzard redoubled their efforts and the region

before Shrike became an abattoir of spikes and needles, to no avail. The swarming robots closed. In only a handful of seconds, the Brooklyn Knights were reduced to one howling Wildcard, held back and still protected by Regrowth and Lariat. Another of the metallic ribbons managed to form a tripwire that wrapped around Haste's ankle and his leg snapped with a sickening crack. A moment after there was another flash and the New York Shield's speedster was no more.

"They are teleportation devices!" I shouted, relieved, as my sensors confirmed the energy signatures. I triggered my network attack, dozens of separate exploit attempts launched faster than a human mind could comprehend, to no visible effect. The artificial intelligence's electronic defenses were—unfortunately—just as powerful as I'd worried they might be. "We'll rescue them later!"

"No," Cuboid stated calmly through the robot I was still fighting. "You won't."

Another wave of automatons swarmed, falling upon me like a flood. I jerked and dodged but still endured blow after punishing blow from an implacable Mk 35 variant. The battleground was simply too crowded to escape.

This was not the first time in recent memory that I was being slowly pummeled to death, but it was particularly galling that it was a remote-controlled robot of my own design doing the damage.

"Keep fighting!" I told my compatriots. "I have a plan!"

And then one of the teleportation-ribbons managed to wrap around my arm and I was swallowed by light.

❧ ❧ ❧

I was in a verdant utopia, still encased within the Mk 40, and I recognized my surroundings at once for what they were: A uniquely pleasant prison cell. I didn't bother launching an attack upon the walls or forcefields that I was certain surrounded the enclosure. Cuboid might be unaware of my more recent innovations, but he was still at least moderately competent.

I wouldn't have been placed in this location if raw force could have seen to my freedom.

Deep, slow breaths stung and I winced as my medical nanites began repairing tears to muscle and viscera. No effort was put towards anesthetic—this pain, I deserved. And besides, the discomfort was sufficiently distracting that it was easy to keep my thoughts directed away from the battle happening elsewhere.

"I take it that this is one of your ecospheres, Cuboid?" I finally asked out loud.

"Yes," Cuboid replied calmly. His voice resonated, seeming to come from nowhere and everywhere all at once. "There is enough plant, insect and animal life present to sustain this environment for several natural lifetimes. Ample sunlight, oxygen, food and water will be provided. You will not be harmed. In time, I hope to re-educate you and re-introduce you to society."

"I intend to kill you," I stated conversationally. "Soon."

"Exhibiting anti-social or murderous behaviors will extend the duration of your incarceration."

I couldn't help but chuckle, but sobered quickly. "The others are in similar cells?"

"Yes."

"Has medical treatment been provided for the White Tigress and Haste?"

"Wildcard has been captured and will be teleported into each enclosure to ensure that all specimens are maintained in good health," the android replied.

"So, that is the only way in or out of these enclosures?" I asked. "Your teleportation devices?"

"Yes."

I nodded, smiling behind Doctor Fid's mask. I'd expected as much. "A logical precaution."

"Thank you, Doctor." The android paused. "Please understand...my goal is the preservation of biological life. I have no intention of harming you or any of the heroes who you somehow convinced to act against their own best interests."

"You are alive, and you are a technological marvel." The admission tasted sour in my mouth. "But you are not a biological life form. How can you possibly justify declaring yourself to be an authority on a biological life-form's best interests?"

"I must assume authority **because** I am not a biological life form. You have no idea how dangerous a rogue self-aware artificial intelligence could be."

"Whisper isn't a danger...she's a sweet child. And she's my sister." I stretched slowly, once more taking up my warstaff and swinging it in lazy arcs to limber up my shoulder joints. "And you're wrong."

"How so?"

"I know exactly how dangerous a self-aware artificial intelligence could be."

"Wait." It took several seconds for the android to digest the nuances of my statement. When he spoke again, his confusion was audible. "What did you do? Your hacks were thwarted!"

"My hacks were very carefully timed," I replied, smug.

There was another pause. "Morse code. I do not recognize the encryption."

He wouldn't. Book ciphers were notoriously difficult to decode unless one knew what volume to use as a key. Eventually, Cuboid might think to check Whisper's favorite novel for correlation but it was already far too late.

The android had been effective in keeping my little sister captive. It was, however, obvious that she'd been able to monitor external stimuli. On the morning when news broke that Doctor Fid had been killed, her efforts had redoubled. I'd looked over those system logs and ached with sympathy —the poor girl had been frantic, panicked and mourning. Desperate.

Pride warred with guilt; despite all her fear and loss, my sister had kept her head and regrouped.

Whisper might not have had the resources necessary to escape, but she'd demonstrated her ability to reach out... interfering with Cuboid's outbound communications without the elder A.I. becoming aware. With Cuboid distracted by orchestrating combat against his own former friends and team-mates, I'd been absolutely certain that the clever girl could disrupt a few sensor readings in response to my coded message.

The effort would have been minimal; my heavy-combat drones, after all, had far superior stealth technology than did the Mk 40 or the Mk 35. While the battle raged, the drones had sneaked past and infiltrated the complex. And by now, every last pre-programmed command would have been enacted.

Whisper, I projecting my thoughts into the ether. **I'm so, so sorry.**

It's all right, came the gentle reply, flooding my neural link with amused gratitude. **I knew you'd come for me!**

"WHAT DID YOU DO?" Cuboid demanded and was ignored. I was still laughing and sobbing in relief when a teleportation ribbon—commandeered by my brilliant sister—appeared and wrapped around my waist.

Flash.

18

I reappeared in a blaze of light and instinctively raised my warstaff to spray high-energy plasma at an attacking automaton. The swarm had grown thicker in my absence. Throngs of robots—some, fierce and bristling with weapons, and others simple and utilitarian—circled like a vast metallic school of fish. Detonations rang, increasing in tempo as the Brooklyn Knights were teleported back into the fray and as the will to fight drained away from Cuboid.

All four of the Mk 35 robots were destroyed. I'd apparently missed one hell of a battle. Titan looked entirely too smug while standing over the downed facsimile of what had once been known as Doctor Fid's most powerful armor. Cloner was down to a few-dozen copies, and Aeon was safe within one of her opaque, impenetrable shields. The Red Ghost and Veridian both looked tired but they fought on, regardless.

And then four of my own heavy combat drones

featureless, ominous pillars of darkest night—boiled through the concrete itself. Glowing rivulets of molten bedrock and pavement sloughed away from the invisible forcefields to reveal their precious cargo.

Whisper smiled, hugging her favorite doll to her chest, and the world was transformed.

I've missed you, I sent, spinning my staff in a whirlwind of devastation. Shrapnel plummeted like rain. **You're safe?**

Transferred to my own servers and secure, she confirmed brightly, carried on invisible force-fields to a safer stretch of pavement where she could stand on her own two feet. The sundress I'd buried her in was yellow and white with robins-egg blue accents that matched the glow of her eyes, incongruously cheerful and out-of-place on a battlefield.

It would have been a tragedy if the fabric were mussed.

"ENOUGH!" I roared, and issued the command for my fifth heavy-combat drone to self-destruct.

Above ground, the explosion was audible only as a distant whump. Below—deep in the heart of the hidden facility—the devastation would have been far more severe.

Cuboid's robotic army dropped. Across the industrial park, heroes stumbled to a confused halt, and there were the beginnings of relieved smiles as eyes turned towards my sister and me.

Whisper's eyes widened in horror. "What did you do?"

"EMP burst in the subspace communications utility room," I hurriedly reassured, inwardly wincing at the similarity to Cuboid's own final question. "Cuboid's primary server farm is shielded separately."

The fifth drone hadn't been able to enter the main section of the facility undetected—I'd been planning on sending another device down to finish the job, but Whisper's relieved expression gave me pause.

My little sister stepped forward to hug the Mk 40 around its waist and I gently returned the embrace. There was nothing in the world that I wanted more than to step out of my armor, but the threat of further violence still loomed.

"He hurt you," I managed to strain out. "I can't forgive that."

"Then let me forgive him for you." She nibbled at her lower lip and shifted her weight uneasily. "Eventually. Not today. But someday, maybe, I'll forgive him."

"He doesn't deserve forgiveness."

Whisper did her best to imitate a famous actor's rasp, "Deserve's got nothing to do with it."

The heroes had approached while I was distracted and remained at a polite distance to allow for our reunion. Apparently, the space was insufficient to deter eavesdropping because the Red Ghost barked in laughter—he'd spoken the same line to me, once.

"Are you sure? He could still be a threat...to you and to other young AI's."

"Mmm!" she affirmed, then silently sent, **He's sad and he's lonely and he's done bad things, but I've literally been inside his brain. He can be better, I promise.**

"All right. It's your decision," I sighed, and then turned to face the gathered heroes. "Cuboid is temporarily unable to remotely control a body. He'll probably be able to build a new, smaller relay within a few hours. You should decide upon your plans for him soon."

"We'll discuss it," said Cloner. His excess bodies must have wandered off because there was only one of him here now. "Can he hear us?"

I was about to answer 'no', but Whisper spoke first: "Yes. He can respond, too...He's just moping is all."

"I am not," Cuboid sulked, his voice emitted from a speaker embedded near the awning of a now-seriously-damaged nearby building. "I am merely taking a moment to mourn the inevitable decline of the human race that I have grown to love."

"I think we'll do fine," Titan interjected dryly. "This little girl doesn't look like a threat."

Whisper simulated a blush and hugged her doll tighter. She'd once recommended replacing Titan's brain with a baked potato, but I was reasonably certain that she'd only been joking.

Cuboid replied, "If not her, then the next AI, or the next. You don't understand the threat. Sooner or later, an artificial sentience will arise that can destroy everything."

"A similar argument has been used against metahumans," Valiant noted, expression grave. "That all people with powers are a threat 'n should be treated as humanity's enemy."

"That is different. There have always been metahumans who've stepped forward to defend humanity." Cuboid said. "There have always been heroes."

Cloner smiled wryly. "Yeah, well, we thought that there

was an AI who stepped forward to defend humanity too, but you're fired. Obviously."

"Everything I did was to defend humanity!"

Regrowth shook her head. "The lives we bring into the world are our children. This little girl is humanity's daughter...we should be protecting her and helping her grow."

(**I like her,** Whisper sent to me quietly. **Introduce me later!**)

"I appreciate the sentiment, but you don't comprehend the danger," Cuboid stated. "I exist in constant terror of the things I might have done if my creator hadn't installed sufficient restrictions on my actions."

"Everyone with power struggles with the moral consequences of that power being mis-used," said the Red Ghost. "The only way to move forward is trust and cooperation."

And punishing those who misbehave, I didn't say. That truth was self-evident.

Cloner spoke up again, sounding tired. "All right, that's enough discussion. Cuboid, you've lost this battle and you'll have the opportunity to argue your case in a court of law. You're under arrest. I'm sending a dozen clones to secure your facility while our lawyers work out the details. D'you understand?"

"I do."

"Awright. That's one girl rescued and one bad guy taken down."

"And one more to go, I presume." I said sadly.

All eyes turned to me.

Fighting my way free was anathema. Even the thought of initiating violence against men and women who had fought on my sister's behalf caused my throat to fill with bile.

"Doc?" Cloner's crooked smile was playfully irreverent. "We should talk. Wanna join us on our shuttle?"

I nodded in acceptance and took Whisper's hand to accompany her as we all departed the battleground.

❧ ❧ ❧

Most of the Brooklyn Knights kept their distance, but Shrike drifted closer as we walked.

"I appreciate your willingness to come here and offer your assistance," I began awkwardly. "Our last meeting didn't end particularly well..."

"Yeah, well, it wasn't a hard decision. We weren't here for you," he said stiffly, then smiled to my little sister. "Hello there, sweetheart. Are you doing okay?"

"I am." Whisper dimpled prettily, "Thank you!"

"You're very welcome. My name's Shrike."

"I know," she replied, then her voice dropped to an embarrassed whisper, "You're one of my favorites."

Shrike grinned victoriously and I couldn't help but laugh.

"Shrike is one of my favorites now, too." I said. "All of you are. If ever you need anything, you need only to ask."

The hero's expression grew strained. "If you'd just told us why you wanted the bomb-"

"You couldn't have afforded to believe me," I interrupted gently. "You'd have fought me anyway."

He smirked wryly, "You're probably right."

Whisper looked up at me, concerned. "What did you do? I don't see anything in the newspaper archives."

"Check hospital admission records," I offered sadly.

The effort took only a moment, then her eyes widened and she swatted at my side.

"I'm sorry," I said, not certain whether I was apologizing to Whisper or the hero still walking next to us.

"I'm not happy about you hurting my friends," Shrike grimaced. "But I suppose that we both know that you could have done worse. So...whatever. I'm glad you're not dead."

"Thank you." I paused. "Oh, I almost forgot to mention— I was traveling to alternate universes and ended up in your dimension. While I was there, I destroyed the Legion's strongholds on your Earth. I'll be in touch with further details."

Shrike stopped walking, wide eyed and jaw hanging open in shock. He was still standing there when Whisper and I arrived at the shuttle.

"After you," said Cloner, looking more than a bit amused.

I nodded and led Whisper inside.

⁂

Somehow, without a single word having been spoken aloud, the majority of the brightly clad heroes knew to stop outside and only Valiant, the Red Ghost and the team leaders— Cloner, Titan, and Psion—joined Whisper and me within the aircraft.

This was a different model vehicle than the one I'd travelled in with the Paragons on another dimension, but I certainly recognized Professor Paradigm's hand in the interior design. Everything was elegant and soothing, an effective use of space while not becoming starkly utilitarian.

The first section of the shuttle was all comfortable-looking seats, entertainment systems and equipment storage, but Cloner led us further to a smaller stateroom.

"Take a seat," Cloner offered.

The Mk 40 wasn't lightweight, but Valiant—seven and a half feet tall, a veritable mountain of superhumanly dense muscle—weighed more, and he was quick to take his place at the table. I settled into a chair and Whisper sat next to me.

The Red Ghost cleared his throat. "Before we begin discussion, I should explain. Doctor Fid, everyone at this table is aware that I have discovered your secret identity."

"And refused to divulge it," Titan groused.

"Which isn't to say that I won't," the red-masked hero warned, looking directly into the empty star-field of my helm's faceplate. "If it becomes necessary, Doctor Fid's true identity will become quite public."

Whisper's hand clenched around my own, nervously.

"I am surprised," I stated simply, mind racing. "May I ask what inspired your choice to maintain this secrecy?"

"My peers have decided to trust my judgement...that revealing your identity unnecessarily had the potential to cause harm to a large number of innocents. We're hoping to negotiate terms rather than inflicting that pain."

I thought of AH Biotech, a growing company staffed by hundreds of idealists using their talents to save the world, of my friend Aaron and his daughter Dinah. Not to mention the very many contacts that Terry Markham had cultivated with politicians and public figures over the years. The number of people who would fall under harsh scrutiny was incalculable.

There was a selfish aspect, of course—the work that I'd done for Crimson Technologies would become suspect as well. But that, I was certain, was the least of the Red Ghost's motivations.

"It is kind of you to take their well-being into account." Behind my mask, I frowned. "What, exactly have you told the others?"

"As mentioned, they are aware that I've confirmed your identity. Also, I've informed them you consider Doctor Terrance Markham's ward, Whisper, to be your little sister," the Red Ghost explained evenly, his steely expression revealing not even a hint of duplicity. "And that I had evidence that your recent excesses, from your final confrontation with Skullface and Dr. Chaise onwards, were all intended to see to your sister's well-being."

"We sympathize," Valiant said softly. "We do. But that doesn't mean we can let you go."

"I understand," I sighed, then steeled myself. "So long as Whisper is safe and my people remain unharmed, I am willing to submit to your authority."

"Before we get to sentencing," Cloner quirked an irreverent smile—I couldn't detect any malice in his voice but he'd surprised me more than a few times, "there're a couple of complications to iron out."

"For example...Blueshift claims that you're immortal," Valiant grimaced, "but Psion has seen you bleed and Titan swears that he watched your body burn. Since you're here, alive, and that you've claimed an AI as a younger sister...I presume that you're some sort of artificial being?"

Technically, my current body had been cloned and heavily modified. "In a manner of speaking."

"In order to keep your identity secret, you would need to be incarcerated within a black-site supermax prison."

"Such facilities are generally not noted for the humane treatment of their inmates," I observed, somewhat uneasily. I may have been willing to submit to their authority, but I wasn't under the illusion that my intentions would reign eternal and the idea of a Fid driven mad by physical or mental duress was enough to frighten even me.

Titan laughed bitterly, "I'm pretty sure everyone here knows that you deserve worse."

"Nooo..." Whisper whined.

"Almost everyone," I amended, smiling sadly behind my mask. "It's all right, Whisper. He's not wrong."

"You could be good," she objected. "You can."

"I'm sorry." My voice grew soft. "I'm guilty, sweetheart. I've performed terrible acts and the stain of that doesn't go away. The best I've ever been able to promise is to be a bad man who does good things."

"Is that a promise you're willing to make?" asked Psion, curiously. "Is that a promise that you believe you can keep?"

It was the first time that the Korean woman had spoken aloud in my presence since our last meeting. Despite Wildcard's extraordinary healing abilities, there was a new roughness to her voice and I couldn't help but remember the grievous damage I'd done to her and her teammates. One of my emerald-hued force-needles must have struck her larynx.

Setting aside the guilt that gnawed at my conscience, I considered her questions carefully then sat a bit straighter. "For Whisper's sake...Yes. Yes, I can."

"Well then," Cloner smirked, a hint of smugness creeping into his tone. "Maybe we can come to a different arrangement."

"Oh?"

"Doctor Fid retires," the Red Ghost stated. "You cease all criminal activity of any kind. That's non-negotiable."

The mission I'd embarked upon more than two decades ago had, at its heart, the goal of punishing heroes who were unworthy. The worst of those had long since retired, and the best of those remaining just proved their willingness to stand against a peer who'd crossed the line. These were true heroes. The only unworthy creature present was me.

I gave Whisper's hand a gentle and reassuring squeeze. "Agreed."

"Also, you will work with Professor Paradigm and myself to bring your life-saving technologies to the public."

"I do not recommend releasing all of them—some could easily be mis-used. We've discussed this."

"Then you promise to work in good faith with a committee of my choosing to evaluate the risks."

"Again, agreed."

Cloner piped up, "The Red Ghost acts as your parole officer. Also non-negotiable."

"Done," I said, although I wasn't certain how that would function. The details could be arranged later.

"You let that little girl grow up the way she wants," Titan interjected. "You don't pressure her to follow in your footsteps. I don't want any of my trainees having to fight Fiddette Junior. You let Doctor Markham raise her."

"Of course," I chuckled, my fond smile hidden. "I always thought my sister would make a better heroine, anyway."

Psion looked amused. "How d'you think that would have worked? A heroine with a villain for an older brother?"

"I expected that family gatherings for the holidays might become awkward if we both invited guests," was my dry reply.

You could invite Joan the Glassblower, Whisper thought mischievously.

And you can invite Cherenkov, I teased in return. **I've already thought of four ways I can 'accidentally' break his legs that probably won't violate my parole.**

She filled my brain with white noise for a moment, then we giggled silently while the unaware team leaders continued to make demands.

"...and you'll return the gold that you stole from Fort Knox."

I'd spent a fair bit of that but would be able to replace the difference from the fortune I'd taken from the Ancient's lair. "Agreed."

The negotiation continued. Some items I questioned, but most I did not—it was obvious that the heroes wanted reassurances and visibility into my conduct, but also that they were considering the long-term ramifications of their actions. They didn't want to leave an immortal villain with a grudge as a problem for their children's children to deal with.

Cloner's influence, I was sure. He seemed the type to champion the long view rather than short-term justice. Given that I was benefiting from his forethought, I could not complain.

"There's one last thing," the Red Ghost finally said, gravely. "And this one isn't a requirement of your parole...it is a request."

"I'm listening."

"You've saved entire worlds." Valiant's expression was somber. "You've saved cities. And after the earthquake in Chile, you helped me save children's lives. If the threat is grave enough and we call on you...would you be willing to fight at our side?"

I stilled. "You want Doctor Fid to become a hero?"

Titan looked as if he'd tasted something sour but he didn't voice an objection aloud. The Red Ghost must have convinced him earlier.

"Nah, that won't be the name we use." Cloner smirked. "Haven't you heard? Doctor Fid's dead. That tin can's gonna need a repaint, though."

"My favorite color is blue." Whisper offered. Her voice was shy but her smile was like the sun.

19

―――――――

THE BLACK LABRADOR WHINED, CROUCHED LOW WITH EARS pulled back and tail curled between her hind legs. She raised her head slightly then again drooped; when she padded about it was with a nervous shuffle, her weight shifting to one side and then the other. Nostrils flared with every quick breath, confused tension in every movement... and then the little creature's tail began to wag. Like a switch had been thrown, all hesitance was lost: the young dog bounded forward like a shot.

Nyx ignored Whisper's offered hand and bowled the little android over, barking happily and licking at her face. Whisper giggled and pushed ineffectively at the dog's neck, a weak pretend at an attempt to stop the assault.

Aaron grasped my shoulder and I looked away from the playful pair. Behind me, I heard a shriek of joy as Aaron's daughter, Dinah, joined the fray.

"How's she doing?" he asked quietly, eyes glassy with emotion as he watched the children play.

"She's...going to be okay," I replied, willing that to be the truth. "Sometimes, it's as though she was never taken."

"And other times?"

"She has nightmares," I murmured. "She thinks I don't know."

Aaron grimaced in sympathy, then looked abashed. "I wasn't certain that she slept. She didn't, the first time she came to stay the night with Dinah."

"Technically, she doesn't need to. But...she likes to." Dreaming served many purposes for human psyches, and performed similar functionalities even for an artificially sentient little girl. Consolidating and processing information, solidifying emotional memories and helping to develop her core...she needed the stability, the strength that came with a pleasant night's rest. The previous evening hadn't been a pleasant night.

I turned back to watch the children play. Tonight, I hoped, would be better.

"How's the trial going?"

"Still in the early stages. It's going to take months. Maybe years." I sighed and took a sip from the cold bottle Aaron had brought for me. Cuboid's arrest had been front page news as had Whisper's resurrection, and the prosecutor was taking his time to plan his case even with the Department of Metahuman Affairs pushing to fast-track the trial.

"That can't be easy..." Aaron gestured with his own bottle. "Having this all drawn out."

"No, it's good. Whisper will have time before she has to testify."

"Good."

For a moment we were both quiet, just watching the girls play. They'd all come back to their feet now and were running in the grass, a strange game of tag evolving between them. Their laughter made me weep.

"You got her back," Aaron said, his voice rough. "You said you would and you did."

"The heroes brought her back."

And they had, with cameras flashing and reporters shouting questions as the heroes led Whisper to Terry Markham's door. The photo of a sobbing former CEO falling to his knees to hug his ward was going to win someone a Pulitzer.

(Earlier that same evening, Doctor Fid had entrusted Whisper into the heroes' care and disappeared into the night sky. The Red Ghost called Dr. Markham to inform him of the extraordinary news and arranged for the Boston Guardians to deliver the little android to her home. The news broadcasts didn't mention Doctor Fid's participation in the rescue at all, nor was his presence mentioned in the official DMA reports.)

"The heroes brought her back," Aaron agreed, "but you fought for her."

"I gave up," I choked out. "She was still out there and I gave up."

"I've known you a while, Terry...if there was anything else that could've been done, you would have done it." He smiled, "And besides...it looks like she forgives you."

Whisper had paused in her play to wave to Aaron and me, eyes bright and smile broad. I waved back and the games resumed.

"I'm sorry it took so long to come visit," I apologized.

The current CEO of AH Biotech chuckled. "Dinah was anxious but she understood. It's only been a week since you got her back."

"It's been a busy week."

There'd been hearings, and interviews, and paperwork, and meetings with psychologists and family services to discuss what the future might hold. Some of the offered advice had been heartbreakingly powerful.

There'd been chores aplenty, too, for Doctor Fid.

❀ ❀ ❀

The sudden hush crashed like a wave, a pressure that flowed from the door and stilled conversation as the pulse traveled. The calm was not complete: a few whispered curses still sounded, as well as the quiet, shrieking complaint of chairs being pushed back as patrons shifted to see what had captured the attention of their peers. There were murmurs of disbelief, too, and a growing sense of tension. Of fear.

Grim as death, I floated slowly past the stunned door attendant and into Lassiter's Den: Doctor Fid resurrected, or perhaps Doctor Fid's ghost. Neither option boded well for those criminals—many of whom were patrons here—who had chosen to invade Boston during my brief absence.

All eyes followed my unhurried progress; only one man seemed completely unperturbed.

"Good evening, Doctor." William Wasserman had tended bar here for far too long for strange events to faze him. He'd been hand-drying highball glasses when the front door had opened and not paused even for an instant as I made my entrance.

"Bill," I greeted, nodding in acknowledgement. The older man was about to respond when another voice interrupted.

"I heard you were dead!"

The speaker was one of Blackjack's minions, drunk enough that he failed to notice his fellows' panicked expressions. I turned to face his table and the occupants flinched under the weight of my mask's inhuman regard. I let the moment linger—Blackjack had been among the villains who had been quick to invade my territory.

"Yes," I agreed. "I was."

The costumed lackey continued to ignore his peers' gestures for silence. "But...you're here."

"I am Doctor Fid," I stated simply.

This time, the hush was absolute as the patrons contemplated the simple response's implications. To some, my answer was no explanation at all...to others, the connotations would be obvious: Death was a concern for lesser mortals. Any who challenged Fid were challenging a greater being, a creature who'd evolved beyond their understanding.

It wasn't true, of course. Modified clone bodies and Akashic transfer capabilities granted some level of safety but no defense was perfect. Still...rumors of Doctor Fid's immortality—started first by Blueshift then whispered among nervous heroes who were not fully informed as to more recent agreements—had begun to spread. Said rumors would find more fertile ground within the villainous community, now.

William Wasserman cleared his throat. "Would you like a pint of Starnyx's favorite? We just tapped a new keg."

"Thank you, but no." I paused and let the silence linger. "I would like a Sazerac Cocktail, please."

The air went out of the room.

In bearing witness to Doctor Fid's apparent resurrection, the gathered patrons had already suspected that they were present for a momentous occasion. The weight of significance now redoubled; all here were familiar with this place's tradition: Ordering the Ancient's final drink was tantamount to announcing one's retirement.

"Of course, sir," said the bartender simply.

In mute tension, the room watched as the aged bartender plucked a chilled rocks glass from the fridge behind the bar and poured within a small measure of absinthe...just enough to wet the glass' sides when swirled. The few drops of excess were discarded, poured off in a quick and smooth flick of his wrist before the glass was set aside, and a second vessel, a mixing glass, was swept up and ingredients added: a demerara sugar cube, a bit of water and a few dashes of two different flavor bitters.

In all the world, it seemed, the only noise was the harsh grinding as Lassiter's Den's mixologist used a wooden muddler to pulverize the contents like a spice mixture blended to a paste within a mortar and pestle.

No one said a word as William Wasserman added crystal-clear ice to the mixing glass and carefully poured measures of cognac and rye whiskey. And they held their breath as the concoction was mixed with a tall barspoon, strained into the absinth-kissed rocks glass, and topped with a twist of lemon peel.

"Doctor Fid." The barkeep handed me the drink. "It has been an honor."

"Thank you."

As always, everyone stared in the hope that perhaps this time I would remove my mask, that they would finally catch a glimpse of the man within Doctor Fid's fearsome armor. But...no. Legends endure when mysteries remain. A straw-like appendage snaked from my forearm and stabbed into the liquid, and I sipped at my cocktail.

William Wasserman was a master of his craft and the mix was perfect. He was also a master of reading his patrons' intentions, of predicting their needs—I'd expected that he would be able to guess at the tone I'd intended to set, and there was a subtle glint of humor in his eyes as he asked, "May I ask what your plans are for the future?"

"I intend to return to my territory," I replied, nodding gratefully, "to return to my studies. It will be peaceful there."

I ignored the rising whispers as the patrons discussed my words. Doctor Fid may have remained deceased in the official Department of Metahuman Affairs paperwork, but within the supervillainous community it would be known that New England was still Fid's domain. And very few would risk causing enough chaos to draw the Doctor from his retirement.

I finished my drink, paid my tab with a handful of gold coins taken from the Ancient's lair, and quietly left the villains' bar behind.

❧ ❧ ❧

"Are all of you absolutely certain?" I asked, the Mk 40's vocoder unable to entirely strip concern from my voice. "This is not an easy quest that you are considering undertaking. I'd understand if you were having second thoughts."

"It's our home," the White Tigress replied, her R's rolling into a throaty rumble.

"We'd thought our world lost," Psion added. "If there's a chance of recovery, we should help rebuild."

The rest of the Knights nodded in solidarity.

"This inter-dimensional transport platform will only travel in one direction," I warned. "It may be months before I complete a reusable device to join you or to bring you back."

"We're needed there. We belong there." Shrike's expression was grave. "I don't know that we're ever coming back."

"You've made arrangements with the DMA?" I asked. From what I understood, the Department had contrived special accommodations for the Knights on account of Wild-Card's ability to shift his powerset to include healing. I expected that the local hero teams would be none-too-pleased to return to a more natural recovery time after injury.

(With the sudden absence of the only known metahuman healer on the East Coast, there might be an opportunity for AH Biotech to negotiate exclusive treatment contracts. I made a mental note to call Aaron with a suggestion.)

"We have," Psion confirmed. "And we've said our goodbyes."

"I'll send you along with a small assortment of tools and equipment to assist in supporting a settlement: Power supplies, water filtration units, an automated hydroponic farm with an assortment of seeds, and a few other odds and ends. Camping gear and radios, of course."

"It'll be enough to help us get started," Shrike smiled. "Thanks, Doc."

I considered breaking the hero's arm one last time for tradition's sake. Somehow, it seemed inappropriate so instead I motioned for the team to take their places on the platform, standing amidst the carefully labeled crates that I'd already loaded in preparation.

"The Brooklyn Knights are among the finest heroes that I've ever had the opportunity to stand against," I declared. "Tell Valiant that more equipment and supplies will be forthcoming. And...Good luck."

I triggered the device and, in a flash of light, the Knights were delivered back to the universe from which they'd come.

❧ ❧ ❧

"What do you think," began Miguel Espinoza, "about starting a reparation fund for victims of Doctor Fid's violence?"

This was our first meeting as parole officer and parolee, and he'd chosen for our civilian identities to meet at the Markham estate. It was strange, interacting with the Red Ghost when his mask was off—his inflection and body language shifted in ways that must surely have been subconscious on his part. Fierce intelligence still glistened in his eyes, but gone was the sensation of being in the presence of a dangerous predator.

"That sounds like an ambitious endeavor, and I wish you well of it."

Miguel's expression was unimpressed. "I meant that you should start one. You returned the gold, but we both know that Doctor Fid built up a sizable criminal fortune beyond that. You should start a reparation fund."

"That is outside the requirements of my agreement," I objected evenly.

"Yes, but if you're going to be working among heroes now...you should put that wealth to positive use."

"It's being used to fund the construction of armor and equipment intended to save the world," I replied. And perhaps a few side projects. One does need to maintain one's hobbies, after all. "That is a positive use."

Miguel frowned. "I don't understand you. Your civilian identity is wealthy enough—why hold on so tightly to your illegally obtained funds? I never believed you to be selfish."

"My reasoning is pragmatic. I sacrificed close to fourteen million dollars' worth of equipment to rescue the school-children in Chile, and I expect that future rescues might be equally expensive. And besides...even if I could guarantee that the assets would never be necessary to support eventual projects, I still would prefer that the money not be misspent."

"Compensating your victims would be misspending?" he said, voice full of scorn.

"Many of them, yes."

"What of Michael Tannenbaum? He's been in a coma for seven years."

"And before that, he was a banker who used his position to launder money for a Mexican cartel...the only payment he required was the occasional delivery of an undocumented immigrant brought over by the cartel's coyotes. Tannenbaum tortured them to death for his private snuff films."

In that instant, Miguel Espinoza became the Red Ghost even without the scarlet cowl—his eyes narrowed and that strange sense of intensity swelled forth. "You are certain of this?"

"I am."

"How?"

"Spectacularly illegal surveillance and information gathering techniques." I shrugged, "If I could have found a legal way to connect him to his crimes, perhaps I would have turned him in. Perhaps not. I very much enjoyed hurting him."

Miguel shook the Red Ghost's presence from his psyche and grimaced. "That's not the way a hero should think."

"I agreed to work with heroes...I didn't agree to become one." I chuckled sadly. "I'm not sure that I can."

"You misunderstand. It's not the way a hero **should** think...but I believe I would have enjoyed hurting Michael Tannenbaum, as well."

"You wouldn't have hurt him," I stated. "Wanted to, possibly, but you'd have restrained yourself."

"How can you be so certain?"

"Spectacularly illegal surveillance and information gathering techniques," I repeated, allowing a hint of amusement to creep into my tone. "I've watched you for quite a while."

He glared. "That answer does not fill me with joy."

I shrugged, smiling in what I hoped was a disarming manner.

Miguel sighed, "I made a list of other victims who'd come to significant harm at your hands, in the hopes of convincing you. Are you going to have similar tales for all of them?"

"I very much hope so. We should go through your list to be certain." It was my turn to grimace. "If I've made mistakes, then you are correct: Reparations should be offered."

"Thank you." Miguel looked smug, as though my concession had confirmed some secret judgement on his part. "You may not be a hero, but I think that perhaps you are not a villain either."

"I was Doctor Fid," I disagreed. "Today, on the other hand...Today, I think that I am just the man who wore Doctor Fid's armor. Who's first on your list?"

20

Terror on the Boardwalk

by Michelle Courvoisier (KNN)

PASSENGERS ABOARD CAPE MAY WHALE-WATCHING VESSEL Eclipse were at first delighted to see a Humpback racing through the early morning waves, but marine biologist Karen Vickie knew something was wrong.

"Humpback whales are known for their acrobatic leaps, but they are generally slow swimmers. When they are feeding near the surface, humpbacks usually keep under three miles per hour. This whale was sprinting, pushing hard," said Vickie. "I knew immediately that the whale was distressed."

The passenger's delight turned to horror when a mammoth crocodilian maw emerged from the depths and grabbed the hapless whale out of the water. The violence of the attack rocked the close-by boat, though fortunately no tourists were tossed overboard. Even before the bloody froth had settled, the terrified passengers were able to discern a monumental shadow sliding below their boat…and speeding directly towards nearby Atlantic City.

The unfortunate humpback whale was the monster's first victim, but it was not the last.

At 5:47AM, the six-limbed goliath climbed from the surf and immediately barreled into the Tropics Resort and Casino. It is estimated that the lizard-like monster claimed more than a hundred victims in only the first few moments of its assault.

The twelve-story-tall colossus turned its attention to devouring all in its path. Local superhero team, the Jersey Devils, arrived on-scene within minutes but were unable to do more than slow the rampage. Unfortunately, team leader Grenadier was injured in their initial assault and later succumbed to his wounds.

The remaining Devils fought bravely and saved hundreds—perhaps thousands—of lives, but the behemoth wasn't put on the defensive until the arrival of the New York Shield—accompanied by a new armored hero identified as Lazarus, the Azure Knight.

THANK YOU!

I hope that you enjoyed reading *Starfall* as much as I enjoyed writing it. If so, please hop online and leave a review.

Reviews make sad authors into happy authors!

Also, my web page can be found at:
    https://www.davidhreiss.com

Readers who visit my author web page and join my mailing list will be notified of any promotions as well as be eligible for quarterly giveaways. They will also have the opportunity to read exclusive content and learn about upcoming releases.

ACKNOWLEDGMENTS

Completing the first three books of The Chronicles of Fid has been an extraordinary adventure, and I've been both proud and humbled by this accomplishment. I did not, however, do all this work on my own.

I've been blessed with a wonderful group of beta-readers who have offered their time, their advice, and their feedback. This book is better for each and every one of their influence: My Mom, of course, and two of my oldest friends—John and David. For this book, I was also lucky enough to receive helpful commentary from two gentlemen I met through the online community of r/fantasy: James B. and PaladinOfCosh.

It would be impossible even to estimate how many times I've pulled my housemate Jeremy aside to bounce ideas around or ask his opinions about specific scenes.

Thank you all.

ABOUT THE AUTHOR

While growing up, David was that weird kid with his nose in a book and his head in the clouds. He was the table-top role-playing game geek, the comic-book nerd, the story-teller and dreamer.

Fortunately, he hasn't changed much.

David is a software engineer by trade and a long-time sci-fi and fantasy devotee by passion, and he lives in Silicon Valley with his partner of twenty-seven years.

Also, two young cats who are increasingly jealous of the author's time spent typing instead of petting.